WHO TOLD THE MOST INCREDIBl

WHY TIGERS AND LEOPARDS DO NOT 1 ... AND OTHER STORIES

Naana J.E.S. Opoku-Agyemang

VOLUME 5

Afram Publications (Ghana) Limited

Published by:
Afram Publications (Ghana) Limited
P.O. Box M18
Accra, Ghana

Tel:	+233 302 412 561, +233 244 314 103
Kumasi:	+233 322 047 524/5
E-mail:	sales@aframpubghana.com
	publishing@aframpubghana.com
Website:	www.aframpubghana.com

First Published, 2015
ISBN: 9964 70 537 9

Edited by: Adwoa A. Opoku-Agyemang
Illustrated by: Peter "Poka" Asamoa

Content   Page

WHY TIGERS AND LEOPARDS DO NOT MIX

Many years ago, the village in which Kweku Ananse and his family lived experienced a severe famine. Ananse, like others in the village, went into the forest to look for food to feed his family. You could see men, women and children foraging the forest for anything they could eat, because their own crops had perished at the hands of the cruel unrelenting sun. After futile trips to the forest his wife advised that her husband should took for employment in a nearby village, while she and the grownup children roamed the forest for their sustenance.

Ananse found a job almost immediately as a cook to Leopard. Kweku Ananse was so adept at the craft of cookery that the aroma of his cooking would bring many animals to the scene. Some were attracted to the scene just to watch him at work, while others came with their corn meal which they ate as they inhaled the appetizing aroma of the food that Ananse prepared. Leopard was really pleased with the culinary expertise of Ananse, and he rewarded him with a big house.

On a few occasions, Leopard boasted to his friend Tiger about the wonderful cook that he had employed. Craving a good meal, Tiger agreed to come to Leopard's house for dinner one day. On the appointed day, Leopard told Ananse that he knew he was a good cook, but he wanted him to outdo himself for his friend Tiger who was coming over for dinner.

What Ananse would do every day was to cook more food than was necessary for Leopard, and he would send the rest to his family in the course of the night. On this particular day when Tiger was coming for dinner, Ananse cooked the most delicious soup he had ever prepared. It was light soup with chicken, well seasoned, to be served with fufu. When the dish was ready, Ananse tasted it and he found it to be most mouth-watering.

He went beyond tasting to actually eating part of the food and after eating each bowlful, he would smoothen the rest of the fufu and rearrange the meal in the bowl. After a couple of courses of the same meal, Ananse realised that the rest of the dish would be inadequate for his master and his guest, and so he ran as fast as he could and sent the rest of the food to his family, trusting in his wits to whip up another meal before dinner time.

Tiger arrived even sooner than expected, and the two friends fell in to a lively conversation, during which they decided to play a game of sword throwing after dinner. Meanwhile, Ananse was in the kitchen, trying to conceive of a strategy to get himself out of the impending disaster. When Leopard walked into the kitchen to find out how much longer they had to wait, Ananse really had a hard time convincing his master not to open the pots. He said that was against his method of cooking. To keep Leopard occupied Ananse asked him to help set the table, which Leopard was happy to do. Ananse busied himself getting out the earthenware bowls and the bamboo cups. When the table was set, Leopard told Ananse that he would go into his room and bring out his swords for sharpening, because he intended to play a game with his friend.

No sooner had Leopard gone to his room than Tiger came to the kitchen to chat with Ananse about his fame as a cook. Ananse was quick to capitalise on this opportunity.

"Thank you for your compliment, but I am a very worried man," Ananse told Tiger, in a most plaintive voice.

"Oh, I am sure you are. Anyone who has to be separated from his family would, too. And in your case they live in a land which is experiencing famine. But, you know, just look at the bright side. You have a good job and you can always..."

"My family is in very good shape," Ananse interrupted Tiger. "I am worried about you."

"You, worried about me? Why so?" asked Tiger, rather surprised.

"I am telling you this in confidence. The whole idea behind bringing you here is that Leopard plans to kill you during the sword game. If I were you, I would flee whilst I had a life to protect."

Tiger's face was suddenly full of fear. Edging towards the door and finding Leopard sharpening the swords and whistling to himself, Tiger bolted through the door and ran as fast as he could.

As soon as he was gone Ananse went to Leopard and asked him if he should move the table outside for the food that Tiger had carried from the kitchen.

When Leopard asked what was going on, Ananse explained that Tiger had taken away all the bowls of food, and so they should look for him.

Leopard was so incensed by the greed of Tiger that, grabbing a sword, he started to give Tiger chase. When Tiger saw Leopard come after him with a sword he knew how right Ananse was and thanked him most fervently in his heart. The faster Tiger ran, the more convinced Leopard became that Tiger had bolted with the food.

Leopard did not catch up with his friend, and so they never cleared the misunderstanding.

These two animals have been avoiding each other since that day.

NEVER SPURN GOOD ADVICE

The season for palm nuts occurs just before the rainy season. At such a time the sun shines with such intensity that you would think it had a bone to pick with mankind. The clouds withdraw from the path of the sun, giving man no protection at all from the rays which continue to pour with diligence. The heat becomes so extreme that even the air which used to move about freely stops in its tracks. If you watch a leaf on any tree carefully, you will discover that it does not even so much as quiver. The atmosphere becomes still, heavy and most uncomfortable. It is the time that babies suffer the most because they cannot sleep well. People spend the night outside of their huts at this time, because the drop in the temperature towards dawn affords them the only respite from the heat. Even skinny people suffer from heat rashes, so you can imagine the fate of heavy people at this time.

During this period of extreme heat and high humidity the palm grove becomes a place which lures all manner of animals. The thicket offers some refuge from the sun, and even more than that, as I have said, it is the time when palm fruits abound.

The fruits, with their crimson and yellow colours and delicious pulp are a great attraction for the animals who know that once the rains start they will have very little, if any palm fruits to enjoy. The palm fruit is known for correcting defective eyesight and for giving smooth skin and shiny feathers. Above all, it is so tasty.

Of all the animals who were fond of the fruits, Parrot was particularly so. He was also aware that Hunter, knowing that these animals liked to congregate at the palm grove, made the thicket his favourite spot for trapping and shooting animals. One day during this season Parrot and Monkey met at the palm grove, and each enquired after the other's families:

"My wife and children are well. It is my greedy mother-in-law that I don't understand. The woman is so overbearing. She is never satisfied with what I can do for her daughter. I get so nervous when she comes to visit," reported Monkey.

"Mine is no better. I remember my own mother telling me to stay away from a woman with a widowed mother, an unemployed brother and a divorced sister. The combination can be lethal, she swore. And I thought I was in love and she was talking too much. If I start narrating my woes you will pity me indeed," commiserated Parrot.

"Yes, Parrot, the elders are right. It is a curse to wish you were someone else's shoes because from the outside you cannot tell if the shoes are lined with thorns. I always thought you had a peaceful marriage. Listen, let us enjoy the palm fruits and forget about our domestic problems for a change. Moreover, it is too hot outside for us to get hot in our minds as well".

The two of them started eating the palm fruits. After they had enjoyed the fruits for a while Parrot began to speak again:

"Good friend Monkey, aren't these nuts tasty?"

"Sure they are, good friend Parrot. God must have been in a very good mood when He made these palm trees. I plan to eat all the nuts."

"Really? Do you have to plan for something like that?"

"Well, what I meant was that I will eat till my stomach bursts. The nuts are so delicious and juicy."

"That is precisely the point. They are so tasty that we run the risk of eating without pausing, and thereby compromising our own comfort and safety. My suggestion is that you should eat just what you can and move on."

"Why so, my friend Parrot? I came here for a purpose, and I intend to fulfil it. Are you trying to get rid of me? Look, if all we did for the entire duration of our lives was to eat these fruits we could never complete the task, so please don't feel intimidated."

"No, monkey, I don't feel threatened at all. I am offering this suggestion for the sake of your safety."

"Parrot, do not upset our good comradeship. Who are you to advise me? My parents gave me all the counselling I needed in my childhood. There is one category of people I have no patience for: I mean those who inaugurate themselves as counsellors of others."

"Monkey, I have been coming to this grove longer than you have. I know what has been happening to animals who stay for too long in here. Remember the old proverb which says that pleasurable things can kill the fool?"

"Oh, so you take me for a big fool? Listen very carefully. I have brains between my ears, just like you do. Don't give advice unless people ask for it. The last time Crocodile had an argument with his wife you condemned him in the presence of the crowd which had come to see what the fuss was all about."

"Crocodile was very upset with me and even called me names which you recall since you were at the scene, but what you may not know is that Crocodile thanks me to this day for my intervention."

"He told me that I saved his marriage, because he was not aware that he had taken the poor woman for granted all those years. He is now sensitive to her and they live more amicably now."

"Parrot, God truly did not curve your beak for nothing. Or did it become arched from giving too much unsolicited advice? Why don't you learn to mind your own business for a change?"

"Believe me, I am saying you should eat enough and move away, for your own safety."

"So does that authorise you to advise me? Don't you have enough thoughtless people in your own family who need your help? Listen, we do not belong to the same family, neither are we related by blood. You are not entitled to tell me what to do, and I don't have to listen to you."

"Well, neither familial nor marital bonds offer the sole basis for friendship. I am giving you a chance to save your life. I insist that you save some of the nuts in the inside pocket of your mouth and move away to a safer place. I have seen a lot of animals fall victim to Hunter's gun because they stayed in the grove for too long. If Hunter finds you here, the sound from his gun will announce the end of your days on this earth."

"Ah, since when did hunters work in broad daylight? They usually work at night and at dawn. Parrot, I don't want to discuss this any longer. My recommendation is simple: leave me alone."

Both of them fell silent and resumed eating the palm fruits. The stillness in the air combined with their own silence to create a ghostly atmosphere, broken only by the chirping of birds as they hopped from tree to tree. Suddenly, Monkey and Parrot heard an unusual sound at the foot of the tree on which they were feeding. They stopped eating, looked at each other and down below, and directed their attention back to the fruits. Unbeknownst to Parrot and Monkey, Hunter had been watching them for a while, and was looking for an angle from which to aim his gun. Hunter had decided that he would get better value for his bullet if he shot Monkey instead of wasting it on Parrot. From behind a tree which had shed all of its leaves, Hunter let out a shot which instantly brought Monkey down from the branch on which he was balanced.

Parrot did not have to say the usual I told you so because with his dying breath, Monkey said: "Parrot, you were right, Parrot; Parrot you were right, Parrot; Parrot you were..."

So you see, it is only the people who love us who give us good advice. We need guidance so that we do not repeat the mistakes others have made. It may be useful to learn from our own miscalculations but not all the time, because some of these errors will leave us no room at all for a second chance. Sometimes we find our counsellors irritating. But remember the case of the Crocodile, and also remember that if only Monkey had eaten a little bit and moved on...

HOW ANGER CAME INTO THE WORLD

A young woman once lived with her parents in a place and time very far from yours and mine. Her name was Pomaa. Pomaa remained unmarried for so long that her parents were very worried. Not that Pomaa was unattractive or that she had no skills; in fact that was part of the problem. She was so attractive and was so unsurpassed in her skill at organising the women of her village in the distribution of fish throughout her country that she had become quite famous for both her beauty and her managerial skills. The only hitch was that Pomaa was also vain. I know that there is a little vanity in all of us, but Pomaa was too, too conceited, and disdainful as well.

Many men sought her hand in marriage, but Pomaa refused to accept any of them. At one time she submitted all her suitors to a wrestling match, and promised she would marry the winner. Some brawny young men entered the competition, each determined to win her hand. At the end of the match, several of the competitors had sustained broken bones and twisted arms.

The winner was so exhausted that he could not lift himself from the ground. Thereupon, Pomaa declared she could not marry a weakling, and so there was no marriage. Remember that during this time there was no anger in the world so nobody got upset with her. The competitors blamed themselves for falling victims to Pomaa's whims, found other preoccupations and soon forgot about her.

After the wrestling match Kwadwo came to ask for Pomaa's hand in marriage, but he found Kwadwo too tall. When Kwabena came, she said he was too short. As of Kweku she said his eyes were too big, while Yaw's eyes were hidden too far away in their sockets. Kofi was too stocky, Kwame too lean and Kwesi too fat. And so she dismissed all the men. Her mother and father were worried because all her age mates were married, and even those initiated two years after her had started to get married while Pomaa was still a spinster. Her mother went to her room one day at dawn and expressed her concern to her daughter:

"Pomaa, your father and I are very worried that you are still not married."

"But mother, why should I get married? Why can't I just have children and look after them?" she asked her mother.

"Pomaa that is the most foolish reasoning I have ever heard. Are you a goat or a donkey just to have a male get you pregnant and walk off? Only animals behave that way. And see what they end up making of parenthood. They even have babies with their own children. What is coming over you? 'Just have children and look after them' indeed! What stupidity is that? And the other thing... what do you plan to tell those children about their father? That you don't remember what he looked like, and that your sons and daughters should follow your example? Of course you can very well look after your children, but who says that parenthood can be bought with wealth? Or are you making a statement about your father?" Her mother was worried indeed.

"Oh, no, mother, Father has been my friend in time of need. At times when no one understands me, he has been there for me. I remember the basket he wove for my akuaba doll when I was a small girl and how he went into the bush to bring me another bird when my pet died and I was crying a lot."

"So why do you want to deprive your children of a similar love? And assuming he was a bad father like that useless younger father of yours, Brafo who has no idea how his children survive, you could still create a home much better than Brafo's.

"I know, mother, but the men here just don't appeal to me."

"What will appeal to you? Listen, there are other aspects of a child's life that only his father can provide. Don't forget that the father gives his child his spirit and that he must be around to nurture it, or the child may not grow up right. Have you considered how you are going to teach your sons how to deal with experiences which only a man can understand? I am worried by the manner in which you dismiss your suitors: Wiredu is too stingy... Dodu is too generous... Amponsa is too loving... Opoku is too patient... Osam smiles too much... Pobi is too polite... What is wrong with you? Are these the standards by which any sensible woman selects a mate? Which human being has no fault or is all virtue?"

"I have heard you, Mother. Tell Father not to worry about finding me a husband. I will find my own and tell you when I am ready to get married," Pomaa assured her mother who soon left her alone.

Pomaa realised that if she did not get married soon she would slip beyond the childbearing age and when she was old, she would have no one to comfort her. If she had brothers or sisters it would not be so bad because nephews and nieces usually love their aunts and uncles more than their own parents.

One bright day Pomaa went to the river to do her laundry. After washing the clothes and leaving them to dry on the nearby rocks she decided to take a nap and lay under the shade of an acacia tree. Soon afterwards she felt the presence of another person and when she opened her eyes, she saw a most handsome man staring at her in admiration. Almost immediately they fell into conversation and the stranger introduced himself as Kokuroko, a prince who had lost his way and needed direction. When Pomaa asked where he was going, Kokuroko said that he had turned down all offers of a spouse in his father's kingdom and had set off to find his own bride. When Pomaa told her own story, they knew they were right for each other, so Pomaa took him home to meet her parents.

Pomaa's parents were happy about the fact that she was going to get married but they were worried about their daughter marrying a man they did not know anything about. Her parents called her aside:

"Pomaa," started her father, "where do you know this man from?

"Had you met him before today?" her mother added.

When she answered both questions in the negative, both parents exclaimed at the same time:

"Ei. Pomaa!!"

Her father wanted to know why she would marry someone she had met barely an hour earlier, and Pomaa answered quite firmly that she had made her choice.

Reluctantly, parents gave in to her wishes. Let us not forget that this was a time when there was no anger in the world.

The marriage rites were performed the day after the handsome man had entered the home of Pomaa. Some of the elders insisted that Pomaa's parents should send messengers to find out about the kind of family the stranger came from before accepting the dowry, but Pomaa threatened to run away with Kokuroko if the ceremony was not performed right away. Later in the day Pomaa set off to travel to her husband's home town, accompanied by four young women who carried baskets of food, crockery, clothing and jewellery.

The party travelled a long way, but not at any time did they pass a single village. When it was dusk Pomaa's husband began to complain of hunger:

"Good wife, I am dizzy with hunger," he informed his wife.

"Good husband, I thought we would have reached your town by now. And I cannot find any village where we can rest for the night or ask to do any cooking. I am sure these young women must be starving too," Pomaa replied.

"You don't have to worry about cooking," Kokuroko informed Pomaa. "Just say 'eat whatever you can find.'"

When Pomaa said those words, her husband brought down her basket which contained smoked fish, yams, eggs, dried meat and game, cassava, cocoyam, plantains and palm nuts and swallowed them all. Pomaa nearly died of shock. She was trembling and was about to shout for help when her husband signalled to her to make no noise. The other women were walking ahead and did not see what had happened.

It was beginning to get dark and so the party decided to rest under a silk cotton tree for the night. The sky was clear and so there was no threat of rain. One of the young women had brought some food which they all shared. The young women soon fell asleep and Pomaa was left awake with her husband whom she now had reason to fear. Her husband spoke again:

"Good wife, I am dizzy with hunger."

"Good husband," Pomaa replied in a quavering voice, "we don't have any more food. You ate at one go the food that I thought would last us for days. And it is so late in the night. How can I provide you with food?"

"Just say, 'eat whatever you can find,'" he ordered.

In a feeble voice Pomaa replied: "Eat whatever you can find," at which command her husband swallowed all the four women who were travelling with them. At this time his eyes turned deep red and his face became distorted. His ears, nose and mouth grew very large, he had hair all over his body and he looked more like an overgrown gorilla now than the normal human being he had been just a couple of hours before.

Pomaa did not remember how she fell asleep but he woke her up at dawn and the two of them continued their journey which lasted another two days and which took them deeper and deeper into the forest. When they got to a place with only a hut with two rooms, the husband said they had arrived at their destination.

"Why, is this a farm house?" Pomaa asked.

"No, this is my home," replied the husband.

Pomaa gathered courage to ask, "And how about your kingdom? You said you were a prince. And why do you look so strange?"

"Kingdom? Ha! I knew you would fall for that, given the hard time you had given all the men of your village. Don't attempt to run away because you can't find help anywhere. My plan is to give you enough food to eat, and when you have put on a lot of weight, I will swallow you too." That was her strange husband's reply. He told Pomaa that she could cook outside and sleep in one room, but that she should never open the door to the other room.

In the daytime when he went out to farm or hunt Pomaa would spend her time crying her eyes out. If only her parents could see her! She had grown very lean and appeared much older that she was. Yet, even in her sorrow she wondered why she should stay away from the second room. She watched Kokuroko's movements closely and discovered that he kept the key to that room under a stone at the foot of the hill before going out for the day.

Pomaa removed the key one day and opened the door when he had gone out. What she saw was enough to blind anyone. There were human skulls, limbs, spines, ribs and more! There was, in the corner of the room, a large drum with human blood, and the room had an awful stench. She thought aloud:

"Is this what has become of me, Pomaa? Is this the man who was so handsome and who was a prince? Is this what I am cursed with? I know that he can tell from the stench all around that I have opened his door and I will soon be on my way to becoming a skull or a rib, so I must run for my life. Come what may, I must save myself from such a miserable life."

Pomaa started running. She ran all day and hid between two trees for the night. Early in the morning she started to run again. She ran for a long time until she felt cramps at the back of her legs; she stopped for a while to rest and to massage her legs. All the time she was aware that her husband would chase her as soon as he came home and found her gone.

In the course of the second morning she met a very old woman who was walking by herself, and she ran to her for help.

The old woman wanted to know what she was doing in such a place, and Pomaa narrated her story. The old woman went on to say that young people always think they know too much, that they are even wiser than their parents. She continued that although some parents act out of greed, most marriages were arranged in the best interest of the young couple.

"Now it looks like you have learnt your lesson," the old woman continued. "Here, take these three eggs. I can already tell that the monster is frantically looking for

38

you. When he comes close enough just throw one egg behind you, and you will see what will happen."

"Nana, thank you very much. May the gods bless you."

"Never mind. From now on show a little respect for the traditions that have guarded us as a people over the years. We modify or change them entirely when there are good reasons for the changes. May the gods go with you."

Pomaa started to run again, and soon she could hear heavy thumping coming from behind her. She turned and saw her strange husband taking long strides and the earth shaking in fear. There appeared a menacing grin on his face as he came closer to Pomaa. She threw one egg behind her, and immediately there arose a thick forest between her and the monster.

That gave her time to run farther away from him. After she had run a few miles and had even rested for a while, she realised that Kokuroko had freed himself from the thick jungle and was coming after her. When she threw the second egg it got transformed into a huge mountain with a very smooth surface. Kokuroko spent a long time climbing the mountain and slipping off. He was seething by this time, and he cursed Pomaa in a language not worth repeating to your ears.

The distance created was so wide that Pomaa even had time to nap. The monster's heavy stomping woke her up, and when he came close enough to touch her, she threw the last egg which broke and formed into a wide river between them.

The monster tried to swim across but he knew he was no swimmer and would soon drown. He waded into the river but it soon reached his nose and he knew it was time to step out of it. Determined, Kokuroko tore off the branch of a tree and floated on it to the other side, and started to chase Pomaa. But by this time Pomaa had reached the outskirts of the town and she ran home, thoroughly exhausted.

Her father was sitting and smoking his pipe when he saw a figure run towards the house and collapse before him. He shouted for his wife who came from the room and both of them turned the person over, only to discover that it was no other person than Pomaa. Her parents bombarded her with questions, hardly giving her time to reply:

"God, who is this?"

"Is that you, Pomaa?"

"Ei, Pomaa, where are you coming from?"

"Where is your husband?"

"Why didn't you ever come home?"

"Where are the young women who accompanied you?"

"Can't you talk?"

"Why are you looking so haggard, Pomaa?"

Pomaa's whole body shook with crying. Her parents allowed her to weep for a while, then her mother said it was enough or else she would get sick. After she had rested for a while, she told her story and still cried some more. Her mother gave her a hot bath and a massage. Her parents planned to teach the imposter a lesson. Soon after she had drunk the hot soup which her mother had prepared, Kokuroko arrived, looking just as handsome as he had looked during his first appearance. Pomaa's parents welcomed him with the customary drink of water and asked him to explain the purpose of his visit.

"Well, my in-laws," began the monster-now-turned-gentleman, "my wonderful wife clearly missed home and being the only child she never stopped worrying about you two. It was a subject of much concern to me too. So I felt it was time for her to pay you a visit. When she left I knew that I could not live without her even for a few days so I also came to be with you all, for a while."

"Where are the four young women who accompanied you to your father's kingdom?" asked Pomaa's father. The monster replied that they had all found husbands in his father's kingdom and that they would be coming to visit soon.

Pomaa's mother gave him food to eat and told him to rest for the night, and that after they had both spent a couple of days with them, he could go back to his father's kingdom with his wife. Meanwhile Pomaa's father had organized the Asafo company to be on the alert with their guns to finish off the monster. As he stepped out of the bathroom later in the evening, the army shot Kokuroko three times, and he fell to the ground and turned into the monster, thus confirming Pomaa's story.

Then something strange began to happen. The monster started to glide on the ground; like fat on a heated surface, he was melting! Initially, people began to flee for their lives. But satisfied that the monster was no longer powerful the people came close to find out what kind of substance was melting from the monster's body. It was pomade with an unusual scent.

Those who took only a little bit of the monster's pomade are the people who are easy to appease and who forgive easily. Those who took more than their fair share of the pomade are those who themselves are not malicious, but who neither forgive nor forget. Those who took too much are the recalcitrant and belligerent ones in the society, while the greedy ones who hoarded the monster's pomade are those with no patience at all, who reach for their guns, spears, bows and arrows and kill others at the flimsiest provocation.

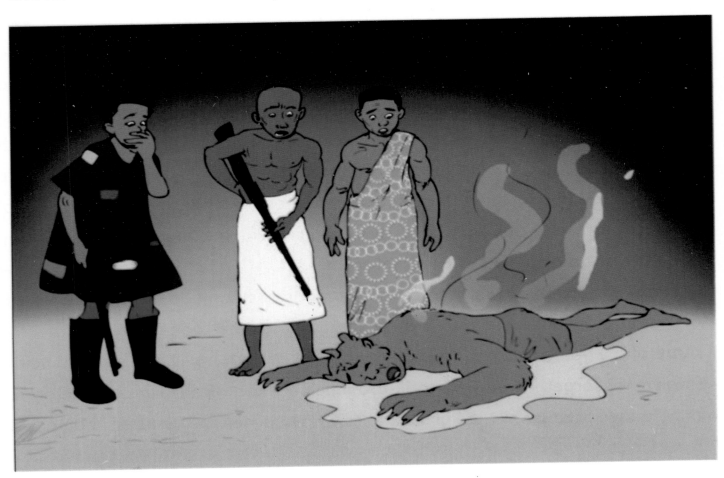

KWEKU ANANSE AND HIS FARM

Kweku Ananse lived in a village with his wife Aso and sons: big-headed Tikenenkene, skinny-legged Nyankronhweaa, huge-stomached Efudohwedohwe, and Ntikuma. This family, like others in the village, were mostly farmers. One particular year, the rains had been good and they had all worked very hard. The farm of the Ananse family was a sight to see. The cassava plants stood tall and leafy; the cocoyam plants showed off their wide leaves, resplendent in their greenness. Contrasting the various shades of green were the red and yellow peppers, the purple, white and light yellow eggplants and the tomatoes in various stages of ripeness. The yam creepers wound themselves snugly around the poles supplied for that purpose; their leaves were brown, signifying that they were ready to be harvested. The farm also had plantain and banana, orange, guava, avocado pear and pineapple plants in fruition.

There was enough food to feed the family for a long time, but we all know by now that Kweku Ananse is often self-centred and that his greed knows no bounds. The thought that everyone else would share in the fruits of their labour did not make Kweku Ananse happy. The sight of his son with the huge stomach, Efudohwedohwe, suddenly gave him nightmares. Ananse knew that boy had an enormous appetite and somehow, he felt there would not be enough food for everyone. Therefore, Ananse's resolution was to devise a strategy to have all the farm produce for himself.

One day Aso and the big-headed Tikenenkene went to the farm to bring home some food. They uprooted some cassava, plucked eggplants and some tomatoes. They also cut off some cocoyam leaves and a bunch of plantains. Just as they were arranging the produce on the wooden platter they had brought with them, they saw skinny Nyankronhweaa running towards them and shouting at the top of his voice:

"Mother! Come home immediately because father is dying!" he gasped.

"What do you mean he 'is dying'? I left the man with a huge bowl of boiled yams and stew which he was eating with relish. How can he be dying so suddenly?" Aso found it hard to believe the bad news.

Tikenenkene told his mother they should just hurry on home and find out for themselves. He hurriedly picked up the platter, carried it on his head and they all started running towards the village.

The crowd of people around their home told them that something serious was going on. Tikenenkene threw the wooden platter along with the produce onto the ground and followed by Aso, they rushed to Kweku Ananse's sickbed. Ananse had put huge dabs of shea butter ointment over his eyes and placed wet towels over his forehead. He was also shivering uncontrollably. Ananse had reduced his speech to hardly audible whispers and from all appearances it looked like the man was in great pain.

"Kweku, my husband, who has done this to you? Who has given my enemies this chance to fling my inadequacies at me?" Aso started wailing.

The neighbours shouted her down, because it is an ill omen to wail when life remains, even in the dying. Ananse really looked so genuine in his deception that people in the room were even afraid to sneeze, thinking his system would not survive the pressure from the air. Ananse then signalled for his wife and sons to come closer. The neighbours withdrew, feeling that Ananse needed privacy with his family before he died. Aso collected her emotions together and fetched a calabash

48

of water for her dying husband to drink, for he needed the water to sustain him on the journey he was about to undertake.

Amid great show of pain and difficulty, Ananse whispered his dying wishes to his family. And what were these wishes? Ananse told them that as soon as he finished talking he would die.

He continued that they must bury him at once in the farm, and that they must not observe the usual rituals of washing the body with herbs, lime and soap; neither must they try to preserve it and lay it in state for the wake-keeping.

He went on that the coffin must neither be nailed nor should the shallow grave be filled. Into the coffin, Ananse directed, must be placed cooking utensils, salt and a water pot. His family must stay away from the farm for a whole year. He made sure that his last sentence trailed off, to give the impression that he did not even have the energy to fully make his wish.

Ananse was so successful in orchestrating his final moments in life that at the time no one thought of asking him questions. Later on Ntikuma was the first to ask his mother what kind of strange wish his father had made, to be buried without rituals and on his farm, along with cooking pots and ladles. Aso told her son that his father, as he knew without any doubt, was a very wise man, that even

Onyankopon sometimes envied Ananse of his wisdom, so they must simply comply with the wish.

With a great show of restraint, Aso quickly closed all the windows and trimmed the finger and toe nails of her husband's corpse. After that she wiped his face with a wet towel and combed his hair. She knew that he did not want the body to be washed, but certainly people would like to look at his face before the coffin was covered. After she had clothed him in his finest cloths, she threw open the windows and started a wail which brought the neighbours and well-wishers to join in the funeral wail. Some wept for the widow and the children, while the funeral reminded others either of their own losses or of the inevitable end of all mankind, and so they wept accordingly.

Some of the relatives and neighbours who were sitting on stools and raised planks discussed Ananse's last wishes. They found Ananse's instructions to be very unusual indeed. Their own experiences with dying wishes had to do with people disclosing important information about family heirlooms, with sharing of property, making a confession or settling an old dispute, to ensure that life would continue peacefully among the living. However, pressure was brought to bear on Aso and her children to grant the wishes of Ananse in order to avoid calamity. The elders explained that a dying man was in closer touch with the ancestors than anyone. Not even the performance of libation brought the ancestors closer to man than the smell of death. As a result, the death wish is really the wishes of the ancestors, and the living must obey them to the minutest detail. The neighbours also told Aso and her sons not to worry about food because they could harvest from their own farms.

Before long, Ananse was carried to his grave by his sons who asked that their father remember them from the land of the ancestors when someone was coming their way. Ananse was buried according to his wishes which soon passed into the narrative and songs of the people of the village.

Soon after this event life returned to normal, and true to their words, the neighbours were most kind to Aso and her children. They provided food and more importantly, a lot of love and warmth in their time of grief. The youth of the village made sure that the Ananse children never missed any of the hunting, fishing or wrestling activities. The boys made a lot more friends, and they also acquired more skills like playing drums and flutes, weaving cloth and baskets, and carving from wood and stone than they did when their father was alive. Indeed the members of the village chose Aso's compound as the venue for storytelling and the mending of farm implements. It also became a place where the women braided their hair and shared information about the medicinal and culinary values of herbs and as well, about how to deal with wayward husbands and difficult children. They were careful to avoid topics that dealt with death or widowhood.

However, Ntikuma was never happy with the whole business, but he was afraid to voice his anxiety, what with the lecture about ancestors and death wishes delivered by the elders. He was concerned that they would think he was unappreciative of their acts of kindness and even worse, that he had no respect for the elders. One day, without telling anyone about his plan, he stole over to their farm. To his dismay, someone had harvested from it. His father's favourite, the cocoyam leaves, were nearly all gone; as well, the eggplants and the okros were also slowly disappearing. He speculated about what was happening. He gathered courage and went about ten feet to the grave; it did not look greatly disturbed. He was satisfied that at least his father was resting in peace. He counted the leaves on a particular cocoyam plant and when he returned the following day, he saw that plant had two leaves too few. He also closely examined the eggplant and the okro, and concluded that someone was taking bits of food at a time from the farm.

The discovery weighed so heavily on his mind that he felt he should share the information. He dismissed Efudohwedohwe of the huge stomach as a confidant because he has no head for secrets. Besides, his sole interest lies with food. Of all the new activities and professions to which they have been introduced, he had shown interest only in the process for preserving game. His brother Skinny Legs?

No thank you. This was not about a marathon. Granted, he is a good runner, but Ntikuma wanted someone to plan with. And then he remembered the problems

Bighead had with thinking and planning and knew that he was instantly disqualified. The only one left was Aso his mother. That woman never ceased to amaze Ntikuma. Even though she was afraid of taking chances, she was nonetheless a very intelligent, beautiful woman. Maybe he could confide in her.

Ntikuma waited until his mother had finished her work for the day and was sitting threading beads while boiling some barks in a pot, when he spoke:

"Mother, something is deeply troubling me, and I think you are the only person I can talk to."

"Ah! Ntikuma, my son, what is the problem?" Aso put down the string of beads and looked anxiously at her son. "You know you can always talk to me. I am aware that you do not always take my advice but that has never stopped me from offering it anyway. I am your mother, you are the first fruit of my womb and you are very special to me. Tell me. Whatever it is   you can always tell me." Aso spoke to her son with such assurance that he felt encouraged to continue: "Mother, I have been to our farm and..."

"Hey, Ntikuma, what are you talking about? I know you are bold but this one beats me. Do you want the whole village to suffer a catastrophe? Or have you forgotten your father's wishes? We have not even celebrated all the funeral rites yet. How can you show such disrespect?" Aso was quite disturbed.

"But mother, you promised to listen," Ntikuma pleaded with his mother.

"I know I did but I did not suspect you had broken such a taboo. Anyway, let me hear the whole story."

"Well, at the farm I discovered that someone had harvested some of our crops. You know Papa's favourite cocoyam leaves? They were nearly gone, and so were the eggplants and other vegetables. The long and the short of it is that someone is taking advantage of the death wish in order to harvest our crops and I mean to find out who it is."

"My son, let me confide this in you. You have always been sensible and I believe I can talk to you like another adult. I have never understood your father's very strange death wish. I hate to admit it but I have been wondering if your father did not simply take advantage of people's respect for the wishes of a dying person just in order to get away with something sinister. Ntikuma, there are times when I ask myself if people are not even mocking us for starting a practice which buries people along with cooking oil and mashing bowls. I am aware that the traditions have been installed by the elders for the good of us all, but I also know that there are times when traditions are amended or even set aside all together, depending on the times and circumstances.

"My grandmother told me that in the olden days when a chief or a very important person died a human being was sacrificed; the ancestors were believed to respond only to human blood, at the demise of royalty. For generations it looked like there was no other way of calling on the ancestors. Then when things began to change animals, especially white sheep, took the place of human beings and were sacrificed. The ancestors still responded. The practice became so prevalent that people almost forgot that actual human beings were once sacrificed like the sheep. The sacrifice of sheep, with time, was modified somehow and sheep of different colours and even goats were sacrificed. Still the ancestors did not complain; they continued to come to our aid when we called for their assistance through the sacrifice of goats and brown, black or multi-coloured sheep.

"Today even animals are rarely used to express our urgent need for the assistance of the departed. When there is a serious occurrence libation is performed, and the ancestors react, as usual. And when you are very desperate and you have no gin, you can even use water, and believe me, the ancestors will not fail you. You see, this tells me that the practices have always been amenable to change, as long as the changes truly reflect the interests of all. What I am trying to tell you, my son, is that I agree that we must find out exactly what is happening, irrespective of the death wish of your father. The neighbours have been very supportive, but why should we continue to eat from other people's farms as if we are unable to feed ourselves?"

Ntikuma then told his mother that he had planted a scarecrow on the farm and had coated it all over with sticky glue, the kind that comes from the rubber tree, and that he planned to catch the thief. After all if the thief had eaten from the farm and survived all this while, then surely they could also harvest their own produce and live.

Meanwhile the thief was no other person than Kweku Ananse, buried in his own farm in a shallow, uncovered grave and with cooking utensils at his disposal. His strategy was to sleep during the day and cook at night. When dusk fell and he knew that most farmers had returned home, he would crawl out of the grave and inspect his traps for game. He was nearly always lucky because the farm knew very little human activity.

The calmness on the farm was an inducement for the deer and the grass cutters who walked right into the traps. Then Ananse would gather fresh vegetables, uproot some cassava and with a piece of the dried game, make a huge pot of soup, pound fufu and enjoy it, while he called the villagers foolish for sticking to customs whose meanings had long evaporated.

One such evening Kweku Ananse was not so lucky and fate caught up with him. After a heavy meal Ananse decided to go for a walk; he had discovered he slept better when his stomach was not so full. After enjoying some pawpaw and after taking in the cool, fresh air for a while, he spotted something that looked like a human being. He moved closer and found that the other person remained at the same spot. Ananse took the scarecrow for a frightened thief and approached the figure:

"Good evening," Ananse greeted the figure, who gave no reply. Ananse misinterpreted the silence of the figure to be his fear of being found on someone else's farm.

"Hey! Don't you know how to respond when people greet you? Didn't your parents teach you that? At any rate, what are you doing on my farm and at such a time? Only a thief goes to someone else's farm at night," Ananse enquired sharply, but the figure was still quiet.

"If you don't reply I will give you a nasty slap. I said what do you want on my farm?" At the lack of response Ananse let loose his right hand and delivered a slap to the glue-coated scarecrow.

"Let go of my hand. Can't you hear me? Hey! Not only are you a thief, you also have no respect for your elders. Look here! Who raised you? Didn't anyone ever teach you to answer questions? And if you were never taught how to answer questions, haven't you observed other people do it so you could do the same? What you don't know is that my left hand is stronger than my right. So, take this one too."

With these words Ananse slapped the dummy, and his left hand similarly got stuck to its cheek.

Ananse gave the effigy a kick, and so his left foot also got stuck to the object. Through the same process his right foot got stuck to the scarecrow.

"Listen, you big fool, if I hit you with my stomach, there will be nothing of you left by the time your relatives come to look for you. Haven't you heard that I am the

father of Efudohwedohwe of the huge stomach? Yes, that's me, the one and only Kweku Ananse... I said, let go of my limbs!" Making good on his threat, Ananse thus ended up with his stomach also stuck to the sticky dummy.

By the time the first cock's crowing was heard, and Ananse was in a panic:

"My friend... Ha! Ha! I know you are surprised at me calling you my friend. I just pretended to be angry with you. In the village from which my forebears migrated that is how they used to find out who true friends were. They insult the friend for a while, and the longer he takes to get angry the better friend he would be. You know, just let me go, and you can come to this farm as often as you want."

(*Silence*)

"I have been here for a couple of months now and you don't have to take the food away to be cooked if you don't want to. I promise to cook for the two of us. Listen, I have smoked meat of every kind - venison, grass-cutter, duiker, bat... I even have monkey meat. And you can choose what you want to eat. I am good at making any kind of soup: groundnut soup, palm nut soup, light soup, green soup. I can also pound and turn the fufu all by myself; and I can also make mashed yam or plantain and add ripe avocado pears to it. If none of that appeals to you, I can tempt you with roasted cocoyam or yam eaten with fresh pepper and salted fish... Good friend, what work do you do? I will offer you free labour, in addition to cooked food of your choice, if only you will release me."

(*Silence*)

Second cock crow.

Ananse was beginning to feel desperate, because he could tell from the coolness of the air that it would soon be morning. He started begging:

"My lord and master, descendant of the parrot who eats palm nuts and allows some to fall on the ground, the gracious and generous one you who feeds orphans and widows and provides shelter to the homeless, the courageous one who singlehandedly kills the leopard and restores peace to the cowardly! I am your humble servant; my life is in your hands. I do not deserve to come so close to you. Please release me, that I may find my proper place..." Ananse was crying now, and calling on his ancestors to come to his aid.

Still the object made no compromise, and when the sky started to clear, Ananse saw that he had been trapped. Nothing hurt him more than the possibility of public disgrace. He decided to plead with whoever found him first.

Soon he heard footsteps, and they belonged to none other than his son Ntikuma.

"Ei! What do I see here? Father! What are you doing stuck to this effigy which I planted to catch the thief?"

"My son, I fathered you. Remind yourself of how the elders express it, that when

the nakedness of the head of your family is shown in public you also suffer the humiliation."

"Father, when we meet my mother and the whole village, you can recite all the proverbs you know to them."

Ntikuma dragged his father home, still bound to the effigy. The whole village, including Aso and her sons, came to hoot at Ananse and remind each other to avoid greed like the plague.

67

Ananse knew he deserved the punishment, but he could not bear the way the people of the village never wasted any opportunity to let him know that they strongly condemned his behaviour. Unable to bear any more derision, Ananse changed into a spider and jumped to the corner of the roof, where he has been living till this day.

KWEKU ANANSE AND THE HAIRY MONSTER

Once upon a time God had a tree. It was a huge, strong tree and it was obvious that no man could fell it with one stroke of an axe. However, God guaranteed that he would make a gift of half of his kingdom and a fattened cow to anyone who was successful at felling the tree with one stroke. The competitor was to do the job all by himself, although he could ask for help before he actually felled the tree. Many men entered the competition, including the carver, the hunter and Kweku Ananse the spider.

The people of God's village felt that the carver stood a good chance at accomplishing the feat, given his expedience with wood. The carver called for the help of a blacksmith, and God paid for the services of the most famous blacksmith in the land. The blacksmith made an axe of a special design, according to the wishes of the carver. The whole town followed the carver to the tree to see how he would fell the tree with one stroke. Once at the foot of the tree the carver took his axe and with all his might, he struck the tree which did not even as much as give the slightest evidence that it had been touched.

The carver had failed, and the townspeople derided him all the way back to the village. He became the subject of such gossip and mockery that he eventually moved to another town with his family.

A few months later, the hunter told God that he wished to try felling the tree. God asked him what he needed and the hunter called for a priest. God paid for the services of the chief priest who assisted the hunter. The hunter wanted the priest to strengthen him spiritually, which he did after the hunter had provided him with eggs, yams, palm oil and honey. The priest gave the hunter amulets to wear around his waist, ankles and wrists for a couple of weeks before the appointed day. When the day came the priest daubed the hunter all over with a white powder and made some patterns on his face and arms with red earth. The hunter also wore a skirt made of raffia and danced his way towards the tree. As in the case of the carver, the townspeople thronged along with the hunter who looked imposing in his raffia skirt and other accoutrements. But the tree was not impressed. Neither was it moved by the prolonged libation which the priest poured. The tree did not even acknowledge the blow which the hunter dealt with all his might. Since no human being merits disgrace, the hunter quickly moved out of town.

So when Kweku Ananse the spider declared his candidacy for the competition the people of the land could not hide their contempt:

"I wonder if Ananse has never seen his reflection against the wall or in the river."

"Talk about ambition!"

"Some people simply do not know what is beyond them."

"Ananse really has no sense of proportion."

"The problem is not that he chooses to do it, but that he is given the chance at all."

"Just compare the strength in his tiny legs and the narrowness of his waist to the strong brawny structure of the carver and especially the hunter, and tell me what chance Ananse has."

When Ananse got home his family was worried. His wife Aso spoke:

"Kweku, my husband, what do you need half of God's kingdom and a whole cow for? We have enough to get by, and if you fail we will be so mocked and degraded that we will have to go and start another village altogether. Think about it again."

"Father," continued his son Ntikuma, "I would not be so worried if the rules allowed you to have help with cutting the tree because then I could offer my help, not that it would make much difference, anyway. I know that you are a very strong man, but I also think that Mother is right. You will only succeed at bringing us all into disrepute. Just consider what will happen to us all."

Determined to win half the kingdom and the fattened cow, Ananse walked away from the argument and headed straight for the house of Nyame. It was in the heat of the afternoon, and after a good meal Nyame was drinking cool water when Ananse called on him and explained his intentions. Nyame actually froze in shock for the space of a few seconds.

"Kweku Ananse, are you sure of what you are saying?" he asked.

"I am certain. Is the cow tethered?"

"But you have not felled the tree, how can we talk of the cow? No one sits down without bending," God told Ananse. "At any rate I like your confidence, and I will give you a chance. What do you need by way of preparation?"

When Ananse asked for a pipe, the counsellors who had assembled gave Ananse up for mad but they advised that he be supplied with the pipe and be given the chance like the other two. On the appointed day no one was willing to waste a whole day to watch something as palpably incredible as a spider cutting a huge tree with one stroke of an axe. Even his family didn't want to be part of an ill-fated expedition. Only the crow decided to go with Ananse and report to God, so the two of them set off for the forest.

At the site, Ananse took his axe and started polishing it while he got into a conversation with Crow. Crow perched himself on top of a tree close to the one Ananse was supposed to fell. After sharpening the axe for a while Ananse asked Crow to go to the village and light his pipe for him. While Crow flew off, Ananse started to hack at the tree from the side opposite to where Crow had settled. As soon as he heard wings flapping in the distance, Ananse pretended to be asleep. Crow spent a long time trying to wake Ananse up. At one point Crow thought Ananse was dead! Ananse explained that he wakes up faster when called from about half a mile away, so next time Crow should call from a distance. Crow agreed.

Ananse picked up his axe and started polishing it while they conversed about this and that. Soon he said that the fire had gone out of the pipe and it needed to be lit again. So off Crow went, while Ananse cut the tree further. He quickly sat down and continued with sharpening his axe when he heard Crow's squawk.

The next excuse was to advise Crow to put the glowing coal on top of the tobacco and not at the bottom. Then, Crow had to go to the village again on account of the pipe because Ananse said he wanted the glowing coal underneath the tobacco and not on top, and that Crow had misunderstood him. Yet another trip had to be made because Crow did not empty the ashes in the pipe before filling it with tobacco. After that it was because Crow had used the tobacco tree beyond the river and not the tree just at the foot of the anthill. Ananse came up with several other reasons why Crow had to be gone for long hours and leave him alone.

Finally, when Ananse saw that the dents he had made were enough to allow him to fell the tree with a single blow, he told Crow that he was ready. Crow knew he had simply wasted the day, and so you can imagine his shock when with one blow, the tree came tumbling down! Immediately, he flew to the house of God and told him the incredible news. God and his counsellors went to the site to verify for themselves. Ananse was carried shoulder high to the palace and given half of God's kingdom and as well, the fattened cow. Nyame and his counsellors started looking at Ananse differently, so that when he requested that no public announcement be made of his success until he had given the order, his wishes were respected.

What we know apart from Ananse's ability to outwit everyone is that he can also be very selfish, even at times when there is no need for it. Ananse decided to eat the cow all by himself, since even his family had discouraged him from entering the competition and his neighbours had made rude remarks about his ambition and the strength in his limbs and so on.

"Just fancy them making a fool of me," he mused as he walked away with the cow. "And who said it was a test of strength anyway? I saw it as a test of wits, and I was right. I can imagine them now giving me appellations and their women singing my praises not because they are impressed but because they want some of the meat. That will not happen. And I thought that after all these years my wife would express a little faith in me. What did I get from her but concerns about becoming a laughingstock and building a new village? As for Ntikuma, I wonder what kind of person he is going to become if he is afraid to take chances..."

Ananse travelled deep into the forest, to a place which even the flies did not know about. There, he quartered the cow, sprinkled salt, pepper and other spices over it before he realised he did not have any fire. So Ananse climbed to the top of a tall tree and saw smoke coiling from a nearby bush. When he went there to get some fire, what did he see?

Ananse saw the hairiest creature he had ever seen, eating in front of a fire. The hair was so thick that it grew like tall grass, covering the ears and eyes of the beast. Kweku Ananse stood and stared for a while, when he found out that in order to eat his food, the brute had to part the hairs over his mouth with his hairy fingers. What any other person would do in such a situation is simply to get some live coals and move on, but certainly not Ananse. He decided that since the monster could not see, he would steal some of his yam.

He quickly entered an eating contest with the monster. When the creature took one piece of yam, Ananse would take another, making sure that their hands did not meet in the pot at the same time. It was obvious that Ananse's appetite was no match for the monster's; nevertheless, Ananse would take the yam as often as did the monster, and he would throw away what he had not finished. Ananse ate the yam until there was only one piece left. Did he leave it for the hairy monster? Oh, No! Ananse struggled with the hairy man over the last piece of yam until the monster understood why his yams had finished so soon.

In addition, Ananse teased the monster and insulted him as he walked away with the fire. The monster did not say much, except, "You wait and see." Ananse

got to where he had quartered the cow, made a fire and started to dry the meat over fire. He also made a pot of soup and got ready to enjoy it. As soon as he directed the first handful to his mouth, the hairy monster appeared and in one gulp, poured the entire pot of soup down his gullet and went away.

Every time Kweku Ananse cooked, the hairy monster would come and eat up all the food. This went on until only the head of the cow remained and Ananse had become desperate. Can you imagine Ananse losing weight? Well, his legs were hardly visible by the time he went home. He called his son Ntikuma:

"My son, I need your help. There is someone in the forest who is harassing me to such an extent that I cannot even bring home the meat I have trapped. You need to come and help me kill a monster that has eaten the meat I was drying for us all.

"But why didn't you bring the meat home so we could all do it?" asked his son.

"Listen, son, do you know something? If we waste time going over such issues, by the time our discussion comes to an end so will the meat."

With these words both of them rushed to the forest where they saw the hairy monster, having eaten too much and resting soundly. With the help of the sharp axe he had used to fell God's tree, Ananse and his son killed the monster and dragged it home. Those who came early to see the monster are the people who retain their thick long hair, while those who were not moved by the news are the people who lose even the thin hair they have and eventually become bald.

THE HAWK AND THE HEN

The hawk often circles in the air, waiting to pounce on a little chick which it carries away for its meals. Is it plain cruelty on the part of the hawk? Why does Hawk feed on little chicks and why is the hen never able to defend her own against him, given that she is at times able to stave off even the cobra? This will help us to understand the behaviour of Hawk, so let us all listen and pass on the story...

Hawk was a fisherman and Hen, a farmer. The two lived close to each other. They were neighbourly and would even borrow an item from each other whenever the need arose.

One evening Hen visited Hawk and they discussed many subjects of mutual interest like the festivals, the recent achievements of the two Asafo companies who managed to save the old man who had fallen into the shallow gold pit and their success at steering the lost canoe to the beach. They were not too happy, however, with the occasional clashes between the various groups.

"Imagine the peace of the whole village threatened over the refusal of one company to allow the other to march past its own part of the village!" Hawk said.

"I think that the gin flowed too freely on that day. These occurrences are rare, unless the first company did not pay the respect due the other," that was Hen's analysis of the near conflict.

"I think we need more forms of entertainment in the village, don't you think so?" asked Hawk.

Hen was enthusiastic. "Entertainment? Why not? At least some of us can learn some more traditional dances and teach those who never learnt them."

The two of them came to the conclusion that if they owned a drum, they could play in the evenings and invite others to join in the fun. They discussed their plan at length and resolved to go to the forest and cut some tree trunks to make a drum.

Before they parted for the night they had agreed that Hen would call Hawk when she was ready so they could leave early the next day.

Come morning, when Hawk had waited for quite some time, he wanted to find out what was keeping Hen so long. When he got Hen's house he saw that Hen was in the process of braiding her hair. The impression was that Hen was not about to leave home. He asked her:

"I have been waiting for so long. Why are you not ready?"

"I don't think I can go with you, Hawk."

"And why not?"

"Because I am busy, and… also… sick, yes, very sick" replied Hen evasively.

"I know you can finish braiding your hair soon enough, and as to the work on the drum, you need not worry too much about that. You really don't have to do the felling of the tree. I just want your company. You can watch while I cut the tree. Look, I have some fresh corn which we can roast for a snack if we get hungry."

"No, Hawk, I really can't go, because I am sick, as I told you," Hen said with a lot of vigour.

"If that is the case, Hen, can I borrow your axe?"

"Hawk, when I am sick my axe also falls sick," said Hen, quite unreasonably.

"I never knew that axes could fall sick. How about your machete?" Hawk asked.

"My machete is also sick."

"Can I borrow your water pot then because this job can take the whole day and you know my water pot got broken last week and I haven't had the time to make a new one," Hawk pleaded with Hen.

"Hawk, what I am telling you is that when I fall sick, everything I own also falls sick so don't go on to ask for my cutlass and my cooking pot as well."

Hawk was completely surprised by Hen's behaviour, and so he turned to other neighbours who lent him the items he needed without much ado.

When Hawk finally finished making the drum on a day at the end of the dry season, he left it in the sun to dry. Then he went to the farm to bring home some groundnuts. While he was at the farm, he heard someone playing a drum, and the sounds coming from the drum told him that the drum was his. Hawk immediately stopped what he was doing and rushed home. There was no one near the drum, which was exactly where he had left it.

He asked Hen if anyone had played his drum and Hen asked him if he was losing his mind, hearing music where there was none. This went on for a couple of times until Hawk nearly believed that he was actually going insane, because whenever he went out to his farm or to the beach to mend his nets he clearly heard someone playing his drum.

Determined to find out who had been playing his drum, Hawk decided to play a trick on the one he suspected to be the culprit. He told Hen he was going to the beach to mend his nets, and that he would be away for a long while. He passed by the front of Hen's hut, so Hen knew that Hawk was away. But Hawk was hiding behind the coconut tree just a few meters from his hut. Soon, Hen came out of her hut and went to get Hawk's drum and started playing it, while singing:

Hawk is a fool,
Indeed he is a fool.
Hawk is a fool,

Indeed he is a fool.

When Hawk wakes up in the morning,

He washes his face upwards.

Oh! It's true he washes it upwards.

Hawk is a fool,

Indeed he is a fool.

She danced while she played, stamping her feet, clapping and flapping her wings to the rhythm of the beat. Hawk waited for a while until Hen had danced herself into a frenzy, when he rushed from behind the coconut tree and pounced on Hen.

"Ooooh! Hen, today I have caught you! Shame on you! You refused to go with me to the forest, not even to watch while I did the hard work of cutting the tree. And then when I wanted to borrow your axe and cutlass you told me they were too sick to work. Have you ever heard of a sick axe and a sick machete since God created seven days? And you almost made me believe I was going out of my mind! So, I am a fool, aren't I! When you start dancing in my soup pot today, the two of us can determine the direction in which we wash our faces in the morning." Hawk was very angry with Hen, who, terrified, was squawking her lungs out.

"Hawk, in the name of your granduncle... the one you loved best... about whom you have told me so much... please let me go... I promise I will never play your drum again..."

"Leave my favourite granduncle out of this. In fact he will be very angry with me if I do not take any revenge for your deception and your meanness."

"Listen, tomorrow we can make another drum..." Hen was weeping.

"Tomorrow? Tomorrow I plan to get sick and my energy will be sick too. Now, you should understand this language better than anyone else. Today you will surely sing and dance in my soup pot," Hawk told Hen pitilessly. The commotion brought out one of their neighbours, the Crow. He asked what the fuss was about, and Hawk angrily narrated the story to him. The old crow, amazed by Hen's behaviour but nevertheless mindful of Hawk's bad temper, advised:

"Hen, you have not done well at all. What made you think of farm implements that fall sick? You have been dishonest and that is unpardonable. However, Hawk, when even your enemy runs to you when his life is in danger, you do not hold his previous offenses against him. You rather show your humaneness by offering protection. You know that if you kill Hen, the little ones who are about to be hatched will experience no life. Therefore, I suggest that you let Hen go for the time being, and when her eggs are hatched, you can take one of her chicks in her place." Hen was so relieved at the reprieve that she quickly agreed to the verdict.

Since that day, Hawk has been feeding on little chicks. Hen can only shout and prance about all she wants but she has never gathered the courage to fight off Hawk because she knows that Hawk is justified in his acts.

THE WOLF FALLS INTO HIS OWN TRAP

Once upon a time there lived two friends, Kweku Ananse the spider and his friend the wolf. We all know that Kweku Ananse knows how to use words and his wits to get out of tricky potentially dangerous situations. I believe you can all recall how he got the two friends, Lion and Tiger, to kill each other so that he could live in peace. The wolf, too, was full of tricks and cunning. These two friends were both very successful hunters. They lived in the same house and shared their catch as well as saved towards acquiring other possessions like cloth and gold.

But what was really going on was that each was planning to get rid of the other so that he could own all that they had acquired together. One day in the rainy season, while Ananse walked over a bridge on his way home from a hunting expedition, he tripped on a banana peel and had a bad fall. What was worse, his gun fell from his hand and into the river which had overflowed its banks Ananse knew that it was futile to attempt to retrieve his gun, and so he limped home sadly.

When he narrated his misadventure to Wolf the latter pretended to sympathize with his friend. In fact he was sorry that Ananse himself had not fallen into the river. He told Ananse to look on the bright side, because he was still alive. He additionally reassured him that whenever he did not feel like hunting, Ananse could borrow his gun. Ananse felt greatly comforted by the concern of his friend. Ananse stayed away from hunting for a number of days while he nursed his sprained ankle back to health. For this, he got a lot of help from a reputed old woman who was the best herbal doctor around. The old woman broke the leg of a chicken and tied the same pounded herb to the chicken's leg as she did to Ananse's foot; she told him that they would both be healed at the same time, which they were.

While Ananse was taking care of his limb, Wolf was planning a way of getting rid of his friend. He summoned the rats and made them dig a deep hole near the end of the path that led to the stream.

When this was completed, he told Ananse that he had been indoors for too long, and so they should go for a walk. Ananse was keen on the invitation, having been cooped up at home for too long. As they walked towards the stream Ananse

told Wolf about the powers of the herbalist and Wolf told Ananse about some of his adventures in the forest.

The two friends suddenly came upon a freshly dug hole, and as Ananse wondered aloud what it was meant for, Wolf aimed his gun at Ananse and asked him to go down into the pit and lay flat on the floor. Ananse was stupefied; he stood as one bereft of his senses, completely taken aback by the behaviour and utterance of his friend. He started to laugh, thinking that Wolf was making poor attempts at a practical joke. But a closer look at the face of his friend told him that it was no laughing matter. Wolf meant business, and he told Ananse that if he played dumb he would shoot him. Ananse had to think very fast about how to get out of such a complex situation. When Wolf repeated the order for the third time, Ananse knew it was time to comply, so he went into the pit and stood in it.

"I want you to lie flat on the ground," Wolf shouted.

Ananse decided to act stupid indeed by pretending that he did not understand the instructions. He raised his hands, and when Wolf shouted at him to be sensible, he knelt down. Wolf told him again in a loud voice that he should lie down flat, at which Ananse stooped in the pit. When Wolf told him to sleep like he does in the night, Ananse told him that he hangs by the roof, so he would have to be moved to the mouth of the pit before he could position himself in like manner. That was when Wolf got so annoyed that he sent his insults to the man and woman who had made such a terrible mistake as to bestow an idiot of a creature like Ananse on humanity. Ananse was not moved by the harsh words; he continued to act as if he had never in his life heard an order to lie flat.

Ananse, as we know, is no fool. He knew that if he lay flat on floor of the pit, Wolf would either simply shoot him or bury him alive with the stones and piles of sand nearby. As he played the fool, he was devising a plan to get out of the pit and make Wolf pay for his treachery. Wolf got so tired and exasperated by the supposed idiocy of his friend that he asked Ananse to come out, so that he would demonstrate what he meant. At this point, Ananse had to stop himself from loudly rejoicing at the chance to pay Wolf back in his own coin. Instead, he meekly crawled out of the pit by using the ladder which Wolf had supplied and stood by, looking as miserable as roasted mushrooms.

Emboldened by Ananse's show of timidity, Wolf jumped into the pit and stretched himself on the floor. The first thing Ananse did was to remove the ladder.

Wolf realised his folly too late, and Ananse started to heap stones and sand into the pit as he buried his treacherous friend. Ananse knew that if he gave in to the pleas of Wolf, then he would not just have acted the fool, he would have lived it.

HOW DO SOME PEOPLE SHOW THEIR GRATITUDE?

In the land where people and animals lived in complete harmony to the extent that they even spoke the same language, there once lived three able, young men who were good friends. These friends were not salaried workers. What they did for a living was to trap animals in exchange for other goods like woven cloth or precious metals.

One day, while out hunting they saw a big grass cutter which they started chasing. The three men ran fast, but the grasscutter ran even faster, dodging between the cassava plants and the smaller trees. Finally, the grasscutter saw a hole and jumped right in. The three men reached the area where the animal had run to and saw a couple of holes in the ground. They decided to try them all. One of the hunters stretched his hand into a hole in an effort to bring out the grass-cutter, and he felt a slight prick on his palm. When his arm began to swell almost immediately, he understood that he had been stung by a cobra. However, he did not disclose what he had experienced to the others. He just told them:

I think the grasscutter is in there but I can't get it out.'

"Why not?" asked the second one impatiently. "Just step aside so that I can bring out the animal."

He also stretched his hand and felt a similar prick. He knew then that his friend did not want to be the only one to suffer.

"Ah! This animal is wise. See how it is moving about in the hole!" he exclaimed.

By this time the third hunter was getting angry with his friends and cut in.

"Why call yourself hunters if you cannot even pull a harmless animal like a grasscutter out of a hole? One hunter cannot get the animal out and another one wants to spin a whole tale about its movement in the hole! Move yourself away so that I can bring the animal out of the hole. You'll see which part ends up on top of your fufu today." He tried to pull out the grasscutter he tried to pull out the grasscutter and was greeted by the sting.

They understood the danger they were in since the sting of the cobra was extremely dangerous. That was no time for asking questions. Their arms were swelling very fast and they had to get home immediately. Only the third one got home. The other two, overcome by the poison, had started vomiting and had collapsed on the way.

As soon as he told his story and indicated where the hole was to be found the third friend also collapsed and died. A search party, made up of men of their

age group, was immediately organized to bring back the bodies of the other two young hunters and kill the menacing cobra. The men armed themselves with guns, cutlasses, clubs and sharpened sticks set off, singing Asafo war songs.

When the cobra heard the war songs he knew he was the object of the search. He immediately started looking for a place to hide. In his wanderings he met a hunter.

"Hunter, please hide me," he pleaded.

"Why? What have you done wrong?"

"We will talk about it later, but you must hide me at once and don't tell anyone that you have seen me."

"I can help, but the question is: where do I hide you? I only have my gun and I have left my sack for carrying game at the other side of the forest, you know, just before the river. If you will walk with me to the..."

"My lord Hunter, let me wind myself around your waist so that you can cover me with your top garment until the search party passes, and then we can talk further," proposed the cobra hurriedly.

Shortly afterwards a group of young men holding guns, cutlasses and sticks approached the hunter.

"Young men, what brings you here in such a state? Is someone missing?" he enquired.

"Papa Hunter, a cobra has stung three strong, able-bodied young men to death," their leader spoke.

"Oh! What a pity! I can just imagine what their mothers are feeling inside of their intestines. Death really has no shame. Does it have to come for three active men and at the same time? Didn't Death see those old people who are brought out daily and dried in the sun like washed clothes?" the hunter sympathized.

"We are looking for the cobra," continued another member of the search party, "in order to prevent him from causing any further harm. Have you seen a cobra around here, somewhere?"

"A cobra? No, I haven't seen a cobra but I just saw the foot marks of the elephant and when I stopped to light my pipe and examine the prints I could see that he was moving away from the river, maybe after drinking..." the hunter continued.

"Papa hunter, we have to be going," the leader concluded the discussion and the party followed him.

When the search party had disappeared into the distance the hunter grinned at the cobra, satisfied about his success at hiding the fleeing animal.

"Now I have to sting you too, until you die" intoned Cobra.

Astonished, the hunter asked:

"Why so?"

The cobra replied by asking another question: "What is the usual way of showing gratitude?"

"What kind of question is that, Cobra?" asked the hunter.

"Oh, are questions of different kinds..."

"Yes!"

"Indeed. And I asked you my kind of question: how does mankind usually show gratitude?"

"By showing a kind gesture either to the person who performed the good deed or to someone else," said the hunter. "How else can anyone acknowledge a good turn?"

"I disagree. Often, mankind forgets its benefactors and even worse, treats them badly. I just do not want to be different, so I will bite you till you die. However, if you can provide witnesses to support your view, I will spare your life."

After some confused thought, Hunter replied that the three animals who would testify on his behalf were Hen, Goat and Lion. So the two of them set off to look for these three witnesses, Cobra still wrapped snugly round the waist of Hunter. Not long afterwards they met Hen, and Hunter called out to her:

"Hen, my friend, please come for a moment." When Hen came Hunter asked her:

"What is the usual way in which mankind shows its gratitude?

Hen kept quiet for a long while and replied:

"I should know the answer. Do you have a little time to spare?" she asked Hunter.

When Hunter said she could take as long as she wanted, Hen told the story of her life:

"I live in a home where I lay eggs and hatch chickens. The people of the house decide how many of my eggs they should use for rituals, how many for food and how many I can hatch. Do I have any control over the fate of my children? Oh, no. The people again decide when to sell them and when to kill them for food. Nowhere is their ultimate contempt for me better dramatized than in how they sometimes slaughter them before my eyes. I am aware that as soon as I cease to lay eggs I will be sacrificed too. And how am I treated for providing so much? Just listen: when the sack of corn lets out a few grains on its own accord and I as much as avail myself of the corn on the ground, the people waste no time in booting me into the air, and I have to go out in search of rotten food. Now tell me, Papa hunter, how does mankind reward a good turn?"

At the end of Hen's story Cobra started to puff with joy, because one witness had confirmed that the reward for gratitude has always been ingratitude. Discouraged, Hunter thanked Hen and went in search of Goat, whom he soon found at the rubbish heap.

"Goat, my good friend, you are a person of great intelligence. I want to find something out and I know you can help me," started Hunter.

The way Hunter began made Goat feel important indeed, because no one had ever referred to his wisdom; he is always reminded of his foolishness. So Goat stopped eating, moved away from the rubbish dump and took Hunter to the shade of the mango tree where he asked of his mission. When Hunter told him why he needed his help, Goat unfortunately proceeded in a fashion similar to Hen's:

"The people I live with get milk from me and kill my children for meat. When I see them display the skins of my kinsmen on their walls or use them as a foot rest, I know that it cannot be anything less than absolute disregard for me. I know that I can be killed any day. Do you know what it is like to live each day, knowing you could be killed and that there is nothing you could do about it? I know we will all die someday, but in my case I will never experience natural death. Some person can decide when to sell me off to another land or when to transform my being from an ordinary, walking, breathing animal into hot, spicy kebab for instance. Hunter, can you imagine this? Meanwhile how am I treated at home by the people who make so much profit from me? You found me eating at the rubbish heap, didn't you? And I hope you did not think that Goat prefers food at the rubbish heap to wholesome food. This is the reason why you found me eating rejected, rotting food: while in the kitchen, even if I as much as bite a piece of the cassava peel that they will eventually throw away, the people reach for the wooden part of the cutlass and hit my horns, pam! Need I say more?"

By the end of Goat's story Cobra was flexing his muscles, feeling triumphant. However, the agreement was that they would call three witnesses, although it was obvious that Hunter had lost the bet. Hunter was desperate, and a glimmer of hope lay in the testimony of Lion. After going back into the forest and walking for a while he met him.

"King of the forest, my friend, I am in deep trouble. There is a bet here and my life is at stake," Hunter told Lion.

"My friend, good Hunter, why do you have to bet your life on anything? What is more precious than your life?" asked Lion, quite surprised at Hunter's statement.

"Lion, we can discuss that later. Meanwhile, this is the question: how does mankind usually respond to an act of kindness?"

Lion started his reply by posing a series of questions:

"Hunter, are you going out of your mind? Why did I find you walking and talking to yourself? Since when did one head alone go into consultation? And, really, how did you place yourself in such difficulty? Who are you betting with?"

"I am not alone; I am with someone."

"Where is he? I cannot see anyone."

So Hunter brought Cobra from his waist and laid him on the ground. He then narrated the story of how he hid Cobra from his pursuers and in return, how Cobra had threatened to kill him because he believed that the usual reaction to acts of kindness is to be ungrateful.

Lion was really furious, especially after Cobra had corroborated Hunter's story. He asked Cobra a number of questions in rapid-fire succession, giving him no chance to answer any of these questions.

"Hey Cobra, just come here for a moment and let's find out what is going on: where do you come from? Do you have elders in your community? Or you all grew tall and left your brains in your knees? Are all the people of your kind so foolish and so thoroughly ill-mannered that they must show a lack of appreciation when someone has been kind to them? Do your people have a word for the conscience in their vocabulary? Answer me! Where did you learn such nonsense from? Show ingratitude for kindness indeed! What kinds of gods do you worship? Or maybe you don't have any?"

Before Cobra could formulate an answer to any of the questions, Lion grabbed him and tore him to pieces.

"And you Hunter," he continued, "you can go home now. The best way you can answer the question to yourself is in how you respond to acts of kindness. Good luck."

Hunter fell to the ground and thanked Lion. He was so exhausted and so relieved that he decided to go home immediately. On the way he met a couple of his relatives who seemed very agitated:

"Papa Hunter, where have you been all day? You only said you were going to set your traps but you have been gone all day. Your wife went into labour again shortly after you left and she is having an awful time. The medicine woman wants the bile of the lion to prepare medicine to ease her pains and to make for an easy delivery," his cousin told him.

Hunter turned and said:

"A lion? Why, I left a lion just a moment ago. He cannot be far off. Let's go and get him."

So the people went to look for the lion, found him and shot him. As he fell he told himself:

"Cobra was right: mankind hardly remembers acts of kindness."

HOW CHIEFS CAME TO POSSESS LEOPARD SKINS

Once there lived a queen who had a beautiful daughter called Mansa. She was called Mansa because she was the third daughter of the queen. The other two, Araba and Ekua, were also good-looking but their beauty paled beside the splendour that was Mansa. Mansa was so beautiful and kind that everyone loved her. She had smooth dark, shiny skin and a good crop of black hair which she always had braided in intricate patterns. Her face was broad, enhanced further by her generous smiles which revealed the gap in her upper teeth. She was of medium build, with buttocks that vibrated slightly to the rhythm of her walk. This delighted her male admirers endlessly; they wished and hoped and dreamt of marrying Mansa someday.

Added to her natural beauty, Mansa was an accomplished potter. She knew the right time to pick the green leaves which she would grind on the stone, in order to extract the desired colour for dyeing. She also knew the right quantities of black substance to add to a mixture of red earth and black soil in order to obtain the right glaze for her pots. For designs she would use broken pieces of calabash,

broomsticks, twigs or her fingers. Younger children loved to spend time observing her at work. Sometimes she would allow them to shape the earth or bring the wood for baking the pots before glazing.

However, all the men but one could only look at her because Mansa was betrothed to a prince, Kwame Arapa, from another village. What nobody knew was that Mansa was in love with Kweku Asamoa, a young, good-looking and intelligent boy from the same village as hers. Kweku was not of royal birth, but unlike Kwame who walked about exuding snobbery and who did not have much regard for women, Kweku was loving, affectionate and he had a lot of respect for Mansa. Kweku confided his feelings about Mansa to his father. His father kept quiet for a long

time before he spoke: "I remember when I first met your mother and I was so unsure of myself. It was the time of the rainy season and my age mates and I..." Kweku soon interrupted him.

"Father, I have heard that story about how you were so nervous, and afraid Mother would say no. What I want is for you to tell me what I can do about Mansa. Father, you must help me."

"My son, first of all I am very happy that you have chosen to talk to me. That is the way it should be because apart from your mother, uncles, fathers and mothers, nobody cares for you more than I do. I also think that given the nature of human relationships, we should marry the people we sincerely care about and who love us in return." Kweku's father addressed the subject directly now. "The case of Mansa, as you know, is very different, because she is betrothed to someone else. Of course if the two of them decide they do not want to get married and the families agree, then we can easily proceed with the marriage rites for the two of you. But as it is..." Kweku's father paused for a while before continuing. "At any rate, you give me some time to consult your fathers and uncles and we'll see what we can do," he reassured his son.

Kweku's father, Opanyin Kwadwo Preko informed his relations about the problem and together they found a way to solve it. First, they got together two bottles of gin and early one morning they set off to the Queen's palace to make their intentions known. They were not prepared for how they were received.

After the usual greetings Kweku's oldest uncle broached the subject through the use of proverbs and aphorisms. When the nature of the visit became apparent to their hosts, they were told, also through the skilful use of maxims, to move themselves out of the precincts if they did not want trouble. They were reminded of their economic status and the fact that Mansa was betrothed to a prince. In short, they should take the rest of the gin away and find someone else for their son.

News reached Mansa and Kweku very quickly. They had decided that if her parents were difficult they would simply run away, which they did. Mansa and Kweku's people searched in vain for them. After a while, they gave them up for dead and performed the necessary funeral rites.

Meanwhile the young couple had gone deep into the forest and built a hut. At first they were afraid and confused, but the animals of the forest were very kind to them. Indeed, they had not known that human beings, plants and most animals

124

could live in such harmony. Kweku and Mansa got on very well, and with time they gave birth to a healthy baby boy.

The little boy, Ankoma, knew only his father and mother, then a lot of animals who were his friends. Although his parents had told him about their past it was all so strange to Ankoma because he had never experienced other people. He spent most of his time trapping smaller animals and learning of the medicinal values of plants from his father. He had been warned to stay away from the larger animals like lions, leopards and foxes because they could be unpredictably wild. Despite this warning Ankoma became friends with the leopard's son, who was about the same age as he was. Leopard's son was training to become a hunter, and the two would meet in their wanderings in the forest.

One day Ankoma came home after collecting some herbs and found that his father had brought home a female leopard which he had killed.

After his mother cooked the meat of the leopardess, Ankoma refused to eat the food. His father was surprised and asked the boy:

"Ankoma, you must try it. It is really delicious"

"No, father, I cannot eat any of this meat."

His parents persisted, but the boy could not bring himself to eat the meat of his friend's mother. His parents did not understand, but they respected their son's wishes.

Ankoma met his friend the next day who gave the sad news of his mother's disappearance:

"She went hunting but did not return, and this is unusual indeed, and my father suspects foul play and means to avenge her death," the Leopard's son told Ankoma.

"Let me tell you the truth at once. My father shot your mother and brought her body home. We nearly had a fistfight when he asked me to help him skin the animal and even eat of the meat. Of course I refused."

"Really? You mean your father is responsible for the death of my mother?" the Leopard's son was shocked.

"Would I lie about a topic of this nature?" responded Ankoma.

Two days after this conversation, Mansa went to pick vegetables for the family's dinner and did not return. At dusk Kweku lit the lamp and went in search of his wife whom he found badly mauled.

The teeth marks told him that the attacker was the leopard. Furious, he went for his gun and looked for the leopard until he found and shot him. Then he tried all the herbs he could but Mansa died in the night. Kweku was so heart broken that he died soon afterwards, leaving Ankoma to fend for himself. The friendship of the two young men became even closer, both of them having lost their parents. Leopard even moved into Ankoma's hut. They looked out for each other and shared everything they had.

A couple of years later, Ankoma felt he must look for his parents' people and get married. He explained to Leopard that his decision had nothing to do with their friendship, but that he had this strong urge to find the relatives of his people and also, to start a family. Leopard understood how Ankoma felt and decided to help. After going away for three days and three nights, Leopard managed to locate the village.

One day Ankoma decided to go home, accompanied by his friend the leopard. On the outskirts of the village Leopard decided to wait and watch events because he knew that he would be killed if he were spotted by the people. The agreement was that Leopard would never forsake his friend. He would protect the entire village from attack by wild animals, and his friend in particular, but for the safety of Leopard, they must keep their friendship a secret.

Ankoma found his way to the palace and introduced himself. At first the people took him for an imposter, but they soon changed their minds when they saw the gold bracelet on his wrist, the same one Mansa had worn when she disappeared. There was much wailing and performing of libation to welcome the lost relative. Ankoma was clothed in beautiful cloths and made to feel part of the royal family. Even though he was settled in the village, he would always steal away at dusk to meet his friend the leopard and exchange news.

Shortly after his reunion with his family, Ankoma met a young woman, Araba, not of royal birth, whom he wanted to marry. His people immediately remembered the story of his mother and did not wish history to repeat itself. Apart from their permission and blessings, they also went ahead and performed the marriage rites, and Ankoma was happy with his bride. The evening of the wedding, just before the bride was officially accompanied to his home, Ankoma went to meet his friend the leopard, as usual. Leopard told Ankoma that he had only one piece of advice for him:

"Never marry more than one woman," he said in earnest. "As a chief, pressure will be put on you to choose another woman for a wife. Believe me, that will bring you untold sorrow."

"Why so? The men with many wives boast of their achievement and they seem to be quite happy with the arrangement. Even the wives are happy. I saw a case where the first wife actually arranged for the husband to marry the second woman," Ankoma told his friend.

"Oh! You have such a child's mind. Can you imagine how much this woman has to divorce her own emotions in order to invite another woman to share her husband? When that happens, you can bet that she is still with him for reasons other than emotional ones. She will only be interested in whatever financial gains she can get. But I am talking about you. Listen to me. Your own people say that the man with many wives dies of starvation and neglect. And apart from this, if those with several wives were to reveal the truth of what they actually experience in their hearts, none of us would ever marry more than one woman. My advice to you is to stick to one woman if you do not want disaster."

Ankoma's relationship with his wife lasted a few years and they even had four children, two boys and two girls whom they named for their fathers and mothers. Araba also knew about the friendship between her husband and the leopard and understood why it should be kept a secret. Life went on quite peacefully until some of the elders began to encourage Ankoma to marry a second woman, Fosua. Ankoma did not find the prompting offensive for long. He married the second, younger woman much to the hurt of Araba. The worst part for her was that Araba was made to bow to custom by her own people who taught her how to pretend that she favoured the terms.

The chief expected the relationship between him and his first wife to remain the same but it was not. Araba became more and more withdrawn, while Fosua enjoyed teasing her through her songs about the old rival who ate up the children in the wombs of her co-wives and who was eventually convicted of witchcraft and abandoned in the forest. Fosua hated the idea of having to take care of Araba's children when she went to buy beads, and of having to cook for so many people. When Araba complained, her husband reminded her that she was older and should know better than to be bothered by the taunts of a child. Araba knew that if she did not keep herself busy taking care of her children and with her trade in beads she would go insane. The rest of society misinterpreted her serenity to be a tacit acceptance of a co-wife.

One day Fosua brought food to her husband and saw him and Araba talking to a leopard. She had been told about it by her husband, but she thought it was one of the stories made to make a chief appear extraordinary. She felt like an outsider, watching the three in what appeared like intimate conversation. Moreover, she suspected that her rival would employ the leopard to cause her some harm, so she decided to report the incident to the elders.

One fateful evening soon after, Leopard was making his way to the usual meeting place. What the leopard did not know was that the hunters were lying in wait for him, and the moment he entered the path that led to the palace he was shot three times. The chief rushed from his room, only to see his lifelong friend gasping for breath. There was nothing the chief could do, except listen to the words of the dying leopard:

"I warned you never to marry more than one woman."

Not only had Ankoma lost the warmth and dedication of Araba, he had also lost his good friend. The chief asked for the skin of the leopard, as a perpetual reminder of their friendship.

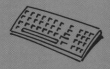

President:	Richard K. Swadley
Publisher:	John Pierce
Executive Editor:	Beth Millett
Director of Editorial Services:	Lisa Wilson
Managing Editor:	Patrick Kanouse
Indexing Manager:	Christine Nelsen

About the Author

Kate Binder is a production artist and freelance writer living in southern New Hampshire. The author of *Teach Yourself QuarkXPress 4 in 14 Days* and co-author of *Photoshop 4 Complete*, she also writes articles on desktop production tools and techniques for *Desktop Publishers Journal* magazine. She can be reached at **UrsaDesign@aol.com**, and her Web page is at **http://members.aol.com/ursadesign**. Her three favorite things (this month, anyway) are Victorian houses, double-chocolate pudding, and stretchy cats.

Dedication

This book is for my parents, who haven't kicked me out of the nest yet and may never get around to it.

Acknowledgments

Thanks to my ever-patient editors, Julie MacLean and Beth Millett, for putting up with me long enough to get another book out the door.

Acquisitions Editor
Karen Whitehouse

Development Editor
Juliet MacLean

Project Editor
Elizabeth Bruns

Copy Editor
Patricia Kinyon

Indexer
Heather Goens

Technical Reviewer
Mike Cuenca

Team Coordinator
Carol Ackerman

Cover Designer
Anne Jones

Book Designer
Jean Bisesi

Illustrator
Bruce Dean

Copy Writer
Eric Borgert

Production Team Supervisor
Brad Chinn

Production Designer
Trina Wurst

Proofreader
Benjamin Berg

How to Use This Book

It's as Easy as 1-2-3

Each part of this book is made up of a series of short, instructional lessons, designed to help you understand basic information that you need to get the most out of your computer hardware and software.

 Click: Click the left mouse button once.

 Double-click: Click the left mouse button twice in rapid succession.

 Right-click: Click the right mouse button once.

 Pointer Arrow: Highlights an item on the screen you need to point to or focus on in the step or task.

 Selection: Highlights the area onscreen discussed in the step or task.

 Click & Type: Click once where indicated and begin typing to enter your text or data.

 Tips and Warnings give you a heads-up for any extra information you may need while working through the task.

2 Each task includes a series of quick, easy steps designed to guide you through the procedure.

1 Each step is fully illustrated to show you how it looks onscreen.

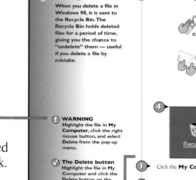
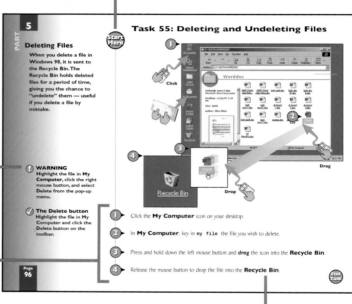

Task 55: Deleting and Undeleting Files

PART 5

Deleting Files
When you delete a file in Windows 98, it is sent to the Recycle Bin. The Recycle Bin holds deleted files for a period of time, giving you the chance to "undelete" them — useful if you delete a file by mistake.

! WARNING
Highlight the file in **My Computer**, click the right mouse button, and select **Delete** from the pop-up menu.

✓ The Delete button
Highlight the file in **My Computer** and click the Delete button on the toolbar.

Page 96

1. Click the **My Computer** icon on your desktop.
2. In **My Computer**, key in `my file` the file you wish to delete.
3. Press and hold down the left mouse button and **drag** the icon into the **Recycle Bin**.
4. Release the mouse button to drop the file into the **Recycle Bin**.

3 Items that you select or click in menus, dialog boxes, tabs, and windows are shown in **Bold**. Information you type is in a `special font`.

Drag

Drop

How to Drag: Point to the starting place or object. Hold down the mouse button (right or left per instructions), move the mouse to the new location, then release the button.

Next Step: If you see this symbol, it means the task you're working on continues on the next page.

End Task: Task is complete.

Introduction to *Easy Adobe Photoshop 5*

Adobe Photoshop 5 is a big, complex program—it's an image editor, a paint program, a Web graphics design tool, and more. It can do a lot for you, but first you have to tame it and make it your own. Learning to use its basic tools will allow you to explore further on your own.

That's why *Easy Adobe Photoshop 5* provides concise, visual, step-by-step instructions for handling all the tasks you'll need to accomplish. You'll learn how to get started in Photoshop 5, how to choose the right color mode for each project, how to adjust scanned images to look their best, how to paint new images with your choice of tools, how to apply filters that can completely transform an image with a single click, and more.

You can choose to read the book cover to cover, or to use it as a reference when you encounter a piece of Photoshop 5 that you don't know how to use. Either way, *Easy Adobe Photoshop 5* lets you see it done and do it yourself.

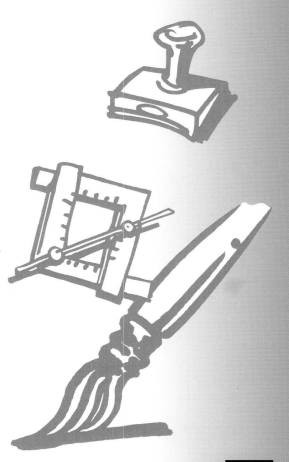

Getting Started

Photoshop is a powerful program with so many features that very few users explore them all. Like any program, though, Photoshop has basic functions that you'll use in almost every project—printing, zooming in and out to view an image, changing an image's print size, undoing commands, and so on. In addition, Photoshop 5 includes features borrowed from page layout programs that help you position elements and measure areas precisely within images.

Part I shows you how to create files, view images in different ways, measure distances and place objects in images, and change images' size and shape. Also included in this part are ways to automate your work, undo one or more commands you've already executed, and apply a series of steps to an entire group of images at one time.

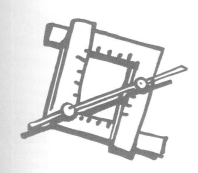

Tasks

Each Photoshop image you create begins with a new file. When you create the file, you specify its dimensions, *resolution*, and *color mode*, depending on the file's ultimate destination (print or onscreen display).

Task 1: Creating a New File

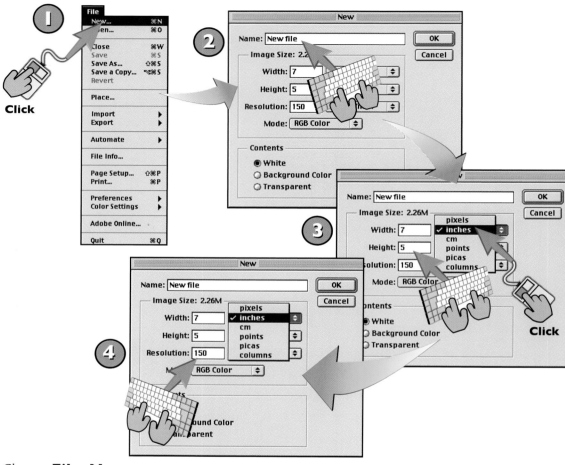

Click

1 Choose **File**, **New**.

2 Enter a name for the file in the New dialog box.

3 Choose measurement units and enter dimensions for the file's width and height.

4 Enter a resolution for the file.

Next Step

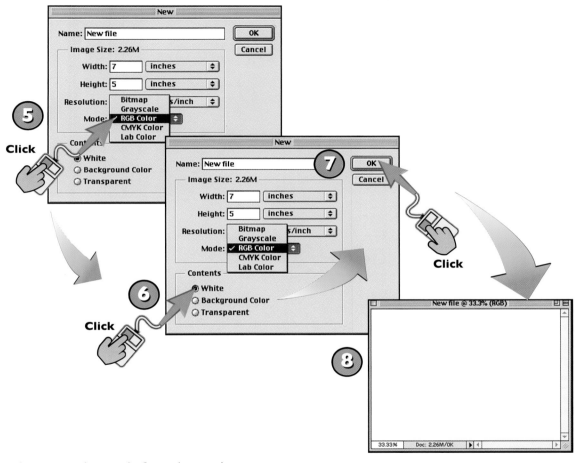

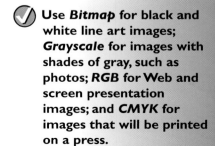

(5) Choose a color mode from the Mode pop-up menu.

(6) Choose a background color for the file.

(7) Click **OK**.

(8) Begin working in the new file's window.

✓ Use *Bitmap* for black and white line art images; *Grayscale* for images with shades of gray, such as photos; *RGB* for Web and screen presentation images; and *CMYK* for images that will be printed on a press.

End Task

Task 2: Moving an Image

With the Move tool, you can move an image within its window or drag it into another image window. For images without multiple *layers*, the Move tool moves the entire image; if there are multiple layers in an image, the Move tool works on individual layers or on linked layers. (For more information about layers, see Part 8, "Working with Layers.")

✓ Hold down the **Shift** key as you drag to move the image straight up and down or left and right.

✓ Using the **Move** tool on an image without layers changes the Background into a layer. To save the file in a format other than Photoshop, choose **Layer, Flatten Image** first to change the layer back into a Background.

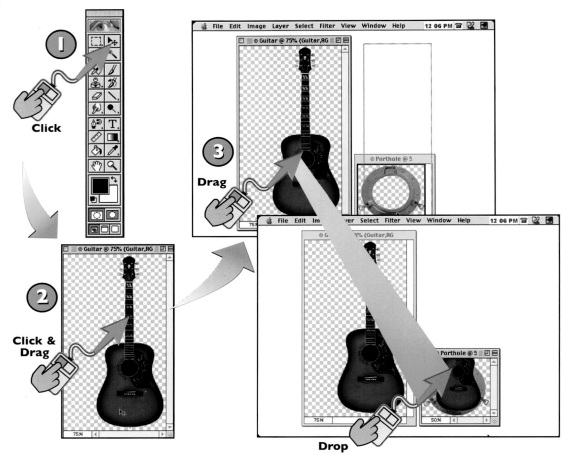

① Choose the **Move** tool from the **Tool** palette.

② Click and drag the image to move it around on its own canvas.

③ Drag the image into another window to copy it into another file.

Task 3: Changing the Zoom Percentage

Start Here

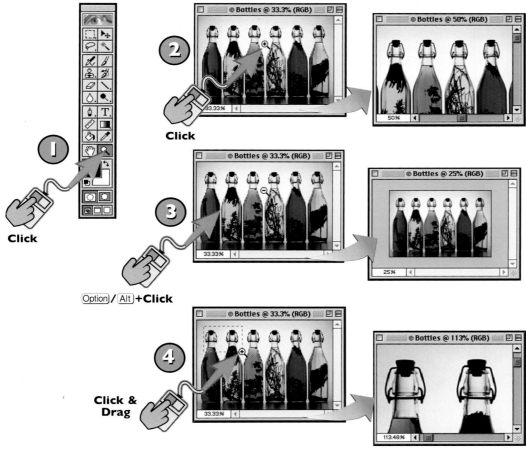

Click

Option / Alt +Click

Click & Drag

Photoshop allows you to view images at any size from 0.01% to 1600% of their actual size. As you work in Photoshop, you'll find that you switch zoom percentages often, zooming in to work on details and zooming out to get "the big picture."

✓ The Zoom tool's magnifying glass cursor will contain a plus sign when you're zooming in and a minus sign when you're zooming out.

① Choose the **Zoom** tool from the **Tool** palette.

② Click in the image to enlarge it (zoom in).

③ **Option+click/Alt+click** in the image to reduce it (zoom out).

④ If you want to enlarge a specific area, click and drag to draw a marquee around the area you wish to enlarge.

✓ To zoom to a specific percentage, click in the zoom percentage box in the lower-left corner of the window, type in a new percentage, and press **Enter**.

End Task

Screen clutter is a constant problem for digital artists. To get rid of the distracting extra windows and backgrounds on your screen, you can view Photoshop images in alternative modes.

✓ If the image is too small to fill the entire screen, a gray background will show around it in Full Screen Mode with Menu Bar.

✓ If the image is too small to fill the entire screen, a gray background will show around it in Full Screen Mode. Palettes will still be displayed.

✓ If palettes start cluttering up your screen, press **Tab** to hide any open palettes; press **Tab** again to bring them back. Press **Shift+Tab** to hide all palettes except the **Tool** palette.

Task 4: Viewing Image Windows in Different Ways

Start Here

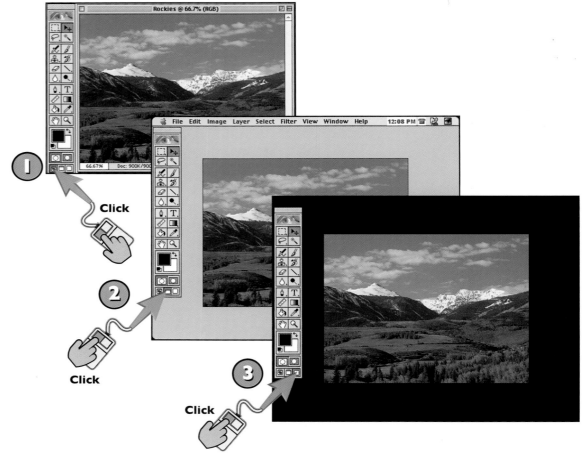

Click

Click

Click

(1) Click the **Standard Screen Mode** button on the **Tool** palette to view the image in a standard window

(2) Click the **Full Screen Mode with Menu Bar** button on the **Tool** palette to center the image on the entire screen without hiding the menu bar.

(3) Click the **Full Screen Mode** button on the **Tool** palette to fill the screen with the image and hide the menu bar.

End Task

Task 5: Viewing Different Parts of an Image

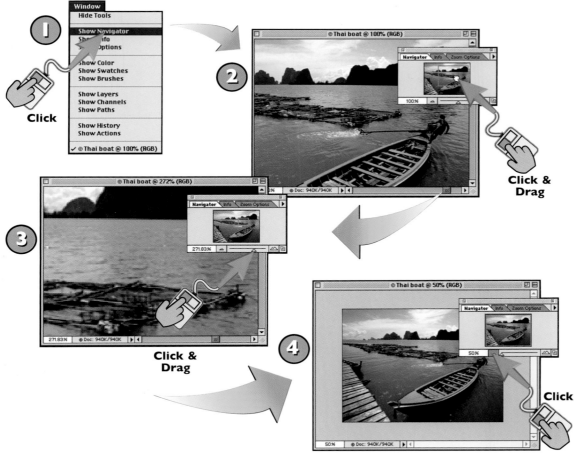

Window
Hide Tools

Show Navigator
Show Info
Show Options

Show Color
Show Swatches
Show Brushes

Show Layers
Show Channels
Show Paths

Show History
Show Actions

✓ Thai boat @ 100% (RGB)

① Click

② Click & Drag

③ Click & Drag

④ Click

The Navigator palette is a handy way to move around a large image quickly and to zoom in and out of the image. Its controls offer several alternative ways to navigate through an image.

✅ If you find you can't drag the red rectangle, it's because the entire image is already showing in the window. You might need to move or hide palettes to see all of it.

✅ For a specific percentage, click in the zoom percentage box in the lower-left corner of the palette, type in a new percentage, and press **Enter**.

✅ The *Grabber Hand* is the easiest (but not always the most efficient) way to view different parts of an image; hold down the **Spacebar** and drag the image around with the hand cursor, just as you'd use your own hand. With larger images, you'd be dragging forever with the Grabber Hand, so try the Navigator palette instead.

① Choose **Window**, **Show Navigator**.

② Click in the **Navigator** palette's red rectangle and drag it to show a different part of the image.

③ Drag the slider to change the zoom percentage.

④ Click the **Zoom In** and **Zoom Out** buttons to change the zoom percentage in specific increments from .01 percent up to 1200 percent.

End Task

The Info palette is Photoshop's clearinghouse location for information about the colors and distances in images. It can display *pixel* colors in eight different ways—including two at the same time—and show measurements in six different units.

Task 6: Viewing Information About an Image

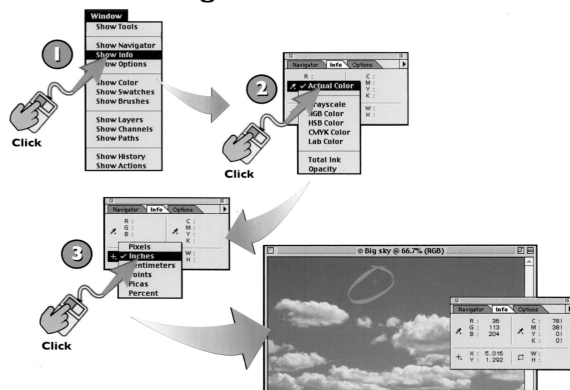

✓ When you move the cursor over the image, the color and coordinates of the pixel under the cursor are displayed in the palette.

✓ The **Actual Color** option in the eyedropper icon's pop-up menu uses the color system corresponding to the image's color mode—*RGB* for an RGB image, *CMYK* for a CMYK image, and so on.

For more information about color modes, see Part 4, "Working with Colors and Patterns."

1. Choose **Window**, **Show Info**.

2. Click and hold the palette's eyedropper icon and choose a color mode from each pop-up menu.

3. Click and hold the palette's crosshairs icon and choose a measurement system from the pop-up menu.

4. Move the cursor over the image.

Task 7: Comparing Different Points in an Image

Start Here

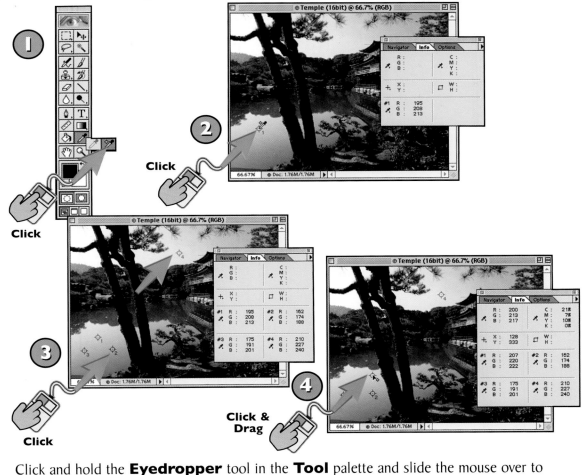

Click

Click

Click

Click & Drag

The Compare tool lets you view information on the Info palette about multiple points in an image. For example, you can determine whether one section of the image is darker or whether two points are at the same vertical position.

① Click and hold the **Eyedropper** tool in the **Tool** palette and slide the mouse over to choose the **Compare** tool.

② Click in the image; the **Info** palette pops up if it wasn't already open.

③ Click at one, two, or three more points; their colors and positions are shown on the **Info** palette.

④ Click and drag any point to compare a different location in the image.

End Task

To change the *color mode* or measurement units displayed on the **Info** palette, see Task 6, "Viewing Information About an Image."

Task 8: Measuring a Distance

Photoshop provides a special tool that you can use to find the size of objects in an image. Like the Compare tool, the Measure tool uses the Info palette to display the results of its calculations, and you can choose to view measurements in different units.

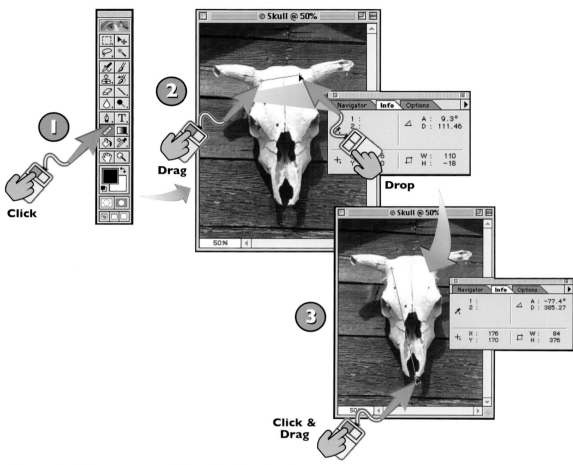

✓ The distance and angle of the line you drew are displayed in the Info palette.

✓ To turn the measuring line into a protractor, **Option+click/Alt+click** on either end and drag out another line. The angle between the two segments of the measurement line is displayed on the **Info** palette.

✓ To change the measurement units displayed in the **Info** palette, see Task 6, "Viewing Information About an Image."

① Choose the **Measure** tool from the **Tool** palette.

② Click and hold at the point where you want to start measuring. Drag to the point where you want to stop measuring.

③ Click either end of the measuring line and drag to measure a different distance.

Task 9: Adding Rulers and Non-Printing Guides

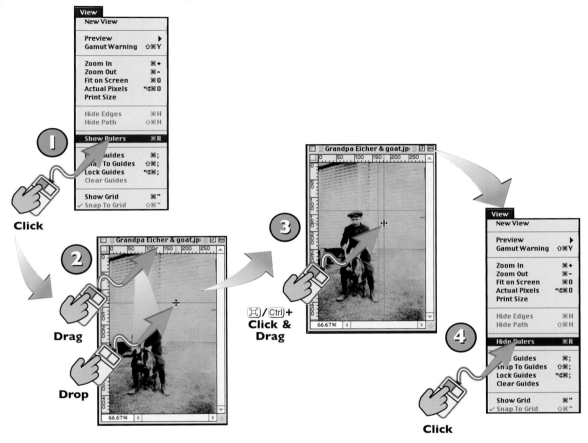

Click

Drag

Drop

⌘/Ctrl+
Click & Drag

Click

Positioning elements in an image can be done more precisely with the aid of rulers and guidelines, like those found in page layout and drawing software. The *rulers* and *guides* don't print, and they don't show onscreen if you view an image in any program other than Photoshop.

✓ To change the ruler's units, double-click the ruler and choose a different option from the **Units** pop-up menu in the **Units & Rulers Preferences** dialog box.

✓ Guides can be even more useful if you choose **View, Snap to Guides**; when you move an object close to a guide, it snaps to the guide's position automatically. Choose **View, Snap to Guides** again to turn off this feature.

1. Choose **View**, **Show Rulers** or press **Cmd+R/Ctrl+R** to display the rulers.

2. Click a ruler and drag to make a guide.

3. **Cmd+click/Ctrl+click** and drag to move a guide; drag all the way to the ruler to delete it.

4. Choose **View**, **Hide Rulers**, or press **Cmd+R/Ctrl+R** again to hide the rulers.

End Task

Task 10: Displaying a Non-Printing Grid

In addition to movable guides, Photoshop can display a grid overlaid on an image. This feature is especially useful when other elements—such as lines or text—will be combined with the image. Like guides, gridlines don't print, and they won't be displayed if you view a Photoshop file in any other program.

✓ You can choose the color, style, and frequency of the gridlines in the **Guides & Grid Preferences** dialog box. Choose **File**, **Preferences**, and choose **Guides & Grid** from the pop-up menu at the top of the dialog box.

✓ The *grid* can be even more useful if you choose **View**, **Snap to Grid**; when you move an object close to a gridline, it snaps to the gridline's position automatically. Choose **View**, **Snap to Grid** again to turn off this feature.

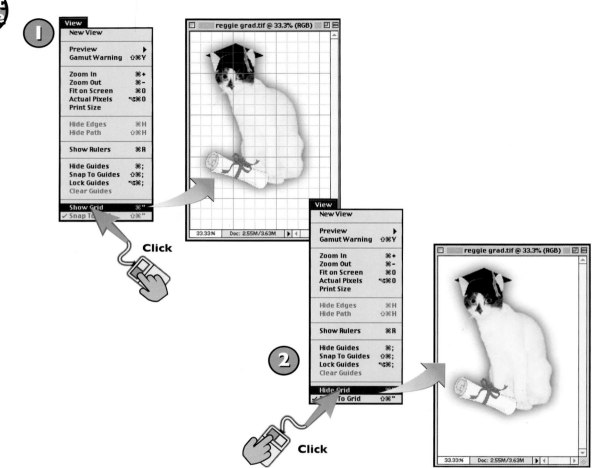

Start Here

Click

Click

① Choose **View**, **Show Grid**, or press **Cmd+"/Ctrl+"** to display the grid.

② Choose **View**, **Hide Grid**, or press **Cmd+"/Ctrl+"** again to hide the grid.

End Task

Task 11: Cropping an Image

Click

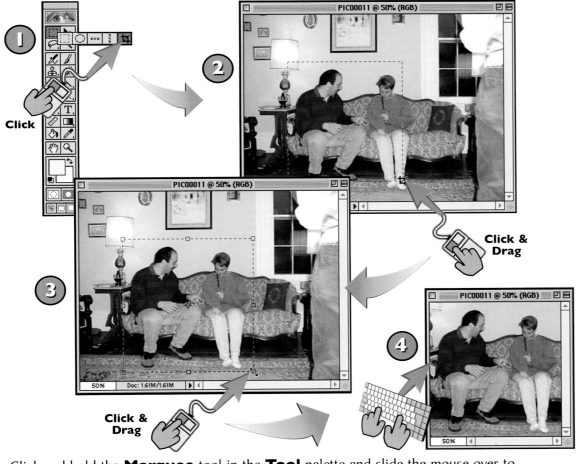

Click & Drag

Click & Drag

Cropping is a procedure familiar to any professional photographer. In cropping, you remove the extraneous portions of an image so that it shows only what you want it to show. Photoshop makes cropping much easier than it is in the darkroom.

1. Click and hold the **Marquee** tool in the **Tool** palette and slide the mouse over to choose the **Crop** tool.

2. Click and drag in the image to define the area you want to keep.

3. Click and drag on the points to adjust the size and shape of the cropping rectangle.

4. Press **Enter** to crop the image, or press **Esc** to cancel the operation.

✓ If you change your mind about what part of the image you want to feature, you can move the entire cropping rectangle by clicking within it and dragging.

End Task

Task 12: Changing an Image's Size or Resolution

Size and *resolution* are closely related in Photoshop, so these two image attributes are controlled via the same dialog box. You can choose to resize an image with or without *resampling* its resolution; if you allow resampling, the resolution of the image doesn't change, and if you don't, the image resolution increases or decreases in inverse proportion to the image's size.

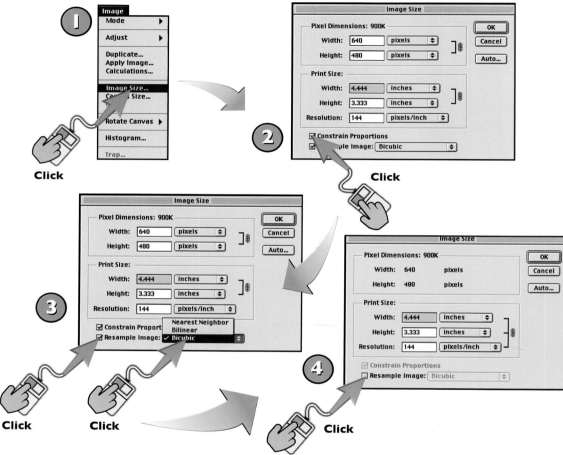

When Photoshop resamples an image, the software adds or subtracts pixels and reassigns pixel colors to create the same image with more or fewer pixels.

1. Choose **Image**, **Image Size**.

2. Click **Constrain Proportions** to make sure the image's proportions stay the same.

3. Click **Resample Image** to change the size but not the resolution; choose **Bicubic** from the **Method** pop-up menu.

4. Click **Resample Image** off to tie the resolution to the image size.

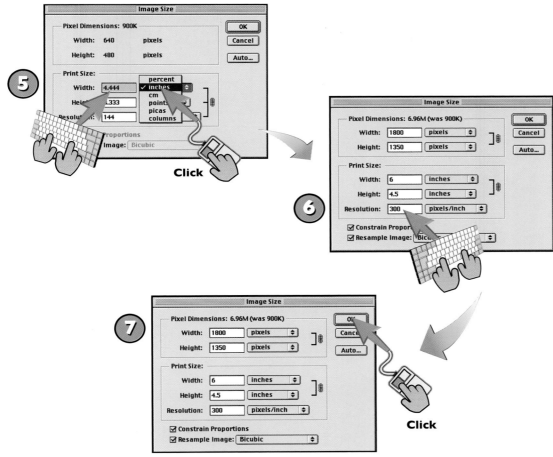

Click

Click

5 To change the size, choose **Print Size** units from the pop-up menus and enter a new width or height in the **Print Size** area.

6 If **Resample Image** is on, enter a new resolution.

7 Click **OK**.

✅ With Resample Image off, if the image is enlarged, the resolution will decrease, and vice versa.

✅ Avoid enlarging an image or increasing its resolution if possible. To accomplish this, Photoshop has to create new pixels in the image, and the software can only guess what color each new pixel should be. Enlarged images are often blurry, with out-of-focus details.

Task 13: Changing the Canvas Size

If an image is the right size but you need more room around the edges to work in, you can add that space by increasing the image's *canvas size*. This operation increases the size of the file without enlarging the existing image elements, filling the new space with the current *background color*.

To change the color of the added canvas area, choose a different background color before changing the canvas size. (See Part 4, "Working with Colors and Patterns," to change the foreground and background colors.)

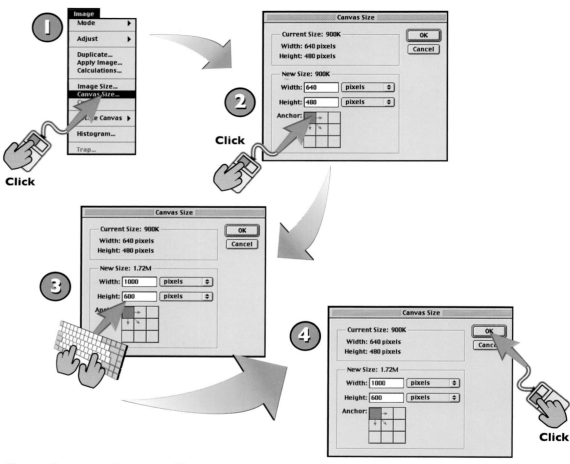

Click

Click

Click

Click

1. Choose **Image**, **Canvas Size**.

2. Click a box in the **Anchor** grid to determine where the extra space will be added.

3. Enter new measurements in the **Width** and **Height** fields.

4. Click **OK** to change the Canvas size.

End Task

Task 14: Undoing the Last Command

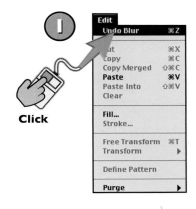

Click

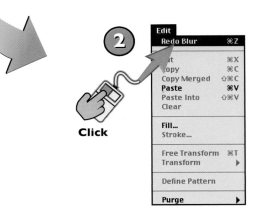

Click

If you change your mind about the command you just executed, you can go back a step by undoing the command. Once you've undone a command, you also have the option of redoing it; flipping back and forth between **Undo** and **Redo** is a good way to see the results of a change you've just made. The Undo and Redo commands always show the action you're undoing or redoing.

✓ The Undo and Redo commands also contain the name of the operation you're undoing or redoing—for example, **Undo Gaussian Blur**, or **Redo Levels**.

✓ You can't undo operations that don't affect the image, such as making changes to the preferences, by using the **Measure** tool or changing the foreground and background colors.

If you need to undo more than one operation, see the next task.

① Choose **Edit**, **Undo**.

② If you change your mind, choose **Edit, Redo**.

End Task

Page
19

Task 15: Undoing More Than One Command

Start Here

Using Photoshop's **History** palette, you can step back though the creation process to an image's original state, or stop at any point along the way. It's a good way to create several variations on an image, or to go back to an earlier stage of the image when you're experimenting with new techniques.

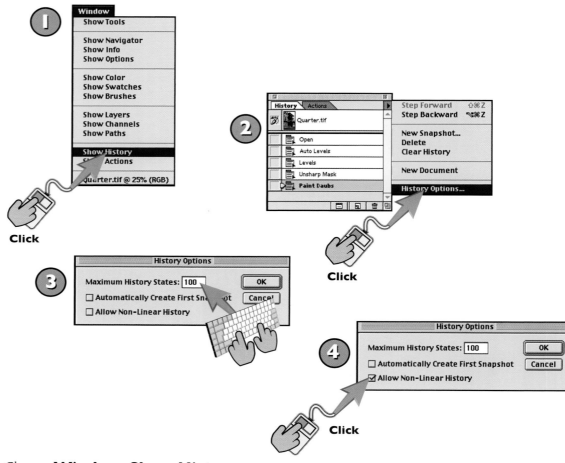

Click

Click

Click

Click

✓ You aren't restricted to reverting the entire image to a previous stage; you can "paint" in the reversion by using the **History Brush** tool. See Part 6, Task 15, "Restoring Part of the Image to an Earlier Stage" to learn how to restore part an image.

① Choose **Window**, **Show History**.

② From the **History** palette menu, choose **History Options**.

③ Enter the number of commands the **History** palette should display.

④ To delete steps in the **History** palette without affecting adjacent steps, click **Allow Non-Linear History**.

Next Step

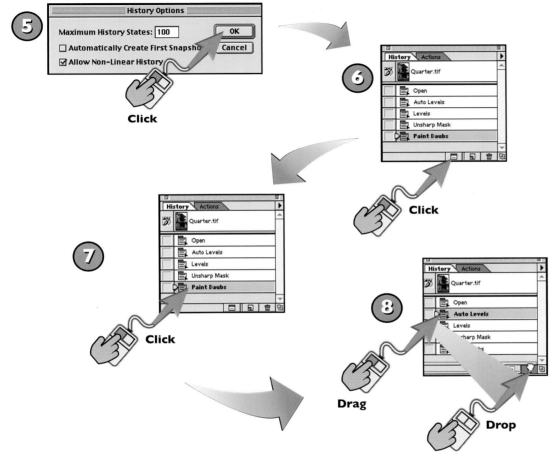

If you're using the **Non-Linear History** option and you go back to an earlier state of the image and make a change, that change is added to the list of changes at the end. **Without Non-Linear History**, all the other changes after the point to which you went back would be deleted. Although **Non-Linear History** clutters the **History** palette a bit, it is a way to leave all your options open.

You can create a new document based on any step in the **History** palette by dragging that step to the **New Document** icon, the lefthand icon at the bottom of the palette. The new document will show the image as it appeared at the completion of that step.

(5) Click **OK**.

(6) Click a command in the list to return the image to its state right after that command.

(7) Click a later command to add the intervening operations to the image.

(8) Drag a command to the trash icon to remove it from the list without removing the command's effect on the image.

Task 16: Automating a Series of Steps

If you find yourself performing the same steps over and over again, you can save a lot of time and effort by creating an *Action* that will perform those steps for you any time you invoke it. Actions are listed in the Actions palette, which has a Button mode that lets you play an action by just clicking its name.

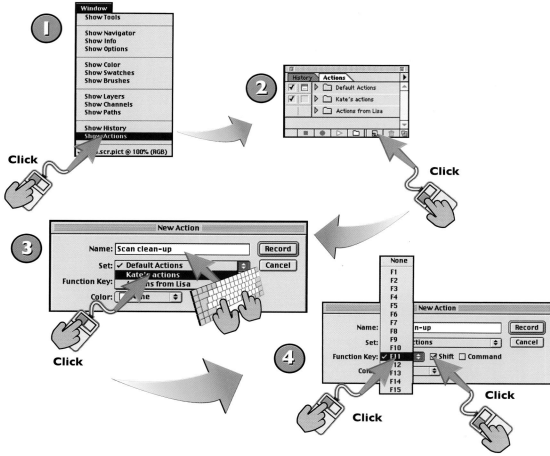

1. Choose **Window**, **Show Actions**.

2. Click the **New Action** button.

3. Enter a name for the Action, and choose a set to which it should belong.

4. Choose a function key that can trigger the action and click to add modifier keys to the function key.

Next Step

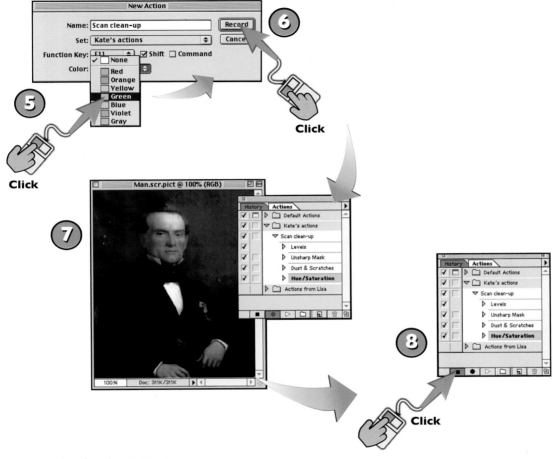

5 Choose a color for the Action's name.

6 Click **Record**.

7 Perform all the steps you want to add to the Action.

8 Click the **Stop** button on the **Actions** palette when you're done recording the Action.

✅ To play an Action, click its name and then click the triangular **Play** button on the **Actions** palette. An alternative method: From the **Actions palette menu,** choose **Button Mode;** in Button mode, you can play actions by just clicking their names in the palette.

✅ You can trade Actions with other Photoshop users. To save Actions, click the set name in the **Actions** palette and choose **Actions palette menu, Save Actions.** To load an Actions file, choose **Actions palette menu, Load Actions.**

✅ The other buttons on the Actions palette allow you to do the following, in order from left to right: stop playing or recording an Action; record more steps within an Action; play an Action; create a new set of Actions; create a new Action; delete an Action.

Task 17: Batch Processing Multiple Images

Start Here

Batch processing allows you to perform the same *Action* on a group of images without having to open each one and set the Action in motion. First you need to create an Action to be applied to each image (see "Task 16: Automating a Series of Steps").

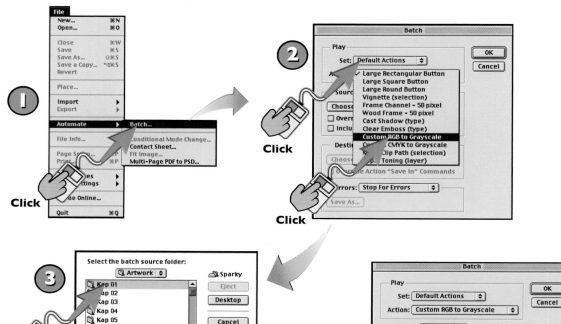

Click

Click

Click

Click

Click

Click

Click

✓ If your batch images are always located in the same place and saved in the same place, you can incorporate the Open and Save commands in the Action. In this case, you'll need to click off **Override Action "Open" Commands** and **Override Action "Save In" Commands.**

1 Choose **File**, **Automate**, **Batch**.

2 Choose an Action set from the **Set** pop-up menu and an Action from the **Action** menu, and then click the **Choose** button.

3 Find the folder of images you want to process, and then click **Open**.

4 Click **Override Action "Open" Commands** to make sure that Photoshop opens only the images in the batch folder.

Next Step

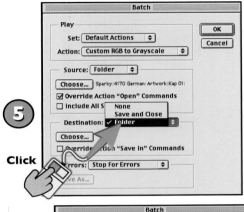

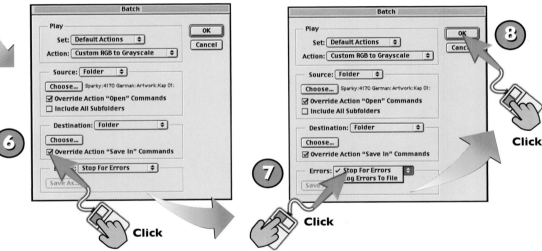

5 Choose **Save and Close** or **Folder** from the **Destination** pop-up menu.

6 If you chose **Folder**, click **Choose**, locate the folder to save in, and then click **Override Action "Save In" Commands**.

7 Choose **Stop For Errors** from the **Errors** pop-up menu.

8 Click **OK** to begin processing.

✓ To keep the original versions of the images and save new versions with the changes, choose **Folder** from the **Destination** pop-up menu; then click **Choose** and select a folder to save the modified images in.

Images have a way of accumulating, whether they're stock images or ones you've created with Photoshop. A good way to get a look at all of your stored images is to make printed contact sheets, a process that Photoshop can automate for you.

Task 18: Making a Contact Sheet

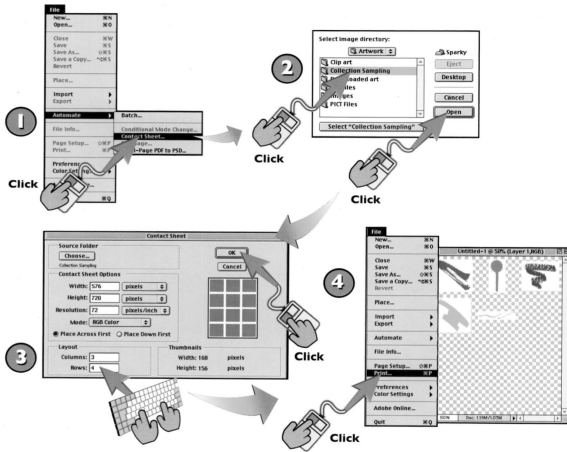

✓ You can change the size of the contact sheets by entering different width and height values in the Contact Sheet Options area; if your printer can handle legal- or tabloid-sized paper, you might want to create contact sheets in those sizes.

✓ Other options for contact sheets include whether images are placed in order from left to right or from top to bottom, as well as whether the contact sheets are created in color or grayscale.

1. Choose **File**, **Automate**, **Contact Sheet**.

2. Click **Choose** and select a folder of images, and then click **Open**.

3. Enter the number of columns and rows for the contact sheets and click **OK**.

4. Print the contact sheet documents Photoshop creates.

Task 19: Freeing Up Memory

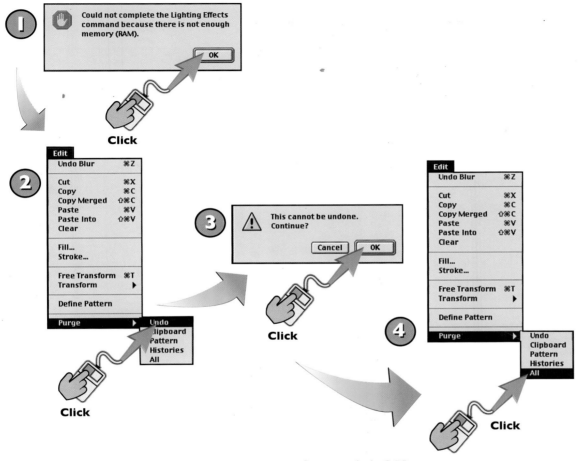

Click

Click

Click

Click

Anyone who's used Photoshop knows that it takes a lot of memory, or *RAM*, to run. Because Photoshop stores the image you're working on in memory, you can run out of memory if you try to work on a large image or apply a complex *filter*. Here's how to free up some of that memory so you can proceed.

✓ **Edit**, **Purge**, **All** clears all four options at once: **Undo**, **Clipboard**, **Pattern**, and **Histories**.

✓ Photoshop's Purge options do have a drawback—you lose access to whatever you're purging. So you shouldn't purge the Clipboard if you'll need to paste whatever's on it later. Also, once you've purged the Undo buffer, you won't be able to undo the action immediately prior to the purge.

(1) When Photoshop warns you that you've run out of RAM, click **OK**.

(2) Choose **Edit**, **Purge** and choose from among the first four options.

(3) Photoshop warns you that you can't undo this operation; click **OK**.

(4) If you still don't have enough memory to perform the desired command, choose **Edit**, **Purge**, **All**.

End Task

Task 20: Printing a File

Sooner or later, everyone needs to print a file, even Web designers. Photoshop offers sophisticated printing options side-by-side with the capability to simply press **Cmd+P/Ctrl+P** and hit **Enter**.

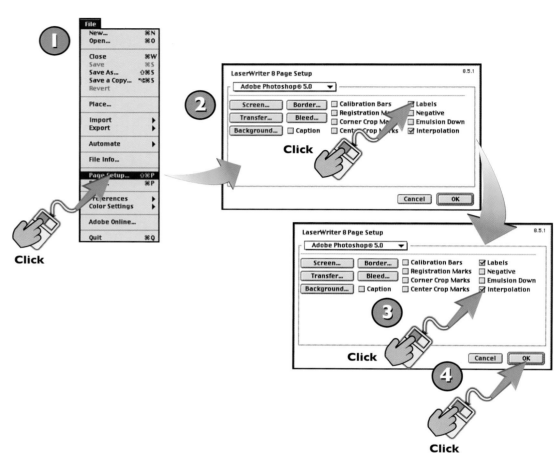

Click

Click

Click

Click

✓ Photoshop offers many complex printing options; for special printing needs, check the Photoshop manual or a more advanced Photoshop book such as *Using Photoshop 5*.

1 Choose **File**, **Page Setup** or press **Cmd+Shift+P**/**Ctrl+Shift+P**.

2 To print the image's filename next to the image, click **Labels**.

3 To improve the appearance of low-resolution images, click **Interpolation** (this option may not work with older printers or with non-PostScript printers).

4 Click **OK**.

Next
Step

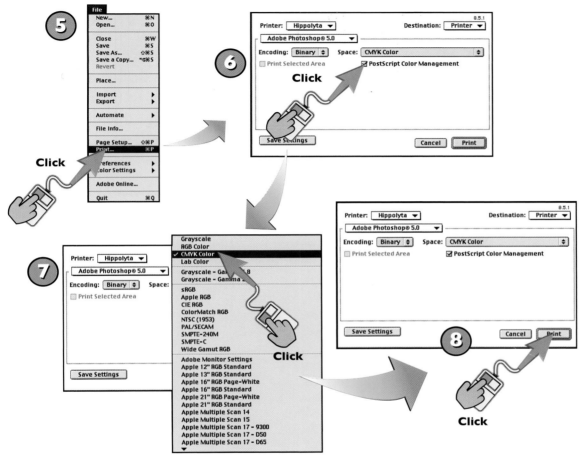

5 Choose **File**, **Print** or press **Cmd+P/Ctrl+P**.

6 If you're printing a color file to a PostScript Level II printer, click **PostScript Color Management**.

7 Choose **Grayscale** or **CMYK Color** from the **Space** pop-up menu, for black and white or color printers, respectively.

8 Click **Print**.

✔ Photoshop prints all the *layers* that are visible; if your image contains layers that you don't want to print, make them invisible before choosing the Print command (see Part 8, "Working with Layers," for more information on making layers visible and invisible).

✔ Always save before printing, in case there's a printing problem that causes your computer to crash. This tip is a good idea when working with any program, not just Photoshop!

PART 2

Opening and Saving Files

All computer files are created equal in one sense—they're all made up of electronic "bits" that can be turned on or off to make a pattern that a computer can read. The tricky part is in knowing which pattern, or *file format,* to use for a given purpose. Photoshop supports dozens of file formats, but most of the time you'll only need to use five or six of these. For print designs, EPS and TIFF are preferred; for Web designs, GIF and JPEG are your best bet.

This part shows you how to open different kinds of files and how to save files in different formats. In addition, Part 2 explains how to change filenames, use filename extensions to identify file formats, and add previews to images so you'll be able to view the images when you import them into other programs.

Tasks

Task 1: Opening a PDF File

Photoshop is famous for its capability to open files in any format, and that includes Adobe Acrobat's Portable Document Format (*PDF*). This is a great way to turn logos or other graphics used in a PDF file into Photoshop images that you can use in creating new documents.

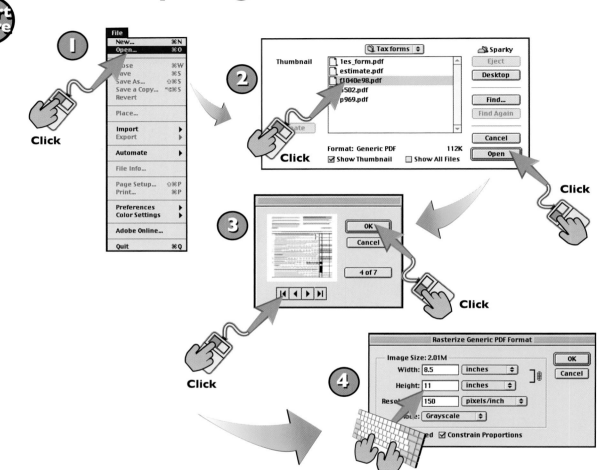

✅ Photoshop can only open one page at a time.

✅ By default, Photoshop enters the document's original measurements in the Rasterize Generic PDF Format dialog box.

① Choose **File**, **Open**.

② Select a PDF file and click **Open**.

③ Click the arrow buttons to choose the page of this document you want to open and click **OK**.

④ Enter the width and height to which you want the page to be converted.

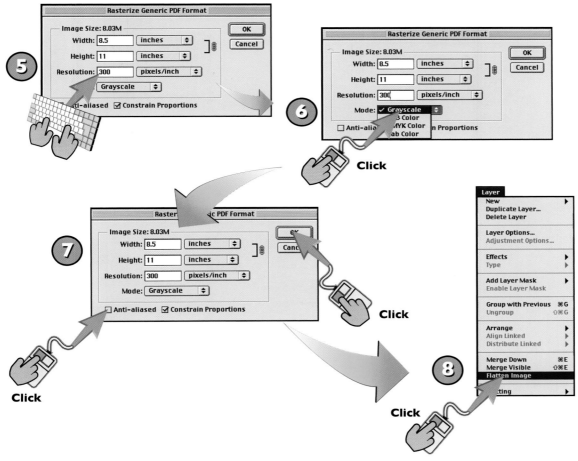

PDF files are *resolution-independent*, so they can be opened at any resolution you like. When Photoshop opens a PDF file, it converts the Acrobat code into individual pixels, a process called *rasterizing*.

Photoshop places rasterized *EPS* and PDF files on a *layer*; before you can save them in a format other than Photoshop's own, you must flatten the layers.

⑤ Enter a resolution—**72** for onscreen use, **300** or more for print use.

⑥ Choose a color mode—**Grayscale** for print or onscreen, **CMYK** for print, or **RGB** for onscreen.

⑦ Click **Anti-aliased** on if the image will be used onscreen, or off if the image will be used in print, and click **OK**.

⑧ Choose **Layer**, **Flatten Image**.

End Task

Task 2: Opening a Photo CD Image

Many stock photography companies supply their images in *Photo CD* format. This multi-resolution format compresses several different versions into each image file, so you have to choose which one you want when you open a Photo CD file.

✓ Each Photo CD file contains up to six images, from a tiny thumbnail to a full-page high-resolution image.

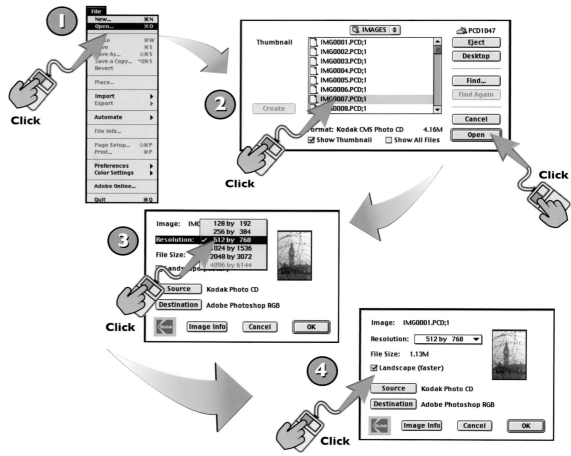

Start Here

Click

Click

Click

Click

Click

(1) Choose **File**, **Open**.

(2) Find the Photo CD file you want to open and click **Open**.

(3) Choose a resolution.

(4) To save a bit of time, click **Landscape** if it's available; the image will open slightly faster.

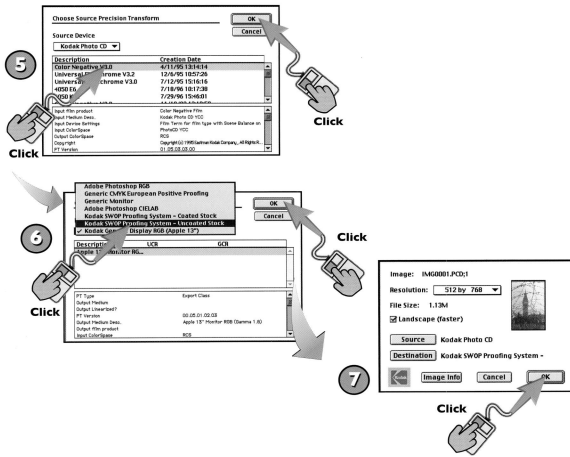

(5) Click **Source** and choose a source profile to match the original film used; if you don't know which profile to use, click **OK** to accept the default.

(6) Click **Destination** to choose a destination profile; unless a listed profile matches your printer, leave this at the default setting and click **OK**.

(7) Click **OK** to open the image.

Task 3: Opening a Vector EPS Image

Photoshop allows you to convert *vector EPS* files, such as those created by CorelDRAW or Adobe Illustrator, to pixel-based images so you can work with them in Photoshop. This is a good way to incorporate EPS images into a Photoshop collage, or to use Photoshop to edit images in ways that you can't do in CorelDRAW or Illustrator.

If the image you're converting is intended for onscreen use, you'll want to choose a low *resolution*—probably 72—and click **Anti-aliased.** *Anti-aliasing* blurs the edges within the image slightly to make them appear smoother at low resolutions.

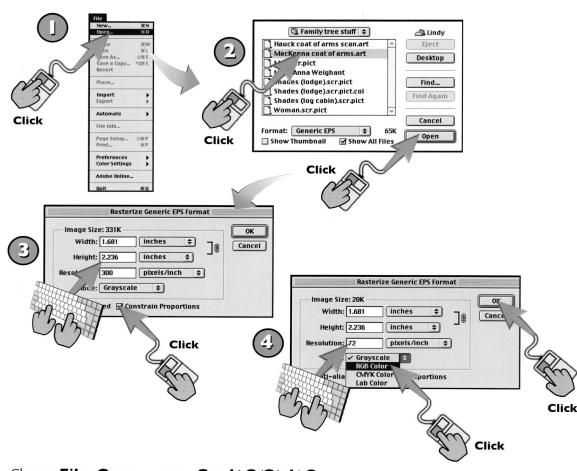

1. Choose **File**, **Open** or press **Cmd+O/Ctrl+O**.

2. Locate the file you want to open and click **Open**.

3. Click **Constrain Proportions** and enter the desired **Width** or **Height** of the image.

4. Enter the **Resolution**; then choose a color **Mode** and click **OK** to open the file.

Task 4: Placing an Image Within Another Image

Start Here

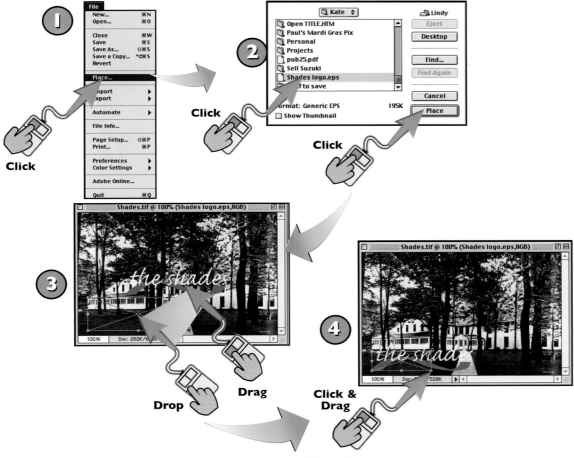

If you want to incorporate **EPS** or **PDF** images into an existing Photoshop image, use the **Place** command. When you place an image, Photoshop inserts it into the existing image on a new layer and allows you to move it and resize it before it's *rasterized*.

① With the existing Photoshop image open, choose **File**, **Place**.

② Locate the file you want to insert and click **Place**.

③ Click and drag to move the placed image.

④ Click and drag on its corners to resize it. When the image is positioned and sized correctly, press **Enter** to rasterize it.

✓ Hold down **Shift** as you drag the corners of the placed image to resize it proportionally.

✓ You can rotate the image by placing the cursor outside a corner until the cursor turns into a curved double-headed arrow; click and drag to rotate.

End Task

Task 5: Saving a File with a New Name or Format

In addition to saving changes as you go along, Photoshop allows you to change the name and format of a file while you're working on it. The Save As dialog box is the same one you see the first time you save a brand new file.

✅ **Depending on the format you choose when you use the Save As command, you may see another dialog box with additional options after you click Save.**

✅ **If the image has layers, you'll need to choose Layer, Flatten Image before you can save in any format other than Photoshop format.**

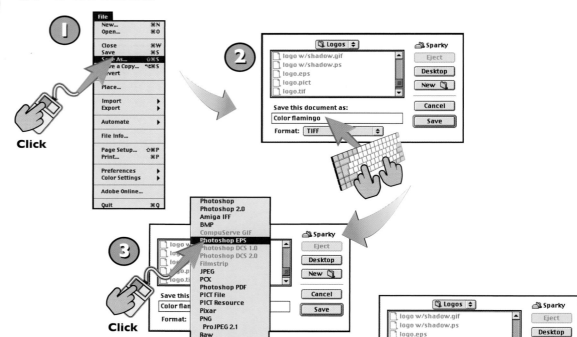

Start Here

Click

Click

Click

① Choose **File**, **Save As**.

② Choose a new location for the file and enter its new name.

③ Choose a new format from the **Format** pop-up menu.

④ Click **Save** to save the file.

End Task

Task 6: Automatically Adding Filename Extensions to Saved Images

Start Here

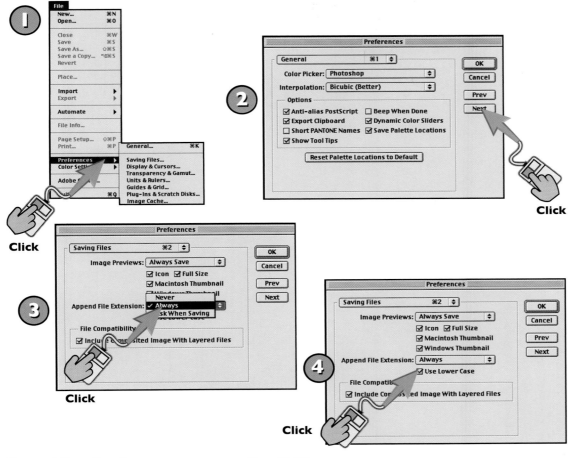

Click

Click

Click

Click

Filename extensions are vital in the Windows/DOS world and can be useful to Mac OS users as well. If you're a Mac OS user, it's a good idea to set your Photoshop preferences so that you can have filename extensions added automatically when you save files. Then Windows systems will be able to identify those files.

✓ If you choose **Ask When Saving**, the **Save** dialog box will have a checkbox labeled **Append**; just click this checkbox and Photoshop adds the extension to the **Name** field.

✓ The **Use Lower Case** option in the **Preferences** dialog box isn't irrevocable; if you choose **Ask When Saving**, a **Use Lower Case** checkbox is also added to the **Save** dialog box, so you can change your mind about lower-case extensions when you save each file.

① Choose **File, Preferences**, or press **Cmd+K**.

② Click **Next** once to switch to the **Saving Files** screen.

③ In the **Append File Extension** pop-up menu, choose **Always** to add extensions automatically or **Ask When Saving** to add a checkbox to the **Save** dialog box.

④ Click **Use Lower Case** if you want extensions to be lower-case letters, and click **OK**.

End Task

Task 7: Exporting a GIF File

The most commonly used format for images on the World Wide Web is *GIF* (Graphics Interchange Format). It's used for simple line art and images with solid colors; photographic images look better when saved in *JPEG* format (see the next task).

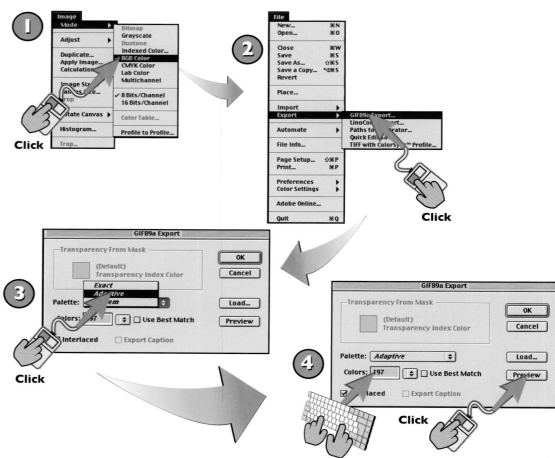

There are three palette options: **Exact,** which won't change the colors at all; **Adaptive,** which reduces the number of colors while trying not to change the image's overall appearance; and **System,** which uses the Mac OS or Windows system palette.

① Make sure the image is in RGB color mode by choosing **Image**, **Mode**, **RGB Color**.

② Choose **File**, **Export**, **GIF89a Export**.

③ Choose an option from the **Palette** pop-up menu.

④ Enter the number of colors you want the image to use—the fewer colors, the smaller the file—and then click **Preview**.

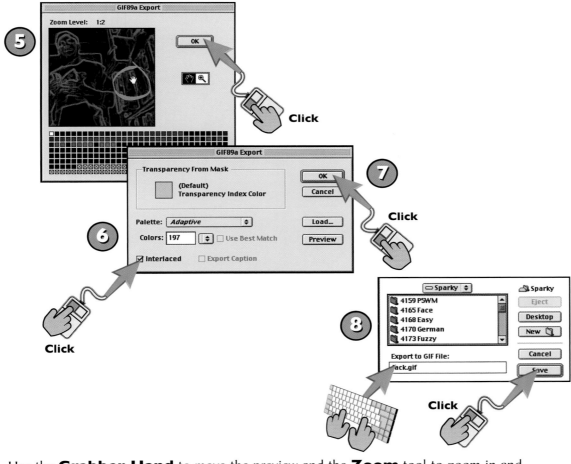

Interlaced GIF files display progressively as they download, starting with a low-resolution version and replacing it with better-looking versions as the image file continues to download. This allows the user to see what the image looks like right away, without having to wait until the entire file is transmitted.

To make a GIF file with a transparent background, copy the portion of the GIF that should be visible and paste it onto a transparent layer; then hide any other layers in the image before choosing the GIF export command.

⑤ Use the **Grabber Hand** to move the preview and the **Zoom** tool to zoom in and out; click **OK** to accept the preview.

⑥ Unless the image will be used as a Web page background, click **Interlaced**.

⑦ Click **OK** to export the image.

⑧ Give the file a name and click **Save**.

Task 8: Saving a JPEG File

JPEG (Joint Photographic Experts Group) is the format most often used for photos on the World Wide Web. It includes powerful *compression* that can create very small image files; however, the more compression you use, the more likely it is that the image will be visually degraded, so it's a good idea to test different compression levels on different images.

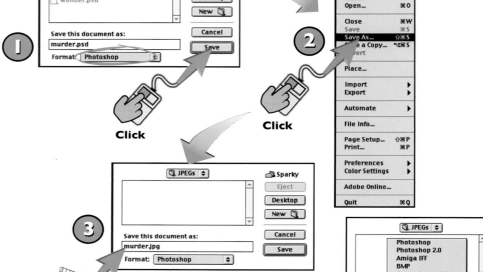

✓ Don't edit JPEG files; they're recompressed every time you save them, so image quality is decreased every time. Return to the original Photoshop file to make changes, and then save a new JPEG file.

① Save the image in Photoshop format to preserve an uncompressed version.

② Choose **File**, **Save As**.

③ Choose a location for the JPEG file and enter a new name for the file with a .jpg extension.

④ Choose **JPEG** from the **Format** pop-up menu and click **Save**.

Next Step

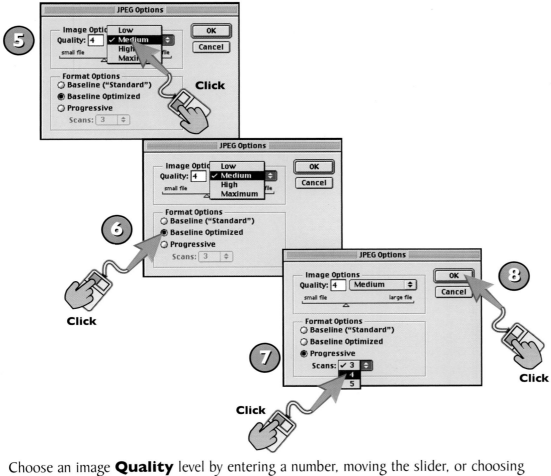

Click

Click

Click

Click

(5) Choose an image **Quality** level by entering a number, moving the slider, or choosing from the pop-up menu.

(6) Choose a **Format Option**: **Baseline**, **Baseline Optimized**, or **Progressive**.

(7) If you chose **Progressive**, choose a number of **Scans**.

(8) Click **OK** to save the file.

✓ Baseline JPEG files are the most compatible with all Web browsers; Baseline Optimized JPEG files are not compatible with all browsers but have better color; and *Progressive* JPEGs start displaying before the entire file is transmitted to the user, like *interlaced* GIF files.

End Task

Task 9: Saving a TIFF File

In print production, the most commonly used file format is *TIFF*. It incorporates *lossless compression*, meaning you can compress a TIFF file without losing any image data, and it's supported by almost every graphics program.

✓ If you're not sure what platform a file will be used on, or if it will be used on both Macintoshes and PCs, choose **PC** in the **TIFF Options** dialog box. Macintoshes can handle files saved either way, but PCs aren't so forgiving.

✓ Very occasionally an older *RIP* will refuse to print images saved with *LZW* compression; in this case, you'll need to resave TIFF files without compression. This is more and more rare, however, so it's best to use **LZW** as a matter of course.

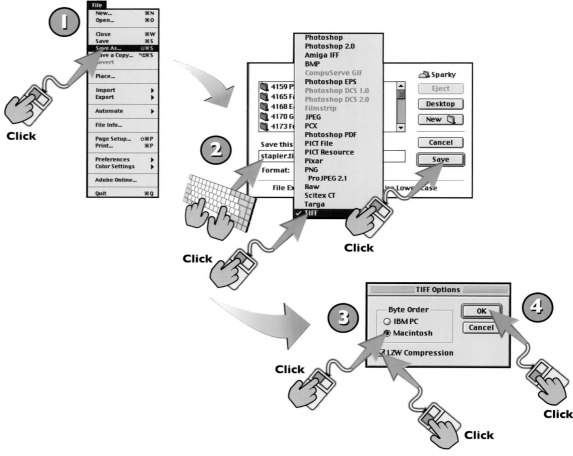

① Choose **File**, **Save As**.

② Give the file a name, choose **TIFF** from the **Format** pop-up menu, and then click **Save**.

③ Click **LZW Compression** and choose the destination platform: **Macintosh** or **IBM PC**.

④ Click **OK** to save the file.

Task 10: Saving an EPS File

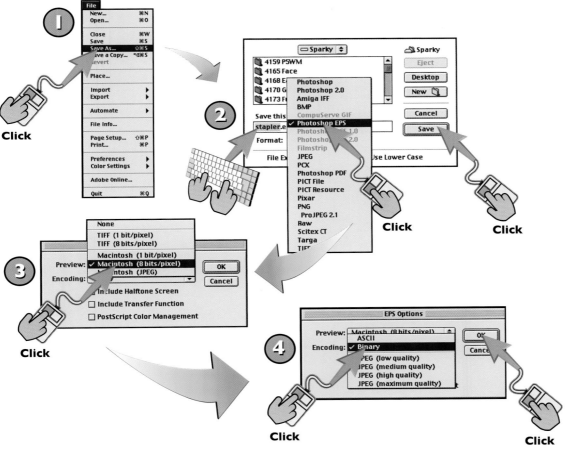

Click

Click

Click

Click

Click

Click

In addition to TIFF, *EPS* files are very common in print production. The name stands for Encapsulated *PostScript*, which means that these files are pre-coded for PostScript printers.

✓ When choosing a *preview* type, use 1-bit for black and white images and 8-bit for *grayscale* or color images.

✓ If an EPS file will be used only on Macintoshes, you can try *JPEG* encoding. It will reduce the size of the file, but it can't be read by some Windows systems (it requires Apple's QuickTime).

1. Choose **File**, **Save As**.

2. Give the file a name, choose **Photoshop EPS** from the **Format** pop-up menu, and then click **Save**.

3. Choose a **Preview** type: **Macintosh** for use on Macintoshes or **TIFF** for use on Windows systems.

4. Choose **Binary** from the **Encoding** pop-up menu and click **OK** to save the file.

End Task

Task 11: Saving a Pre-Separated DCS EPS File

DCS stands for Desktop Color Separations; it's a pre-color-separated format, which means that *color-separated* film outputs faster when you use this format because images don't have to be separated in the *RIP*. DCS images are contained in five files, one for each *process color* and a composite that you can import into a page layout program.

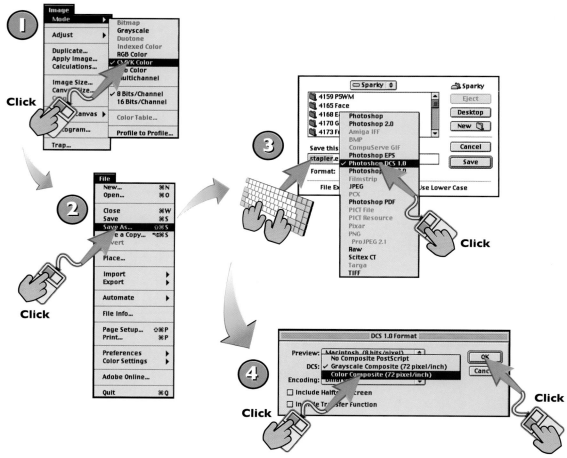

Other than the DCS composite options, the other choices in the DCS 1.0 Format dialog box are just like those in the EPS Options dialog box (see Task 10, "Saving an EPS File.")

Photoshop DCS 2.0 is a more sophisticated version of the DCS format that supports spot colors and can create a smaller single file, as opposed to the multiple files of DCS 1.0.

1 Make sure the image is in CMYK mode by choosing **Image**, **Mode**, **CMYK Color**.

2 Choose **File**, **Save As**.

3 Give the file a name and choose **Photoshop DCS 1.0** from the **Format** pop-up menu.

4 Choose a **DCS** composite option—none, grayscale, or color—and click **OK** to save the file.

Task 12: Adding Previews to Saved Images

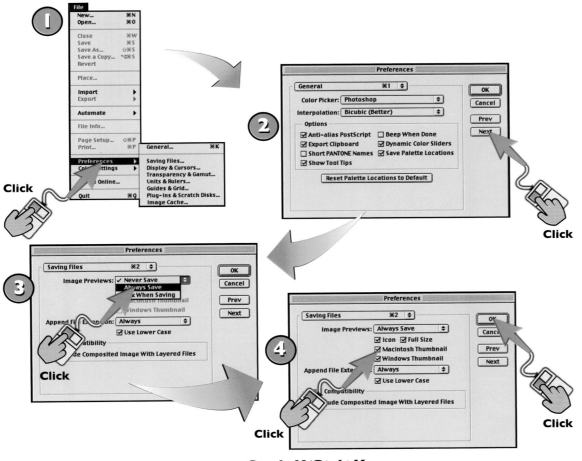

Image *previews* allow you to see what files look like before you open them. Icon previews are custom file icons on the desktop that show a tiny representation of the image; thumbnail previews are viewable in Photoshop's Open dialog box; and full-size previews are low-resolution versions of the image for applications that can't open high-resolution files.

✅ For Windows users, the **Ask When Saving** option adds a checkbox to the **Save** dialog box; check the box if you want to add a preview. For Mac OS users, three checkboxes are displayed, one for each type of preview; click the boxes for the previews you want to add.

✅ If file size is a concern, you might want to skip adding previews and icons—they can make your Photoshop files much bigger. Files without previews and icons can still be placed in other applications like QuarkXPress, and they can still be opened and edited in Photoshop.

1 Choose **File**, **Preferences** or press **Cmd+K/Ctrl+K**.

2 Click **Next** once to switch to the **Saving Files** screen.

3 Choose an option from the **Image Previews** pop-up menu: **Never**, **Always**, or **Ask When Saving**.

4 On Mac OS, choose the types of preview you want to include and click **OK**.

Making and Saving Selections

Most operations in Photoshop start with a *selection*. Any time you want to apply an effect to part of an image rather than the entire image, you need to select the portion of the image you want to work on. Photoshop allows you to select parts of the image that don't touch each other, and you can combine selections in various ways. You can make selections in several ways—such as by painting over the area you want to select or by using the Pen tool to draw a precise outline of the area to be selected. You can also save selections for future use.

Part 3 shows you how to create selections with Photoshop's selection tools, how to save and restore selections by using channels and paths, and how to select areas based on their color. This part also covers ways to modify selections once they're created.

Tasks

Task 1: Selecting a Geometric Area

To apply changes to a single area of a Photoshop image, first you have to select that area. Photoshop's Marquee tool offers the simplest, quickest way of selecting an area, and it comes in both rectangular and elliptical versions.

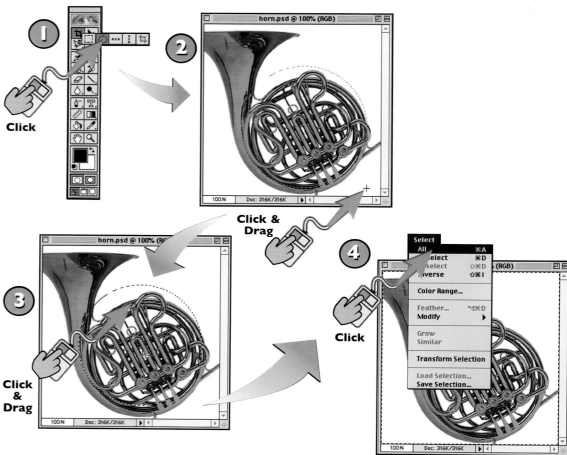

Start Here

Click

Click & Drag

Click & Drag

Click

✓ The animated dotted line surrounding a selected area is referred to as the *marching ants* by most Photoshop users.

✓ To choose from the different Marquee tools, click and hold the visible one and choose a tool from the "fly-out" tool menu that appears.

(1) Choose the elliptical or rectangular **Marquee** tool from the **Tool** palette.

(2) Click and drag to define a selection—hold down **Shift** as you drag to make the selection perfectly circular or square.

(3) Click and drag in the selection to move it.

(4) To select the entire image, choose **Select**, **All** or press **Cmd+A/Ctrl+A**.

Task 2: Selecting an Irregular Area

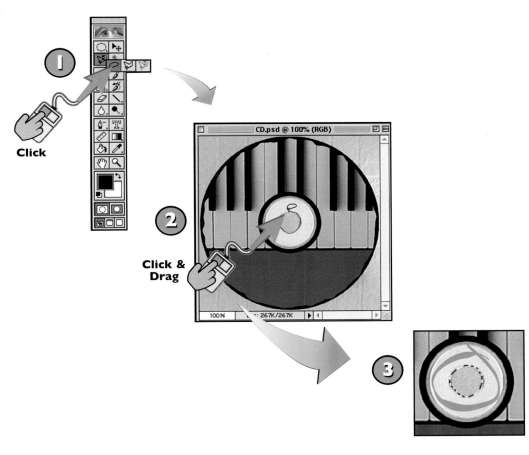

Click

Click & Drag

You can select an irregular shape by using the Lasso tool to draw around the area you want to select. The bottom end of the lasso's "rope" is the "tip" of the tool.

✓ To make precise *selections* around objects, try the Magnetic Lasso tool; see Part 3, Task 5, "Selecting an Object Magnetically," for instructions.

✓ The Polygonal Lasso tool creates selections from straight line segments. Click anywhere you want a corner and double-click to make the last corner— Photoshop automatically connects your starting and ending points. Or return to your starting point; when the Polygonal Lasso cursor adds a little ° symbol, let go to close the shape.

① Choose the **Lasso** tool from the **Tool** palette.

② Click and drag in the image to select an area.

③ Release the mouse button to create the selection—Photoshop connects your starting and ending points with a straight line.

End Task

Task 3: Selecting an Area of a Fixed Size or Shape

To make a *selection* of a specific size or shape, you use the Marquee tools, modifying them so that they can create only that size or shape when you click in the image.

Start Here

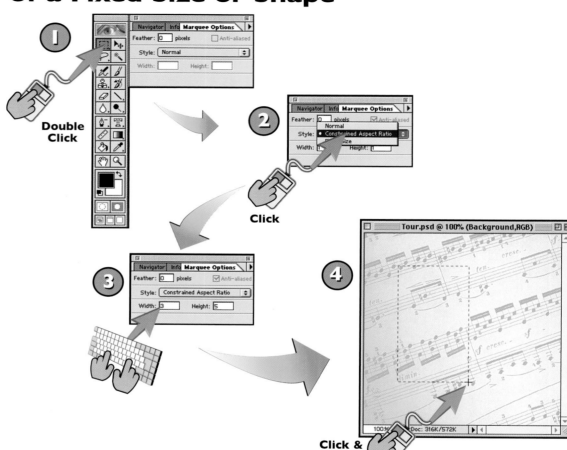

Double Click

Click

Click & Drag

✓ Fixed-size selections are useful as measuring tools, too; to make sure objects in an image are all within a certain size, set the Marquee tool to that size and just click each object to make sure it falls within the *marching ants*.

1 Double-click the **Marquee** tool in the **Tool** palette to display the **Marquee Options** palette.

2 To select an area with specific proportions, choose **Constrained Aspect Ratio** in the palette's **Style** pop-up menu.

3 Enter a ratio for the **Height** and **Width** of the selection.

4 Click and drag in the image to make the selection.

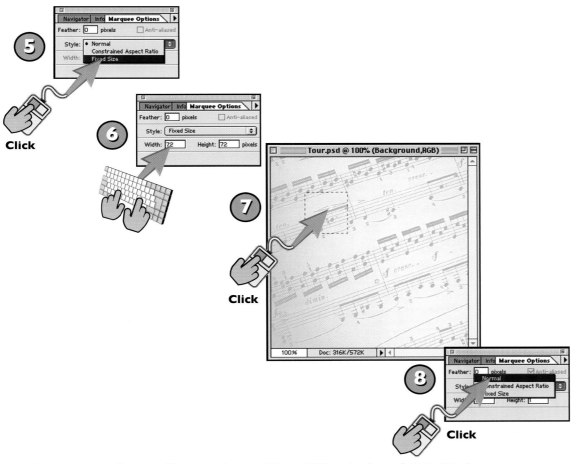

Click

Click

Click

5 To select an area of a specific size, choose **Fixed Size** in the palette's **Style** pop-up menu.

6 Enter the **Height** and **Width** of the selection in pixels.

7 Click in the image to make the selection.

8 Choose **Normal** to return the Marquee tool to its normal behavior.

✓ **Fixed-size or -shape selections can be moved around in the image just like any selections; it's often easiest to click anywhere to make the selection and then drag it to surround the area you want selected.**

End Task

It's not often that you need this capability, but when the need arises to make stripes, or to delete just a fringe of pixels along the edge of an object, Photoshop provides a tool to let you do it. The single-column and single-row **Marquee** tools select just what their names imply.

Task 4: Selecting One Column or Row of Pixels

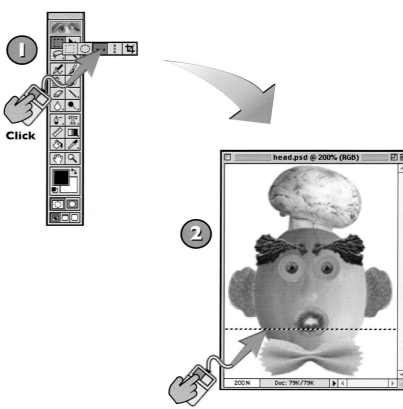

✓ Dragging with the single-column or single-row **Marquee** tool moves the *selection*, rather than enlarging it, because you can't select more than one column or row with these tools.

① Click the **Marquee** tool in the **Tool** palette and slide the mouse over to select the single-column or single-row Marquee tool.

② Click in the image to make the selection.

Task 5: Selecting an Object Magnetically

Start Here

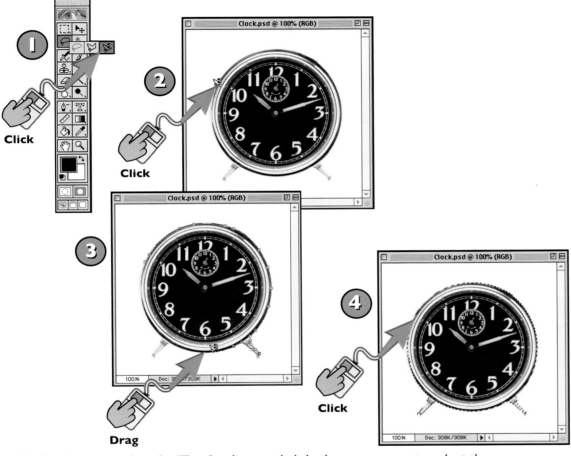

Click

Click

Clock.psd @ 100% (RGB)

Clock.psd @ 100% (RGB)

Clock.psd @ 100% (RGB)

Drag

Click

Selecting hard-edged objects is easier than it used to be with **Photoshop 5's** new **Magnetic Lasso** tool. This tool finds the edges between areas of different colors and draws *selections* along those edges.

✓ You can override the Magnetic Lasso's choice of where to place its selection line at any point by clicking where you want the selection to go; the selection won't be created until you double-click or click again on your starting point.

✓ If the Magnetic Lasso seems to be rounding off corners, double-click the **Lasso** tool in the **Tool palette** to bring up the **Magnetic Lasso Options palette** and make sure **Anti-aliased** is off.

✓ You'll know you've reached your starting point when the Magnetic Lasso's cursor adds a ° —then click to close the selection.

1 Click the **Lasso** tool in the **Tool** palette and slide the mouse over to select the **Magnetic Lasso** tool.

2 Click (without holding down the mouse button) near an edge of the object you want to select.

3 Drag the cursor around the edge of the object.

4 Click again at the starting point to create the selection.

End Task

Task 6: Creating a Selection by Painting

Based on an analogy with the prepress technician's rubylith, Photoshop's Quick Mask feature allows you to paint a transparent reddish image over your existing image that can then be converted to a *selection*. Because you can paint in Quick Mask mode with less than 100 percent opacity, pixels selected this way can be partially selected, so that whatever effect you apply to them is only partially applied.

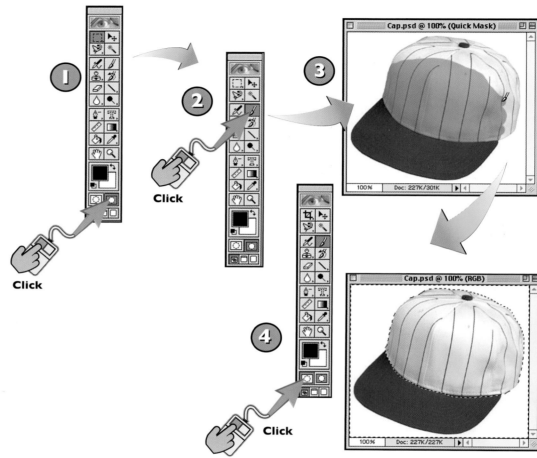

Start Here!

Click

Click

Click

✓ To begin using Quick Mask with part of the image already masked out, select the portion of the image you want to keep before entering Quick Mask mode.

1 Click the **Quick Mask Mode** button on the **Tool** palette or press **Q**.

2 Choose a painting tool from the **Tool** palette.

3 Paint over the portions of the image that should not be included in the selection.

4 Click the **Standard Mode** button or press **Q** again to return to normal selection mode.

End Task

Task 7: Selecting the Inverse of a Selection

Start Here

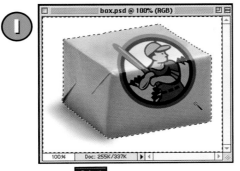

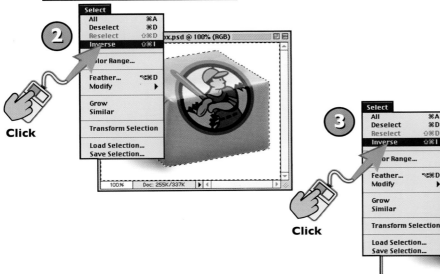

Click

Click

Probably one of the most confusing commands in Photoshop, the Inverse command is very different from the Invert command (which reverses the colors in the image to create a negative). The Inverse command inverts a selection instead, selecting the parts of an image that were not included in the original selection.

① Make a selection by using any method.

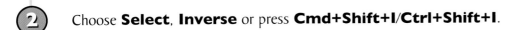
② Choose **Select**, **Inverse** or press **Cmd+Shift+I/Ctrl+Shift+I**.

③ Press **Cmd+Shift+I/Ctrl+Shift+I** again to return to the original selection.

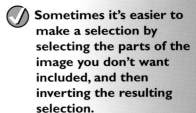
Sometimes it's easier to make a selection by selecting the parts of the image you don't want included, and then inverting the resulting selection.

Task 8: Selecting an Area of the Same Color

Using the Magic Wand tool really does feel like doing magic. Clicking with this tool selects all the pixels in an area that are the same— or nearly the same—color as the pixel on which you directly click.

Start Here

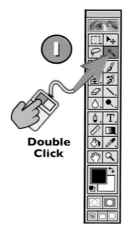

Double Click

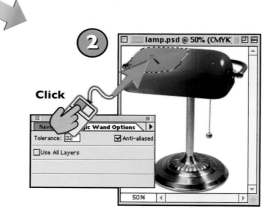

Click

✓ Use the Magic Wand together with the Inverse command to select objects on a plain background. First select the background with the Magic Wand, and then press **Cmd+Shift+I** to invert the *selection* so that the object itself is selected.

Double-click the **Magic Wand** tool in the **Tool** palette to select the Magic Wand and display the **Magic Wand Options** palette.

Click in the image to select a group of pixels of the same color range.

Next Step

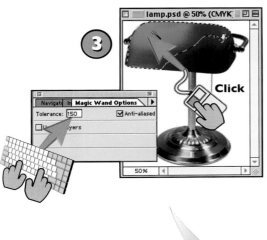

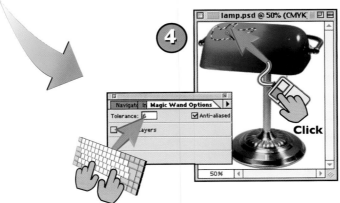

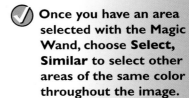

3 To broaden the color range to select more pixels, adjust the **Tolerance** setting on the palette upward, and then click again in the image.

4 To narrow the color range to select fewer pixels, adjust the **Tolerance** setting on the palette downward, and then click again in the image.

✓ **Once you have an area selected with the Magic Wand, choose Select, Similar to select other areas of the same color throughout the image.**

When you need to select the same color all over an image, the Magic Wand tool isn't enough. Photoshop gives you a way to do this: the Color Range command. You can adjust the tolerance of the selection via a preview, so that the final selection is just what you want.

Task 9: Selecting Multiple Areas of the Same Color

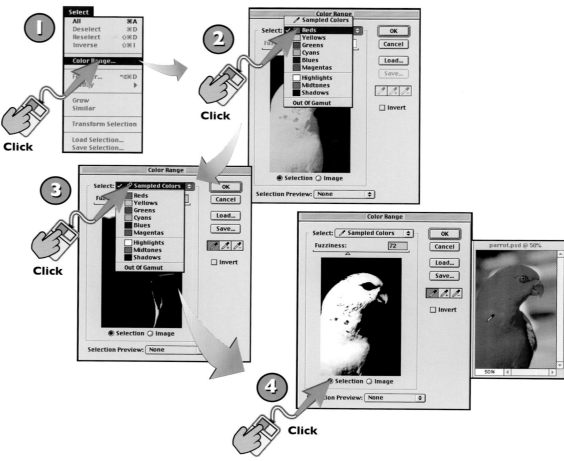

The Fuzziness slider performs the same function as the Magic Wand's Tolerance setting; it determines how close to the original color a pixel has to be for it to be included in the selection.

1. Choose **Select**, **Color Range**.

2. To select a specific range of colors, choose a color from the **Select** pop-up menu.

3. To select a color chosen from the image, choose **Sampled Colors** from the **Select** menu.

4. Click the **Selection** radio button to preview the selected area in the dialog box.

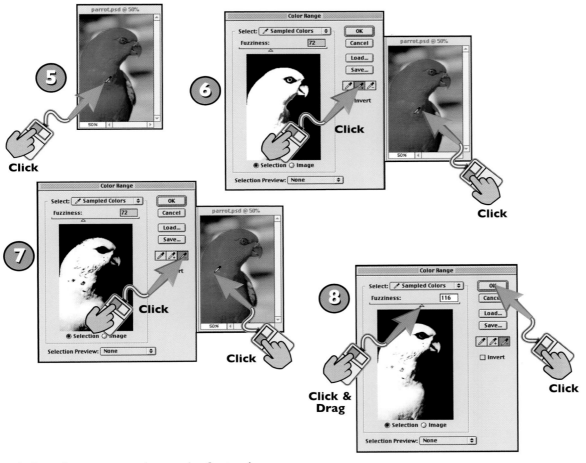

5 Click in the image to choose the first color.

6 To add more colors to the selection, click the **plus eyedropper** and click other colors in the image.

7 To remove colors from the selection, click the **minus eyedropper** and click other colors in the image.

8 To select more or fewer pixels, drag the **Fuzziness** slider right or left respectively, and then click **OK** to create the selection.

Task 10: Creating a Selection from Type

In Photoshop, sometimes type is more than just text—you can make it glow, spin, tremble, or just about anything else. Some type effects start out with a type-shaped selection rather than actual type, so Photoshop includes the **Type Mask tool** to create such selections.

✓ Unfortunately, the Type Mask tool doesn't offer a preview, so you can't see how big the type mask selection will be as you create the type. But the text you used remains in the Type Tool dialog box, so if the type mask isn't the right size, just click again with the Type Mask tool and change the size in the dialog box.

✓ For more information about creating type and using the options in the Type Tool dialog box, see Part 9, "Creating and Editing Type."

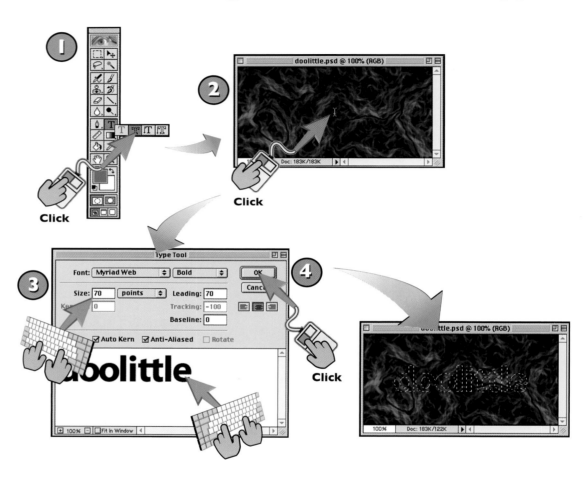

Start Here

Click

Click

Click

Click

(1) Click the **Type** tool in the **Tool** palette and slide the mouse over to choose the **Type Mask** tool.

(2) Click in the image to open the **Type Tool** dialog box.

(3) Choose a font and size for the type, and then enter the text.

(4) Click **OK** to create the selection.

End Task

Task 11: Adding to a Selection

Start Here

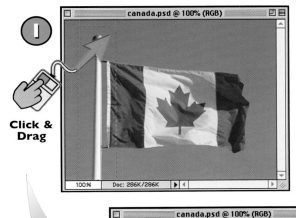

Click & Drag

In Photoshop, the **Shift** key almost always means "add." That holds true when creating selections as well; with a selection active, holding down the **Shift** key enables you to add more selected areas to the selection.

Shift+Click & Drag

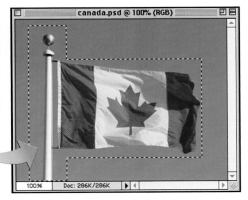

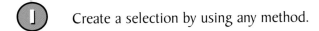

Create a selection by using any method.

Press **Shift** and make another selection with the same tool or a different one.

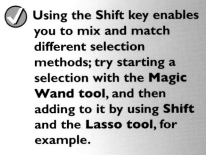
Using the **Shift** key enables you to mix and match different selection methods; try starting a selection with the **Magic Wand tool**, and then adding to it by using **Shift** and the **Lasso tool**, for example.

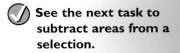
See the next task to subtract areas from a selection.

End Task

Task 12: Subtracting from a Selection

If things get out of hand when making a selection, you don't need to start all over again. You can deselect portions of a selected area by holding down the **Option/Alt** key.

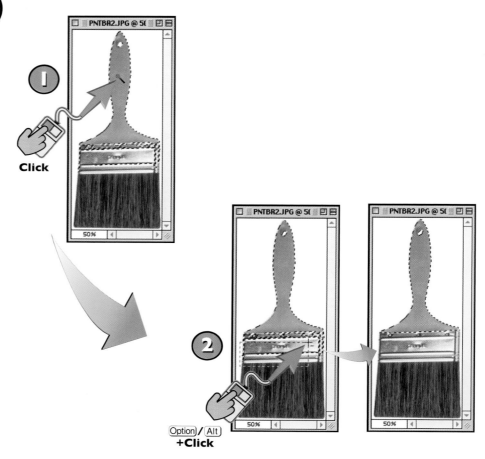

Click

Option/ Alt
+Click

✓ The Magic Wand tool often selects a larger area than you really want; use the Option key to clip off those unwanted portions of the selection.

✓ By alternating among different selection tools and by using the **Shift** and **Option** keys, you can quickly select any area of an image; don't be afraid to mix and match these different selection techniques.

① Create a selection by using any method.

② Press **Option/Alt** and select the "extra" area with the same tool or a different one.

Task 13: Making a Selection Smaller or Larger

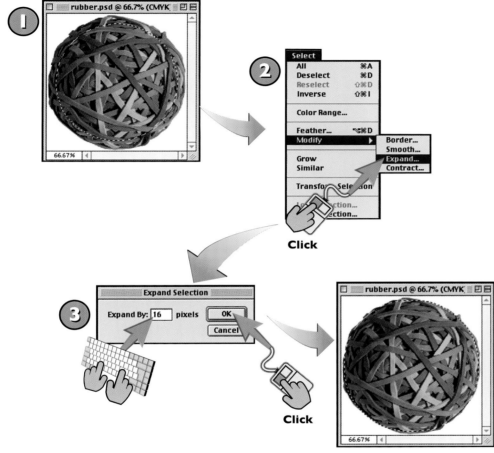

Click

Click

Sometimes a selection is perfectly shaped, but not the correct size. In this case, it's easy to add a bit around the edges, or shrink the selection a bit. The Expand and Contract commands work with selections created by using any method, and you can use them as many times as you need to adjust the selection perfectly.

1. Create a selection by using any method.

2. Choose **Select, Modify, Expand** to enlarge the selection or **Select, Modify, Contract** to shrink it.

3. Enter a number between 1 and 16 pixels and click **OK** to adjust the selection.

 An unfortunate idiosyncrasy of the Expand command is that it cuts off corners of rectangular selections, so if you use it, you no longer have a rectangular selection.

Task 14: Selecting the Non-Transparent Areas of a Layer

A selection made up of a layer's opaque *pixels* is called that layer's *transparency mask*. You can select a layer's transparency mask even if that layer isn't currently active or visible, so it's a good way to duplicate a shape on another layer. You can also combine transparency masks from more than one layer into a selection.

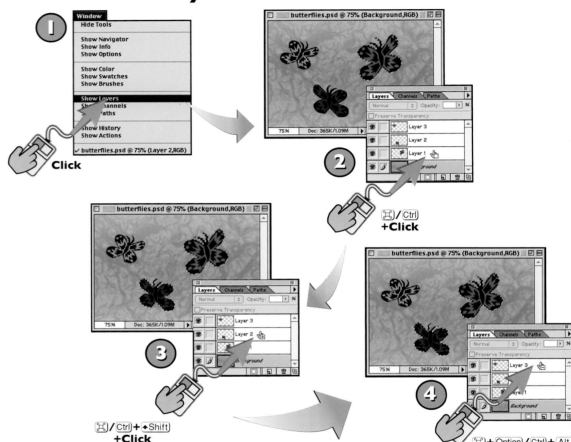

Start Here

Click

⌘/Ctrl +Click

⌘/Ctrl+⬆Shift +Click

⌘+Option/Ctrl+Alt +Click

✓ If an image's background layer is not made transparent when the image is created, you can't select that layer's transparency mask.

① Choose **Window**, **Show Layers**.

② **Cmd+click/Ctrl+click** on the name of the layer whose transparency mask you want to select.

③ **Cmd+Shift+click/Ctrl+Shift+click** a layer name to add that layer's transparency mask to the selection.

④ **Cmd+Option+click/Ctrl+Alt+click** a layer name to remove that layer's transparency mask from the selection.

Task 15: Selecting a Border Area

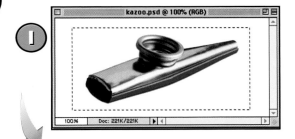

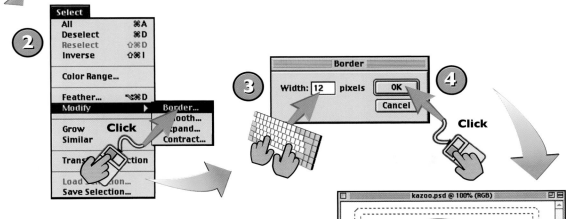

Suppose you don't want to apply a change to an entire selected area—just to the edges of it. Photoshop allows you to do this by changing the selection to a border selection.

(✓) A border selection is automatically *feathered*, meaning that the pixels along its edges are only partially selected. Effects you apply to a feathered selection will gradually fade out from the center.

For more information about feathered selections, see Task 18, "Feathering the Edges of a Selection."

① Make a selection by using any method.

② Choose **Select**, **Modify**, **Border**.

③ Enter a number of pixels for the border **Width**.

④ Click **OK** to select the border area.

Task 16: Transforming a Selection

Once a selection is made, you can resize and reshape it in a number of ways by *transforming* it. To transform the pixels in the selected area of the image, you use the Transform commands in the Edit menu. But for transforming the shape of selection marquees themselves, you use the Transform Selection command in the Select menu.

The cursor changes as you hold down modifier keys and move over different handles. A black arrowhead means you're about to move the selection; a gray one means you're applying perspective. A white arrowhead indicates skewing, a double arrow indicates resizing, and a curved double arrow indicates rotating.

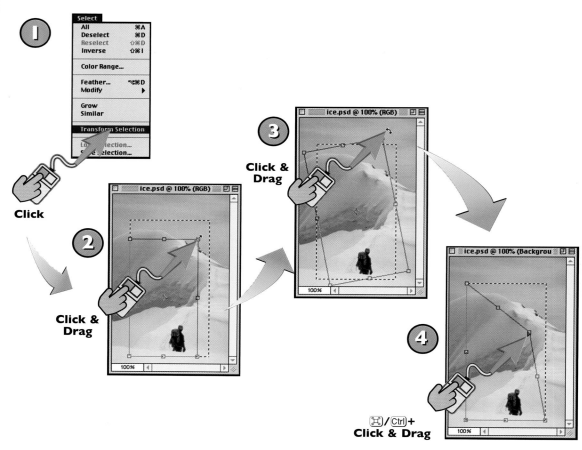

Start Here!

Click

Click & Drag

Click & Drag

Click & Drag

⌘/Ctrl+
Click & Drag

1. Create a selection by using any method and choose **Select, Transform Selection**.

2. To scale the selection, click any handle and drag.

3. To rotate the selection, click and drag outside the selection border.

4. To reshape the selection, **Cmd+click/Ctrl+click** and drag any handle.

Next Step

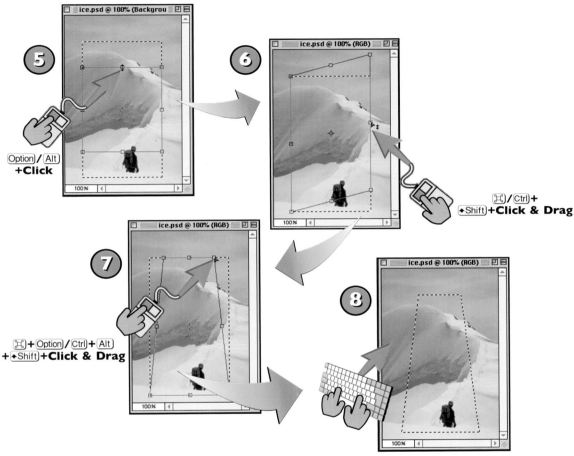

(5) To reshape the selection symmetrically, **Option+click/Alt+click** and drag any handle.

(6) To skew the selection, **Cmd+Shift+click/Ctrl+Shift+click** a side handle and drag.

(7) To apply perspective to the selection, **Cmd+Option+Shift+click/Ctrl+Alt+Shift+click** a corner handle and drag.

(8) Press **Enter** to apply the changes or **Esc** to cancel them.

✓ It's usually hard to picture the effect of these transformations on a selection without trying it; a good exercise is to make a selection and experiment with the different transformations until they make sense.

✓ For more information on transforming a selected area, see Part 6, "Editing Images."

Task 17: Smoothing a Selection

Selections—especially those made with the **Magic Wand** tool or the **Color Range** command—often have rough edges and little "bubbles" of unselected pixels within selections. An easy way to fix this problem is to use the **Smooth** command, which removes small extraneous selections outside the main selection as well.

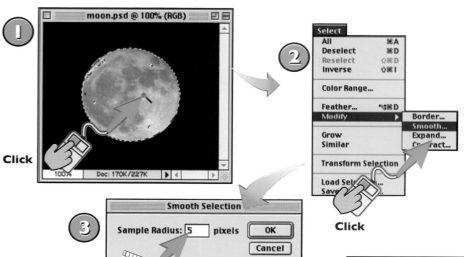

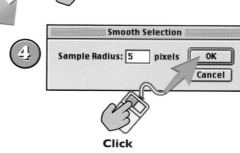

Click

Click

Click

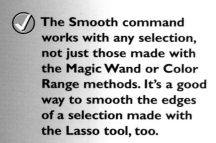

✓ **The Smooth command works with any selection, not just those made with the Magic Wand or Color Range methods. It's a good way to smooth the edges of a selection made with the Lasso tool, too.**

Make a selection by using any method.

Choose **Select**, **Modify**, **Smooth**.

Enter a number of pixels for the **Sample Radius**—this is the smallest "bubble" that will be smoothed out.

Click **OK** to smooth the selection.

Task 18: Feathering the Edges of a Selection

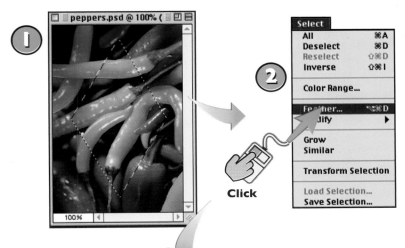

Select
All	⌘A
Deselect	⌘D
Reselect	⇧⌘D
Inverse	⇧⌘I
Color Range...	
Feather...	⌥⌘D
...lify	▶
Grow	
Similar	
Transform Selection	
Load Selection...	
Save Selection...	

Click

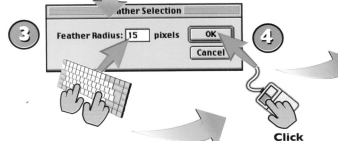

Feather Selection

Feather Radius: 15 pixels   OK   Cancel

Click

One of the neatest tricks Photoshop has to offer is the fact that pixels in an image can be partially selected, so that whatever changes you make to the selected area are only partially applied. A feathered selection is one whose edge pixels are partially selected—think of it as being like a cloth that's wet all over, but wetter in the center and almost dry around the edges.

✓ The Feather Radius determines how deep the feathered area is—how far it extends from the edge of the selection.

✓ After you apply a feather to it, the selection may appear to shrink and become more rounded, but you won't really see the effect until you make a change to the selected area, such as filling it with a color.

① Make a selection by using any method.

② Choose **Select**, **Feather**.

③ Enter a **Feather Radius** in pixels.

④ Click **OK** to feather the selection.

Task 19: Hiding and Deselecting a Selection

Photoshop's *marching ants* are helpful in defining the selected area, but they can be distracting when you're trying out changes for that area. Hiding the selection marquee can help. You also need to remember to deselect, or drop, a selection when you're done with it.

Start Here

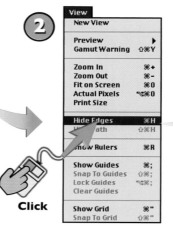

Click

Click

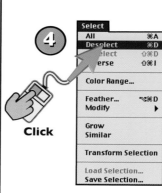

Click

To save a selection for future use before you drop it, see the next task, "Saving a Selection as a Channel."

① Make a selection by using any method.

② To hide the marching ants, choose **View, Hide Edges** or press **Cmd+H/Ctrl+H**.

③ To show the marching ants, choose **View, Show Edges** or press **Cmd+H/Ctrl+H** again.

④ To drop the selection, choose **Select, Deselect** or press **Cmd+D/Ctrl+D**.

End Task

Task 20: Saving a Selection as a Channel

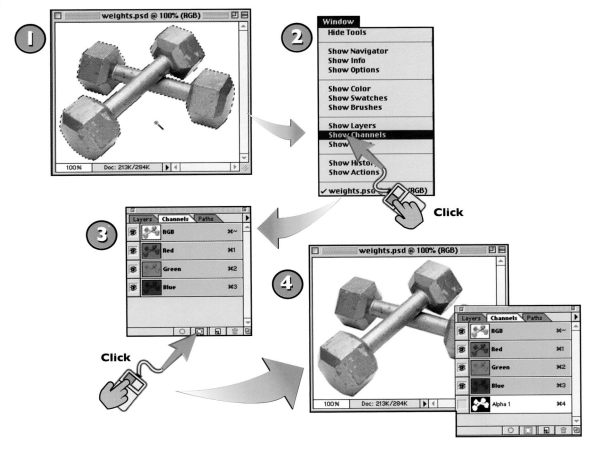

Click

Click

You can save selections as channels so that you can reactivate them if you later need to select the same area. Photoshop translates a selection into a grayscale image representing selected pixels with white, nonselected pixels with black, and partially selected pixels with gray.

---

1. Make a selection by using any method.

2. Choose **Window, Show Channels** to display the Channels palette.

3. Click the **Save Selection as Channel** button on the palette.

4. Press **Cmd+D/Ctrl+D** to drop the selection.

✓ You can see the channel Photoshop created from your selection by clicking its name in the Channels palette—Alpha 1, if it's the first selection you've saved. To view the image again, click the top channel in the palette or press **Cmd+~/Ctrl+~**.

✓ To reactivate the selection from the channel, see Task 24, "Creating a Selection from a Channel."

End Task

Task 21: Pasting into a Selection

In addition to defining the area that will be affected by editing changes, selections can be used to define the area into which you can paste objects. This is actually a quick way of creating a *layer mask*.

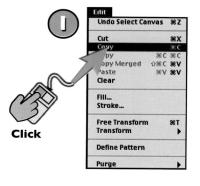

Click

Click

⌘/Ctrl+
Click & Drag

✓ Once you've created a layer mask, you can modify it to change its effect on the image. See Part 8, "Working with Layers."

✓ Holding down **Cmd/Ctrl** temporarily turns whatever tool you're using into the Move tool, with which you can move the image on the current layer. Let go of the **Cmd/Ctrl** key to return to the original tool.

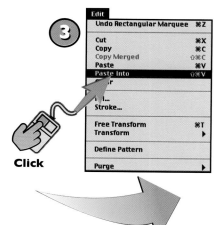

1 Cut or copy the image you want to paste.

2 Make a selection in the new image by using any method.

3 Choose **Edit**, **Paste Into** or press **Cmd+Shift+V/Ctrl+Shift+V**.

4 **Cmd+click/Ctrl+click** and drag to move the pasted image within the area defined by the selection.

Task 22: Removing "Fringes" from a Selection

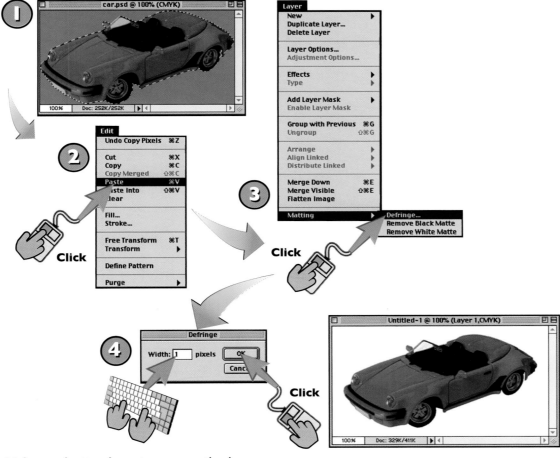

When you make a selection and then move it or paste it, sometimes bits of the background colors come with it. Photoshop has a command designed specifically to remove those fringes from a pasted or moved selection.

✓ Rather than clipping the edges of the pasted selection, Photoshop changes the pixels around the edge to colors that more closely match the colors of the selection.

✓ The Remove Black Matte and Remove White Matte commands work similarly on selections copied from black or white backgrounds.

(1) Make a selection by using any method.

(2) Copy the selection and then choose **Edit**, **Paste**.

(3) Choose **Layer**, **Matting**, **Defringe**.

(4) Enter the **Width** of the area to be affected and click **OK**.

Task 23: Using the Channels Palette

Photoshop's images are made up of channels—one for each color component of an image, and one for each selection you've saved for later use. Channels can also be used to indicate what areas of an image should be transparent when it's saved as a GIF file.

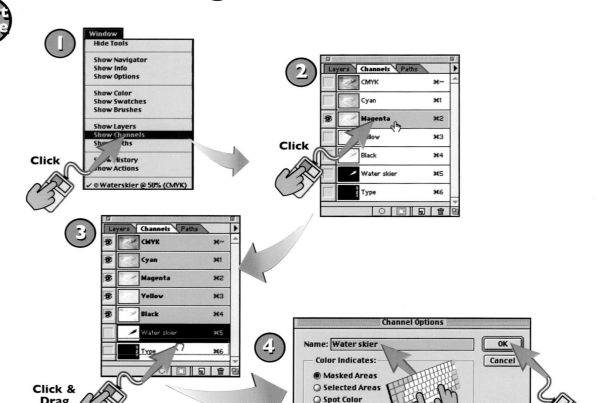

Click

Click

Click & Drag

Click

✓ The Channels palette works like the Layers and Paths palette, and by default it's grouped with them. You can view any of the three by clicking the appropriate tab at the top of the palette.

1. Choose **Window, Show Channels** to display the Channels palette.

2. To view a channel, click its name in the list.

3. To move a channel in the list, click and drag its name.

4. To change a channel's name, double-click it, enter a new name, and click **OK**.

Task 24: Creating a Selection from a Channel

Start Here

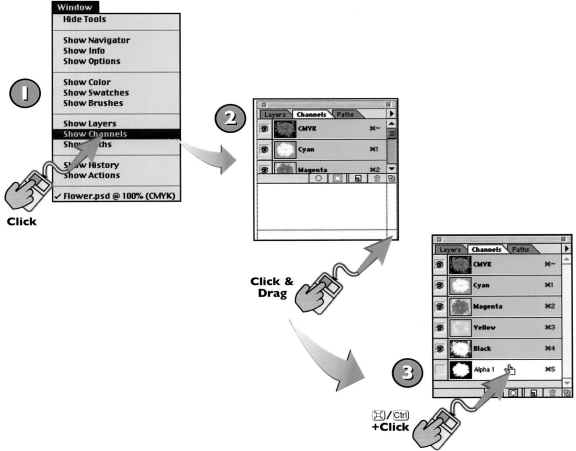

Click

Click & Drag

⌘/Ctrl +Click

When you save a selection, Photoshop creates a grayscale representation of it and places that image in an *alpha channel*. These channels enable you to save selections for later use. You can recreate the original selection based on the channel.

✓ This technique also works with the color channels, not just alpha channels. Depending on the image, this can be a good way to create a selection of the image's background.

✓ An alternative method of loading a selection from a channel is to click the channel's name and click the **Load Channel as Selection** button at the bottom of the **Channels** palette. Then click the first channel in the list to view the entire image again.

1 Choose **Window, Show Channels** to display the Channels palette.

2 Resize the palette if necessary so you can see the name of the channel you want to use.

3 **Cmd+click/Ctrl+click** on the name of the alpha channel to load the selection.

End Task

Task 25: Creating a Selection from Multiple Channels

Photoshop provides several ways that you can combine the selections stored in alpha channels. You can add and subtract channel selections from each other or from a prior selection, and you can choose to select the places where two or more channel selections intersect.

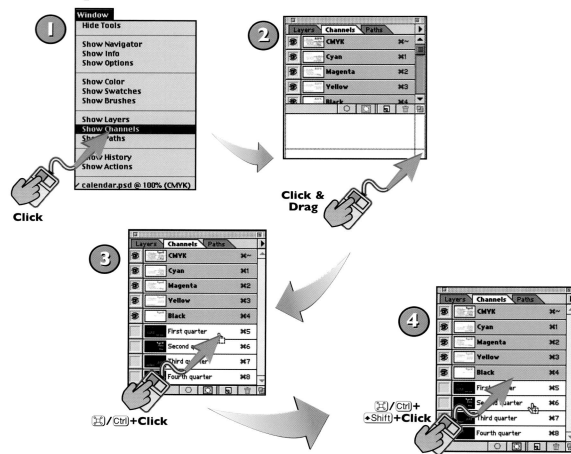

Start Here

Click

Click & Drag

⌘/Ctrl+Click

⌘/Ctrl+ +Shift+Click

✓ The procedure for adding and subtracting channel selections to and from the current selection is the same as that for adding and subtracting layer transparency selections (see Task 14, "Selecting the Non-Transparent Areas of a Layer").

1 Choose **Window**, **Show Channels** to display the Channels palette.

2 Resize the **Channels** palette so you can see all the alpha channels.

3 **Cmd+click/Ctrl+click** on a channel to load its selection.

4 **Cmd+Shift+click/Ctrl+Shift+click** on the name of another channel to add that channel to the selection.

Next Step

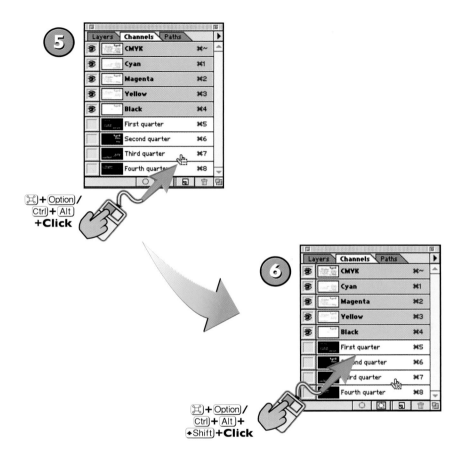

⑤ **Cmd+Option+click/Ctrl+Alt+click** the name of another channel to remove that channel's selection.

⑥ **Cmd+Option+Shift+click/Ctrl+Alt+Shift+click** a channel name to select the intersection of that channel and the active selection.

✓ If you have a hard time remembering all these keyboard shortcuts, there's an easier (but more time-consuming) way to combine channel selections. Choose **Select, Load Selection,** choose the channel you want from the pop-up menu, and click the radio button next to what you want to do with that channel.

Task 26: Viewing Multiple Channels at the Same Time

Ordinarily, when you work on an image in Photoshop, you're viewing just the image channels, not the alpha channels. But you can choose to overlay the alpha channels on the image, so you can see how they relate to it.

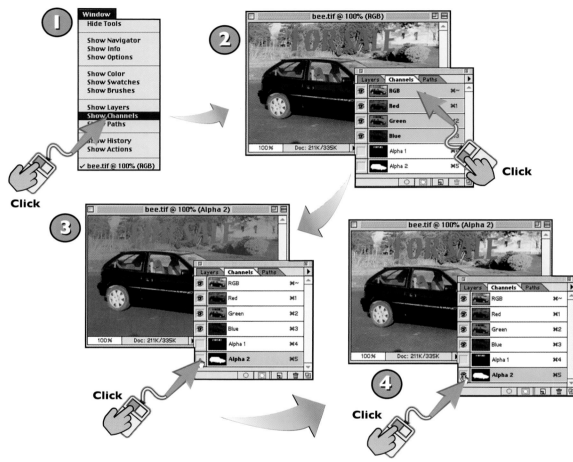

Click

Click

Click

Click

✓ If viewing overlaid channels looks familiar, that's because they look like Quick Masks (see Task 6, "Creating a Selection by Painting"). In fact, Photoshop treats a Quick Mask as a temporary channel, and it's listed in the Channels palette while you're working on it.

① Choose **Window**, **Show Channels**.

② Click the first channel in the list to view the image alone.

③ Click in the blank square next to any alpha channel you want to view as an overlay.

④ Click the eye icons next to each channel to hide the overlaid channels.

Task 27: Viewing Channels in Color

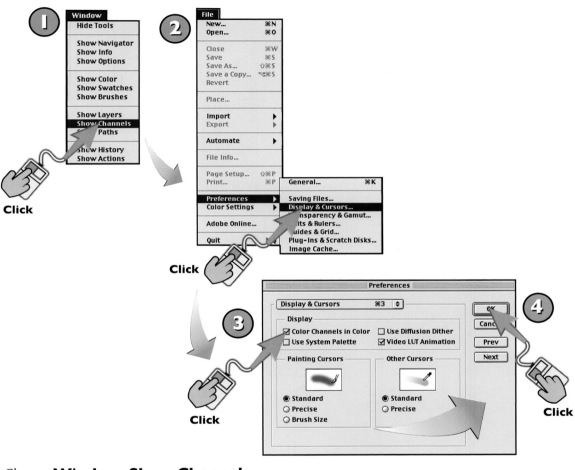

By default, Photoshop displays the color channels in grayscale, so they look like film-based color separations. It's sometimes easier to understand just what each color channel is contributing to an image, though, if you view them in the colors that they represent.

Click

Click

Click

Click

✅ Viewing color channels in color has no effect whatsoever on what the image itself looks like—it's just an easier way to comprehend the color information contained in each channel.

1. Choose **Window**, **Show Channels**.

2. Choose **File**, **Preferences**, **Display & Colors**.

3. Click **Color Channels in Color**.

4. Click **OK** to apply the change.

✅ Because this setting is in the Preferences menu, it's global—that is, it applies to every image you open, rather than just the current image.

Another way to save and create selections in Photoshop involves the use of Bézier paths, like those used to draw objects in CorelDRAW, Adobe Illustrator, and Macromedia FreeHand. Paths are organized in a Paths palette that's grouped with the Channels and Layers palette.

✅ When you create a path, it's saved temporarily in the Paths palette as "Work Path." To keep this path, you must double-click its name in the palette and give it another name.

✅ The essential difference between using paths to define a selection and using channels to do the same thing is that when you use paths, you draw them. When you use channels, you essentially paint them, so the difference is similar to the difference between drawing software like Illustrator and painting software like Photoshop.

Task 28: Using the Paths Palette

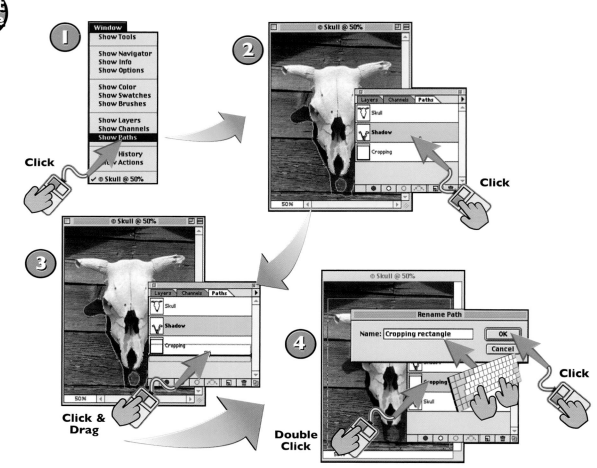

(1) Choose **Window**, **Show Paths** to display the Paths palette.

(2) To view a path, click its name in the list.

(3) To move a path in the list, click and drag its name.

(4) To change a path's name, double-click it, enter a new name, and click **OK**.

Task 29: Converting a Selection to a Path

Start Here

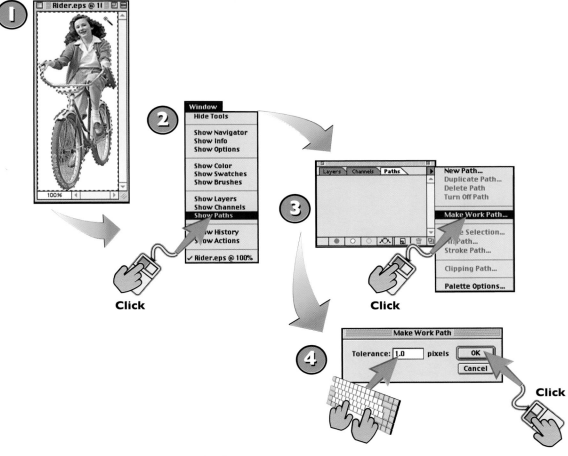

1

Rider.eps @ 1:

100%

2

Window
Hide Tools

Show Navigator
Show Info
Show Options

Show Color
Show Swatches
Show Brushes

Show Layers
Show Channels
Show Paths

ow History
ow Actions

✓ Rider.eps @ 100%

Click

3

Layers Channels Paths

New Path...
Duplicate Path...
Delete Path
Turn Off Path

Make Work Path...

e Selection...
. Path...
Stroke Path...

Clipping Path...

Palette Options...

Click

4

Make Work Path

Tolerance: 1.0   pixels   OK
                         Cancel

Click

The most comprehensive way of altering a selection is to convert it to a path, edit the path, and then convert back to a selection. This gives you precise control over every angle and curve in the selection's shape. To convert paths to selections, see Task 31, "Converting a Path to a Selection."

1 Make a selection by using any method.

2 Choose **Window**, **Show Paths**.

3 Choose **Paths palette menu**, **Make Work Path**.

4 Enter the desired **Tolerance** in pixels and click **OK**.

✓ The Tolerance number in the Make Work Path dialog box indicates how precise you want Photoshop to be in creating the path. Lower numbers make more accurate—but more complex—paths.

✓ You can also choose a path in the **Paths palette** and click the **Load Path as Selection** button at the bottom of the **Paths palette**.

End Task

Page 83

Task 30: Drawing a Freehand Path

Drawing your own paths is the best way to create clean paths without the extra points you sometimes get by converting selections to paths. It can be hard to get the hang of working with the Pen tools Photoshop provides for creating and editing paths, but practice makes perfect.

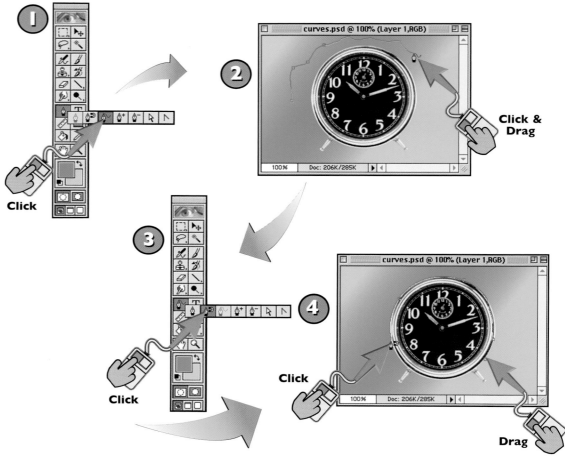

(1) To draw a freeform path, click the **Pen** tool and slide the mouse over to choose the **Freeform Pen** tool.

(2) Click and drag to draw a path.

(3) To draw a path around the edges of an object, click the **Pen** tool and slide the mouse to choose the **Magnetic Pen** tool.

(4) Click where you want the path to start and drag the cursor along the edge of the object to automatically create the path.

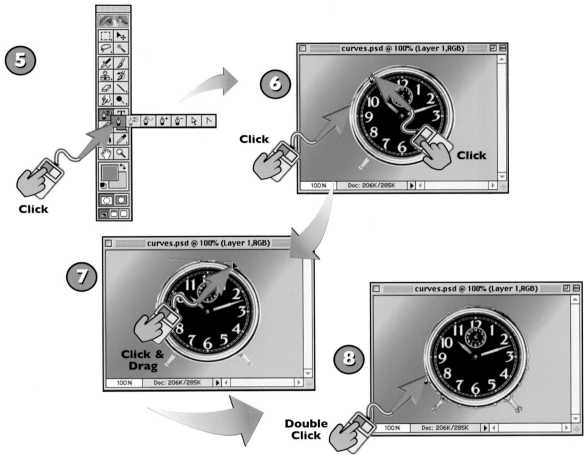

You can copy and paste paths just as you would in a drawing program, and a path can consist of more than one path element—in other words, you can create two or more closed paths within one Photoshop path.

When you click and drag while creating a new point, you're moving that point's curve handles to change the angle of the path. Bézier paths are defined mathematically by the positions of the points and each point's curve handles.

When you save images in EPS format, you can use a path to define the area of the image that should print; any pixels outside that *clipping path* don't show up when the image is imported into another application. Click a path name and choose **Paths palette menu, Clipping Path** to choose a clipping path.

5 To draw a more structured path, choose the main **Pen** tool.

6 Click to start the path, and then click at the next place you want to add a point.

7 Click and drag while creating a point to change the angle of the path.

8 With all three tools, double-click to close the path, or click again on the starting point.

Task 31: Converting a Path to a Selection

Just as you can create a path from a selection, you can convert a path back into a selection. The selection will follow the path exactly, but the path may not have followed the original selection exactly because of a high tolerance setting.

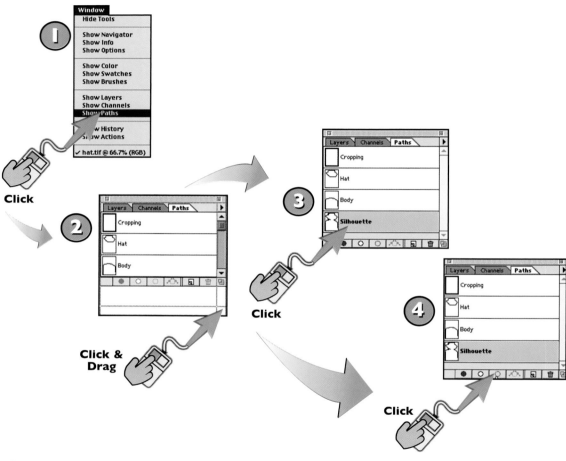

Start Here

Click

Click & Drag

Click

Click

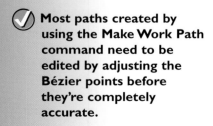

Most paths created by using the Make Work Path command need to be edited by adjusting the Bézier points before they're completely accurate.

① Choose **Window**, **Show Paths** to display the Paths palette.

② Resize the palette if necessary so you can see the name of the path you want to use.

③ Click the name of the path.

④ Click the **Convert Path to Selection** button at the bottom of the palette.

End Task

Task 32: Saving Paths in Adobe Illustrator Format

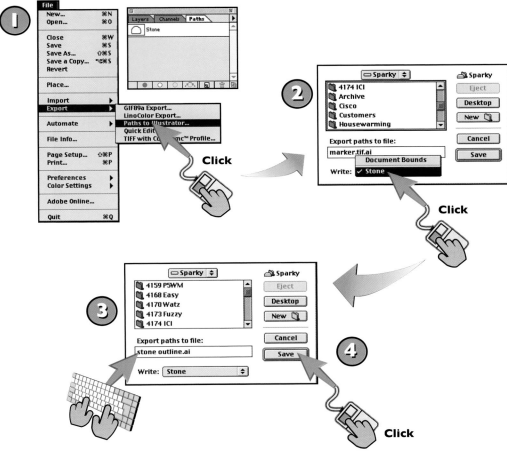

Click

Click

Click

If you're used to working in Illustrator, you may want to export Photoshop paths to Illustrator format as the basis for a separate image in Illustrator. You can choose to export one path, all paths, or a rectangular path the same size as the document (Document Bounds).

---

① Choose **File**, **Export**, **Paths to Illustrator**.

② Choose the path to export from the **Write** pop-up menu.

③ Enter a name for the file in the **name field**.

④ Click **Save** to save the Illustrator file.

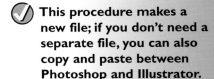

This procedure makes a new file; if you don't need a separate file, you can also copy and paste between Photoshop and Illustrator.

Working with Colors and Patterns

Mixing colors in Photoshop is, for most people, "the fun part." With Photoshop's support for several different color modes, you can create and use any color you can think of. It's important to know ahead of time how an image will be used so you can mix colors in the right mode (CMYK for print projects, RGB for onscreen ones); some RGB colors can't be reproduced in print, and the same thing goes for some CMYK colors onscreen.

Part 4 shows you how to mix colors, use colors already present in an image, use spot colors that will print on a single printing plate, and swap one color in an image for another. In addition, this Part explains how to create and use repeating patterns that will tile seamlessly for use as monitor wallpaper or Web page backgrounds.

Tasks

At all times, **Photoshop** has two active colors—the foreground color and the background color. You paint or draw with the foreground color, and if you erase pixels on the Background layer, the space is filled with the background color.

Task 1: Changing the Foreground and Background Colors

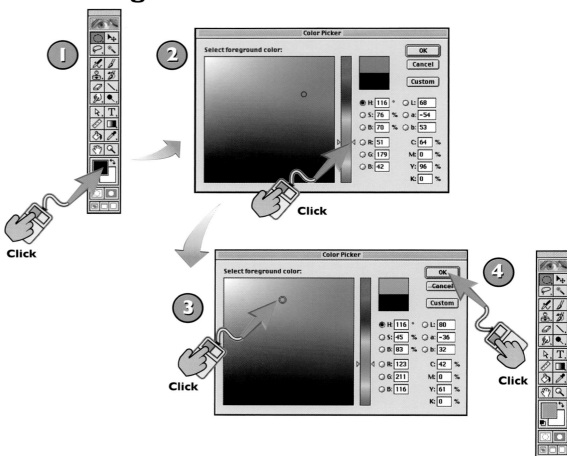

Start Here

Click

Click

Click

Click

✓ You can also enter colors numerically by entering numbers in the fields in *RGB*, *HSB*, *Lab*, or *CMYK* values.

✓ You can switch quickly to black foreground, white background by pressing **D** for default colors.

① Click the **Foreground Color** or **Background Color swatch** in the Tool palette.

② Click in the **color slider** to choose a general range of hues.

③ Click in the **color field** to choose lighter or darker versions of that hue.

④ Click **OK**.

End Task

Task 2: Choosing a Color from an Image

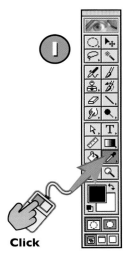

Click

Click

Option/Alt+**Click**

The easiest way to mix a new color is not to mix it! You can choose a color from any pixel in an image by using the Eyedropper tool. This is a good technique for when you're "repairing" a scanned image, and it's a great way to choose harmonious colors for type.

✓ Sometimes you don't get the color you're expecting when you use the Eyedropper tool; that's because many colors in an image are made up of different-colored pixels grouped together. Try clicking a few pixels over from the first place you clicked.

✓ You can access the Eyedropper any time you're using a painting tool, such as the Airbrush, Paintbrush, or Pencil, by Option+clicking/ Alt+clicking to choose a foreground color.

① Click the **Eyedropper** tool in the **Tool** palette.

② Click in the image to choose a foreground color.

③ **Option+click/Alt+click** in the image to choose a background color.

Task 3: Choosing a Spot Color

Photoshop allows you to use and print spot colors as well as process colors. Each spot color is made up of a single ink when printed, rather than a mix of process ink colors. To use spot colors, you need to have printed swatchbooks showing how the colors look on paper.

✓ You can convert an existing channel to a spot channel by double-clicking its name in the **Channels** palette and clicking the **Spot Color** radio button. Then choose a spot color as in step 4.

✓ Images that contain spot color channels must be saved in DCS 2.0 format to retain the spot color data. See Part 2, "Opening and Saving Files," for more information on saving DCS files.

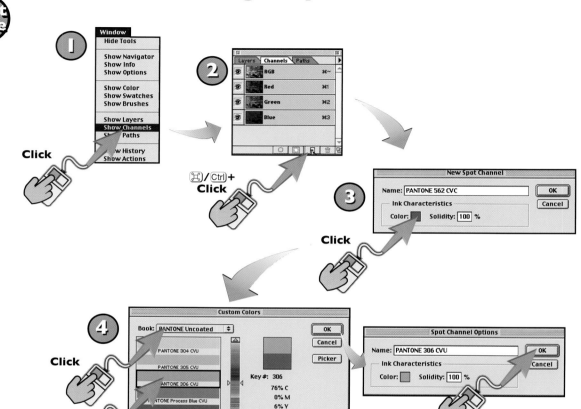

1 Choose **Window**, **Show Channels** to display the **Channels** palette.

2 **Cmd+click/Ctrl+click** the **New Channel** button.

3 Click the **Color** swatch to display the **Color Picker**.

4 Choose a swatchbook and a color, and then click and drag in the **swatch area** to choose a color. Click **OK** in the Color Picker, and then click **OK** in the **New Spot Channel** dialog box.

Task 4: Using the Colors Palette

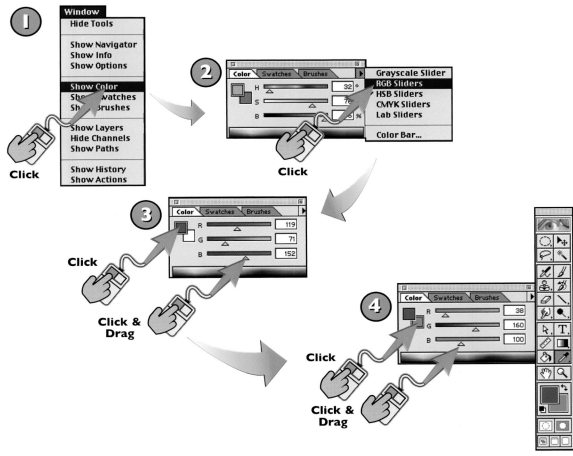

If you change colors frequently, it's faster to use the Colors palette. It offers you access to the same color models that the Color Picker dialog box uses, and it can be left on the screen all the time for quick access.

Start Here

Window
Hide Tools

Show Navigator
Show Info
Show Options

Show Color
Show Swatches
Show Brushes

Show Layers
Hide Channels
Show Paths

Show History
Show Actions

Click

Grayscale Slider
RGB Sliders
HSB Sliders
CMYK Sliders
Lab Sliders

Color Bar...

Click

Click

Click & Drag

Click

Click & Drag

✓ The "highlighted" color swatch in the Colors palette is the one with a box around it.

✓ With each color model, you have the option of dragging the color sliders or entering numbers; if you prefer to enter numbers, press **Tab** to move to the next field and **Enter** when you're done.

① Choose **Window**, **Show Color**.

② Choose a color mode from the **Color palette menu**.

③ If it's not highlighted, click the **foreground swatch** and mix a foreground color.

④ Click the **background swatch** and mix a background color.

Task 5: Previewing CMYK Output Onscreen

Printed output uses cyan, magenta, yellow, and black inks on paper, a very different way of reproducing color from the red, green, and blue light that computer monitors use. When you're designing for printed output, one way to see how colors will look on paper is to use the **CMYK Preview** option.

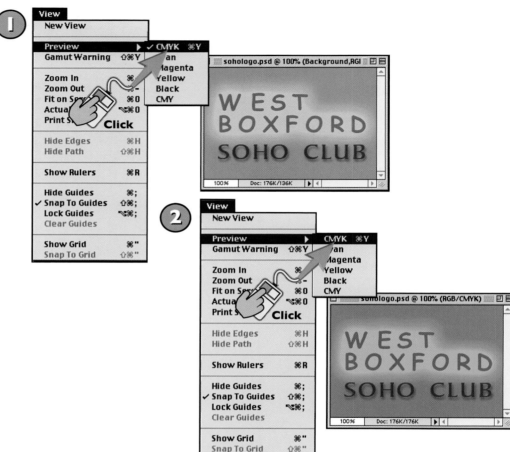

✅ CMYK preview mode gives you an idea of which colors will be affected by conversion to CMYK, but it doesn't necessarily show exactly how they'll look when printed.

① Choose **View**, **Preview**, **CMYK** or press **Cmd+Y/Ctrl+Y** to turn on the CMYK preview.

② Choose **View**, **Preview**, **CMYK** again to turn off the CMYK preview.

Task 6: Replacing a Color with Another Color

Start Here

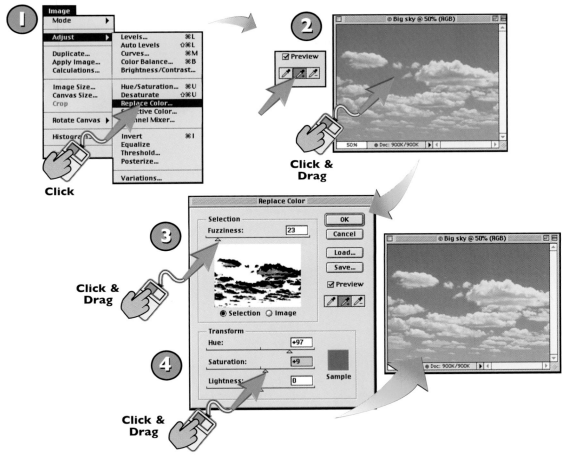

Click

Click & Drag

Click & Drag

Click & Drag

Here's a way to exercise some of that famous Photoshop magic. With the **Replace Color** command, you can turn a green sweater red or make a yellow flower blue. You use a thumbnail preview of the image to see which colors you're changing.

✓ It's okay if light areas of the image are partially selected (light gray) in the Replace Color dialog box's preview; that means that reflections of the color you're changing will change as well.

✓ The Replace Color dialog box works much the same way as the Color Range dialog box does (see Part 3, Task 9, "Selecting Multiple Areas of the Same Color"). The key to good results in both techniques is lots of practice with the Fuzziness slider and the eyedropper tools.

1 Choose **Image**, **Adjust**, **Replace Color**.

2 With the **plus eyedropper tool**, click and drag in the image to select the colors you want to change.

3 Drag the **Fuzziness** slider to adjust which colors are selected.

4 Drag the **Hue**, **Saturation**, and **Lightness** sliders to change the color, and then click **OK**.

End Task

Task 7: Creating a Seamless Pattern

Repeating patterns can be used for Web page backgrounds, computer desktop patterns, and many other design projects. This technique produces a pattern with no edges—the viewer can't tell where the pattern tile begins and ends. You need to start with a squarish image that you want to turn into a repeating pattern.

✓ Only one pattern can be defined at a time, so it's a good idea to save each file you used to create a pattern. You can always redefine the pattern by opening the file and performing step 7.

✓ For information on the Airbrush tool, see Part 5, Task 4, "Painting Soft-Edged Shapes." For information on the Rubber Stamp tool, see Part 5, Task 7, "Cloning Areas." And for information on the Smudge tool, see Part 6, Task 8, "Smudging an Area."

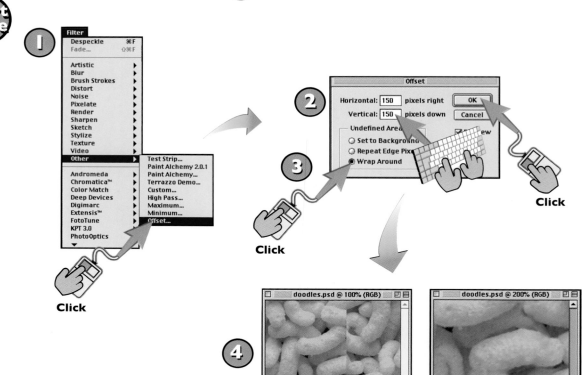

1 Choose **Filter**, **Other**, **Offset**.

2 Enter **Horizontal** and **Vertical** values that are about half the size of the image.

3 Click the **Wrap Around** radio button, and then click **OK**.

4 Edit out the hard edge lines with the **Smudge**, **Rubber Stamp**, and **Airbrush** tools.

Next Step

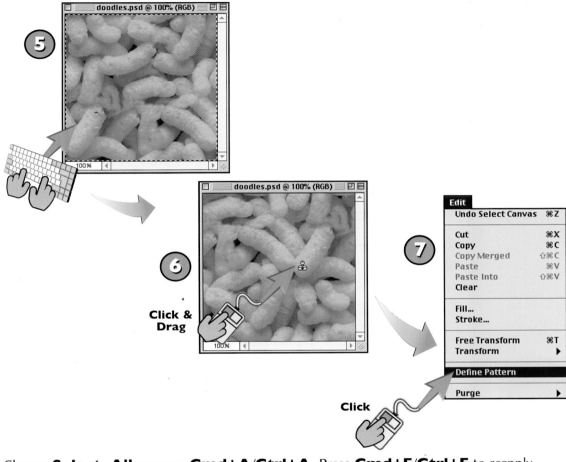

Click & Drag

Click

Edit

Undo Select Canvas	⌘Z
Cut	⌘X
Copy	⌘C
Copy Merged	⇧⌘C
Paste	⌘V
Paste Into	⇧⌘V
Clear	
Fill...	
Stroke...	
Free Transform	⌘T
Transform	▶
Define Pattern	
Purge	▶

(5) Choose **Select**, **All** or press **Cmd+A/Ctrl+A**. Press **Cmd+F/Ctrl+F** to reapply the **Offset** filter.

(6) Clean up any remaining hard edges at the center of the image.

(7) Select all (**Cmd+A/Ctrl+A**) and choose **Edit**, **Define Pattern**.

✓ When editing out edge seams, use a light touch and a medium-sized, soft-edged brush. Many short strokes usually look much more realistic than one long one.

You can only define a pattern when part of the image is selected, and the selection has to be rectangular.

End Task

Task 8: Filling an Area with a Pattern

Filling an area with a pattern is much simpler than creating the pattern in the first place. The Fill command offers Pattern as an option, along with Foreground Color, Background Color, Black, 50% Gray, and White. Before filling with a pattern, you must define a pattern, as outlined in Part 4, Task 7.

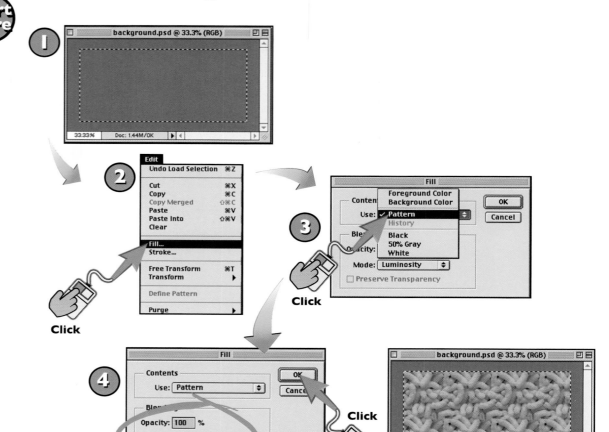

The Fill dialog box's Mode menu refers to blending modes, different ways of blending new colors with the image's existing colors. Most of the time you will use Normal, but experimenting with the other modes will yield interesting results.

1. Select the area you want to fill.

2. Choose **Edit**, **Fill** or press **Shift+Delete/Shift+Backspace**.

3. Choose **Pattern** from the **Use** pop-up menu.

4. Enter an **Opacity** percentage, choose a **Mode**, and click **OK**.

Task 9: Converting a Color Image to Grayscale

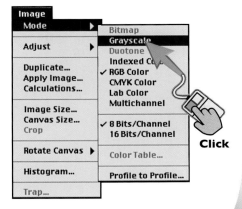

Click

A lot of the color images in the world end up getting printed in grayscale, rather than in color. If you're going to do this, you'll get better results by converting the image in Photoshop so you can make any needed adjustments to the image.

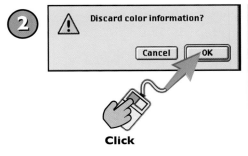

Click

✓ See Part 7, "Adjusting Colors and Tones," for ways to adjust an image for best reproduction.

✓ An alternative method for creating grayscale images is more complicated but can produce better results with problem images: Convert the image to Lab Color mode, discard the a and b channels, and convert it back to Grayscale mode.

① Choose **Image**, **Mode**, **Grayscale**.

② Click **OK** in the alert box.

Task 10: Creating a Duotone Image

Duotones use an extra ink color to add to an image's richness. They range from images that appear gray, but with increased warmth and detail, to images with pronounced color. Variations on duotones include tritones and quadtones, using three or four inks.

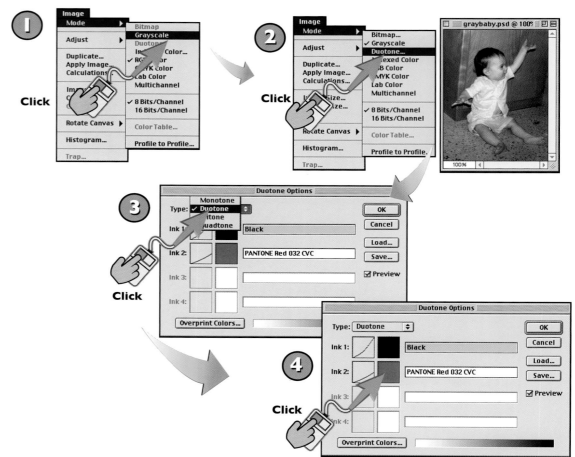

Start Here

Click

Click

Click

Click

1. If the image is in color, choose **Image**, **Mode**, **Grayscale** and click **OK**.

2. Choose **Image**, **Mode**, **Duotone**.

3. Choose a **Type** from the pop-up menu.

4. For each ink color, click the **color swatch** to choose a color.

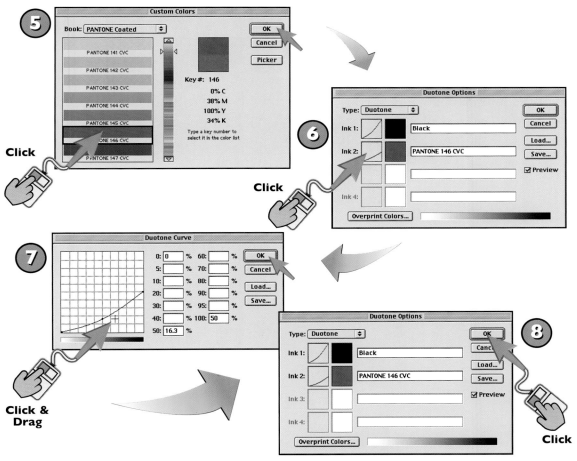

Once you've created a duotone, you can convert it to CMYK or RGB mode for a simulated duotone image that can be used on the Web or in four-color process printing.

The tricky part when creating duotones is adjusting the ink curves. The corresponding percentages in the modtones should add up to about 50%; for example, at the 50% point, you might want 30% coverage of the spot color and 20% coverage of black.

(5) Specify a color in the Color Picker and click **OK**.

(6) For each ink color, click the **curve swatch** to adjust the ink coverage.

(7) Drag the **curve**, watching the image window, to adjust the amount of color used for each brightness level, and then click **OK**.

(8) Click **OK** in the Duotone Options dialog box to apply the duotone.

End
Task

Page
101

Painting Images

Photoshop's painting tools include paintbrushes, airbrushes, and pencils, along with special tools such as an eraser, a rubber stamp, and a line tool. With this tool set, you can create any image you can imagine, as well as retouch and add to existing images. Each painting tool has individual settings that you can change, such as the pressure with which the tool is applied, and each offers a selection of brush sizes and shapes from which to choose.

Like any operation in Photoshop, you can paint throughout an image or within a selection. Part 5 shows you how to use each of the painting tools, how to select and modify a brush, how to clone areas of an image with the rubber stamp tool, how to create gradients, and how to erase part of an image.

Tasks

Task 1: Filling a Selection with a Color

To fill a large area with color rather than painting the whole area, you can select the area and fill it with the color. The Fill dialog box includes White, Black, and 50% Gray options, as well as Foreground Color, Background Color, and Pattern.

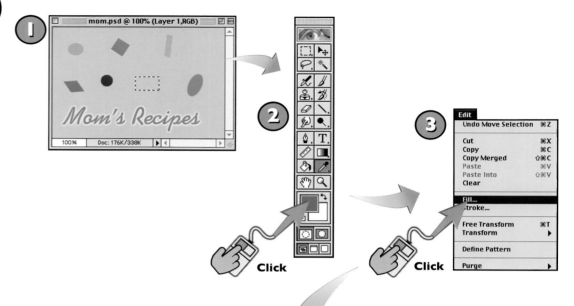

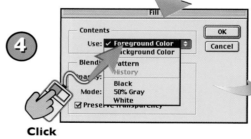

Click

Click

Click

✓ To fill the selected area with transparent color, lower the Opacity setting in the Fill dialog box.

✓ To fill an area with a pattern, see Part 4, Task 8, "Filling an Area with a Pattern."

① Make a selection by using any method.

② Change the foreground color to the color you want to use.

③ Choose **Edit**, **Fill** or press **Shift+Delete/Shift+Backspace**.

④ Choose **Foreground Color** from the **Use** pop-up menu and click **OK**.

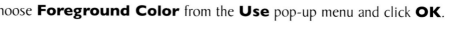

Task 2: Choosing a Brush

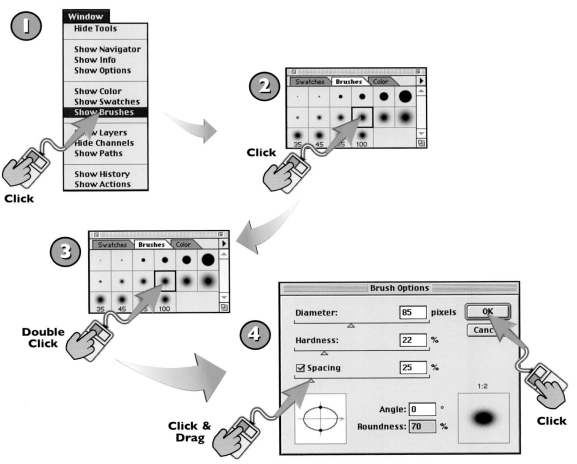

Each of the painting tools allows you to use different "brushes" that can vary in width and hardness. Soft-edged brushes make a fuzzy stroke; hard-edged brushes make a crisp stroke.

You can create a new brush by choosing the **Brushes** palette menu, **New Brush.** The Diameter setting determines the size, Hardness makes the brush soft or hard, and Spacing determines whether the brush "skips" as you paint with it. The Angle and Roundness fields let you make angled, flat brushes for calligraphic effects.

① Choose **Window**, **Show Brushes** to display the Brushes palette.

② Click a **brush** to select it.

③ Double-click a **brush** to change its attributes.

④ Adjust the brush's **Diameter**, **Hardness**, and **Spacing**, and then click **OK**.

Task 3: Using Different Brush Cursors

By default, Photoshop's painting cursors are small pictures of the type of tool you're using. Two other types of cursor—Precise and Brush Size—allow you to paint with greater precision.

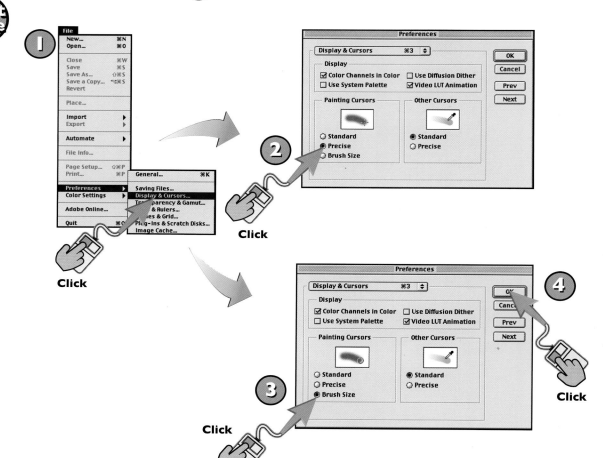

(✓) You can use Precise cursors at any time by pressing Caps Lock. Turn Caps Lock off to return to Standard Cursors.

(✓) The Other Cursors section allows you to specify Precise cursors for tools other than the painting tools.

(1) Choose **File**, **Preferences**, **Display & Cursors**.

(2) In the Painting Cursors area, click **Precise** to use a crosshairs cursor.

(3) Click **Brush Size** to use a circular cursor the same size as the brush in use.

(4) Click **OK** to make the change.

Task 4: Painting Soft-Edged Shapes

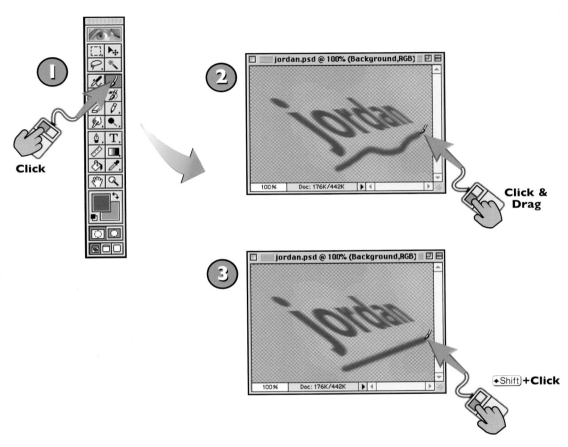

Click

Click &
Drag

↑Shift+Click

Two of Photoshop's painting tools create soft-edged lines: the **Airbrush** and the **Paintbrush**, which work like their real-life counterparts. Airbrush and Paintbrush strokes are *anti-aliased*, meaning the edge pixels are semi-transparent so they blend with the surrounding colors.

1. Click the **Paintbrush** or the **Airbrush** in the **Tool** palette.

2. Click and drag in the image to draw a line.

3. Click and **Shift**+**click** to draw a straight line between two points.

 To change the size of the lines drawn by the Paintbrush and Airbrush, choose a different brush from the Brushes palette (see Task 2, "Choosing a Brush").

Task 5: Painting Hard-Edged Shapes

The Pencil tool is used for drawing clean, sharp lines in Photoshop. It's often most useful for filling in a pixel here and a pixel there in scanned images. Pencil strokes are not *anti-aliased*, so they don't blend in with the surrounding colors.

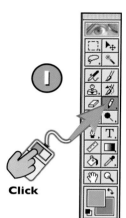

Click

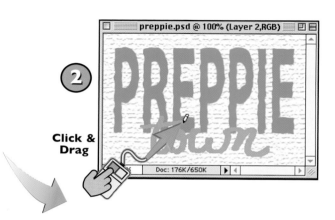

Click & Drag

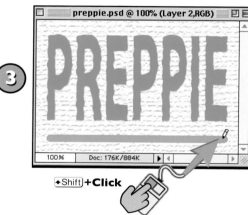

◆Shift+**Click**

✓ To change the size of the lines drawn by the Pencil, choose a different brush from the Brushes palette (see Task 2).

✓ You can restrict Pencil lines to 90- and 45-degree angles by holding down the Shift key as you draw.

1. Click the **Pencil** in the **Tool** palette.

2. Click and drag in the image to draw a line.

3. Click and **Shift+click** to draw a straight line between two points.

Task 6: Drawing Lines

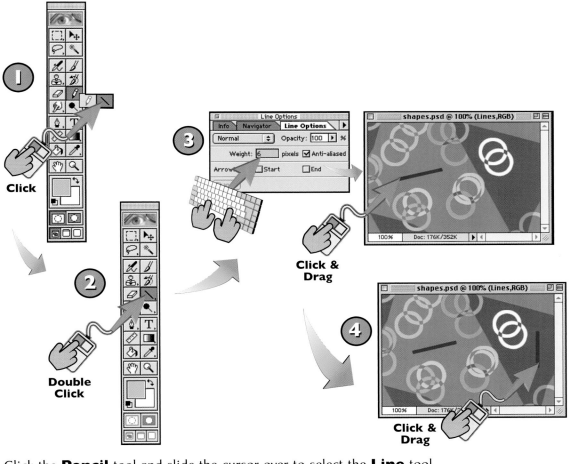

Photoshop's Line tool draws straight lines between two points. The lines can be *anti-aliased* or not, depending on your preference, and you can also restrict them to 45-degree increments if you choose.

① Click the **Pencil** tool and slide the cursor over to select the **Line** tool.

② Double-click the **Line** tool to display the **Line Options** palette.

③ Enter a **Weight** for the line and then click and drag to draw a line.

④ Hold down **Shift** as you draw to restrict lines to 90- and 45-degree angles.

✓ The Line tool is considered a painting tool, so you can access the Eyedropper tool by pressing **Option/Alt** when the Line tool is active.

✓ To determine whether lines are anti-aliased or not, double-click the **Line** tool and click **Anti-aliased** on or off in the **Line Tool Options** palette.

Task 7: Cloning Areas

To clone areas of an image, you use the **Rubber Stamp tool. It allows you to reproduce elements by specifying an origin point and painting in a "clone" of the area around that point elsewhere in the image.**

Start Here

Click

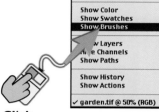

Click

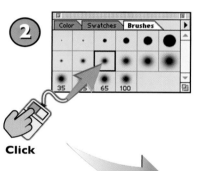

Double Click

✓ **To clone from just the active layer, click off Use All Layers in the Rubber Stamp Options palette.**

① Choose **Window**, **Show Brushes**.

② Choose a small or medium-sized brush with soft edges.

③ Double-click the **Rubber Stamp** tool in the **Tool** palette to select it and display the Rubber Stamp Options palette.

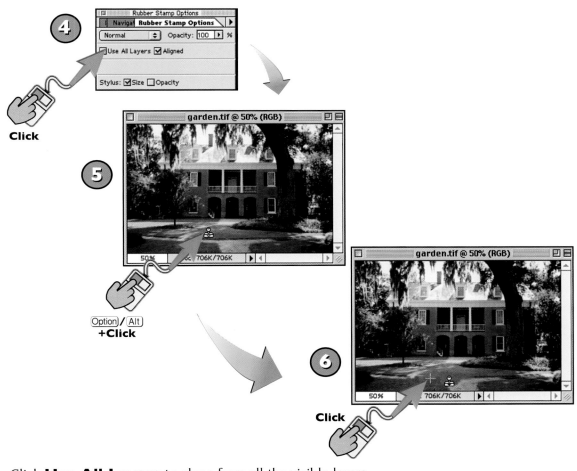

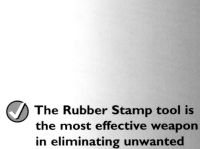

Click

Option / Alt
+Click

Click

4   Click **Use All Layers** to clone from all the visible layers.

5   **Option+click/Alt+click** in the image to choose the point to copy from.

6   Click anywhere else in the image to paint in a cloned image.

☑ The Rubber Stamp tool is the most effective weapon in eliminating unwanted elements from scanned photos. Use it to clone sidewalk right over an offending dog, for example.

☑ When working with the Rubber Stamp tool, use several small strokes instead of one large one for more realistic results.

Task 8: Applying a Gradient to an Image

Gradients, in which one color fades into another, are among the most impressive, yet the easiest, effects Photoshop offers. The Gradient tools allows you to choose from dozens of pre-built gradients and five shape variations.

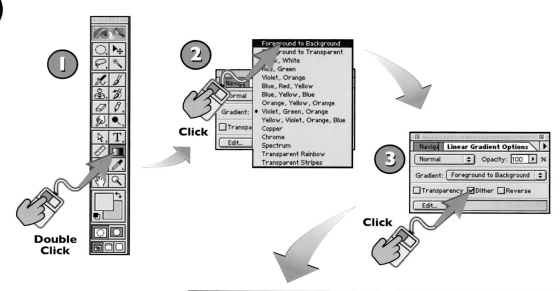

Start Here

Double Click

Click

Click

Drag

Drop

✓ By default, Photoshop uses the foreground color for the beginning of the gradient, where you first click and hold, and the background color for the end, where you let go.

✓ To use a different gradient shape, click the **Linear Gradient** tool and slide the mouse over to choose the **Radial, Angle, Reflected,** or **Diamond Gradient** tool. They all work the same, just with different shapes.

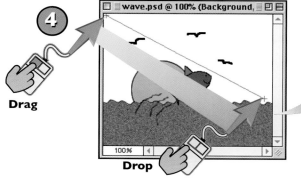

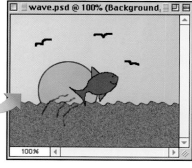

(1) Double-click the **Linear Gradient** tool to display the **Linear Gradient Options** palette and select the tool.

(2) Choose a Gradient type from the pop-up menu.

(3) Click **Dither** to create a smooth blend without banding.

(4) Click and drag in the image to create the gradient.

End Task

Task 9: Creating a New Gradient Type

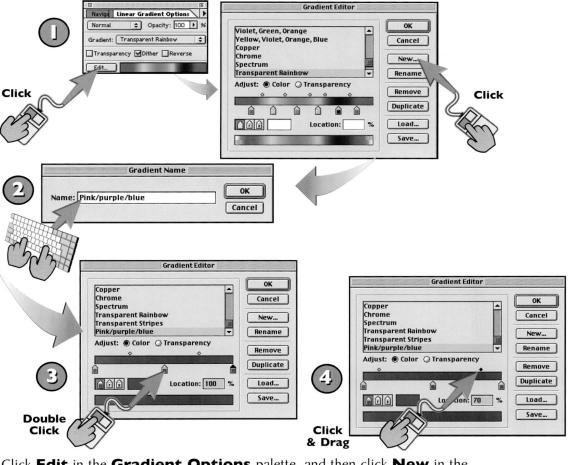

Click

Click

Double Click

Click & Drag

In addition to the built-in gradients, you can create your own, specifying the colors and intensity you want to use at each point in the gradient.

1 Click **Edit** in the **Gradient Options** palette, and then click **New** in the **Gradient Editor** dialog box.

2 Give the gradient a name and click **OK**.

3 Double-click the "houses" below the upper gradient slider to change their color; click once below the line to add a new "house."

4 Drag the diamonds above the line to change the point at which the color changes, and then click **OK**.

In addition to creating your own gradients, you can edit the ones that are already there (the ugly Red, Green one is a good candidate for this). You can always get the originals back by choosing **Reset Tool** from the **Gradient** palette menu.

Task 10: Adding a Stroke Around a Selection

Rather than trying to paint perfect circles and rectangles, you can stroke a circular or rectangular selection to create hollow shapes. Photoshop can place the stroke inside, outside, or centered on the selection marquee.

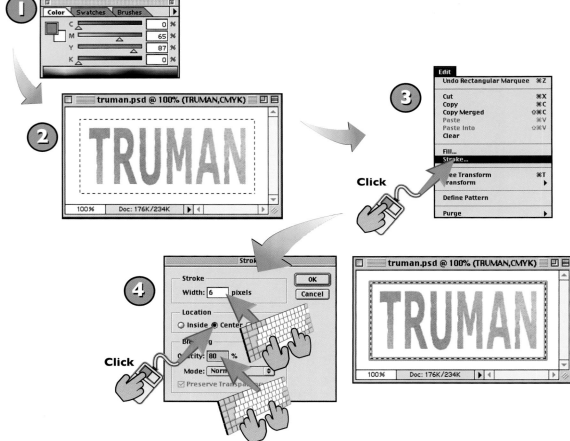

✓ The Mode menu allows you to apply a stroke by using different blending modes to combine the stroke color with the image's existing colors; experiment with different modes for different effects.

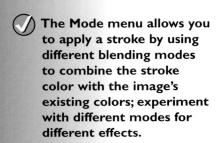

1 Choose a foreground color to use for the stroke.

2 Make a selection by using any method.

3 Choose **Edit, Stroke**.

4 Enter a **Width** for the stroke and click in the **Location** area to determine its location. Enter an **Opacity** percentage and click **OK**.

Task 11: Erasing Part of an Image

Start
Here

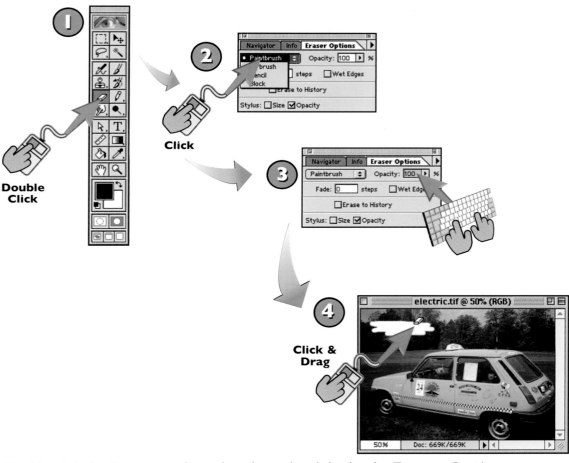

Double
Click

Click

Click &
Drag

The Eraser tool does just
what it sounds like: erases
pixels. It can work like a
square block eraser, the
kind used in older programs
like MacPaint, or it can
operate like a paintbrush,
airbrush, or pencil, for more
specialized erasing tasks.

The Fade setting on the
Eraser Options palette lets
you place a limit on the
erasing power of each
"stroke" of the tool. When
you enter a number of
steps other than 0, the
eraser stroke fades out as
it goes.

The block eraser always
erases the same amount of
space on your screen, so it
erases bigger areas of the
image the more you zoom
out and smaller areas the
more you zoom in.

1. Double-click the **Eraser** tool to select the tool and display the **Eraser Options** palette.

2. Choose an eraser type from the pop-up menu.

3. Enter an **Opacity** or Pressure percentage other than 100 to partially erase pixels.

4. Click and drag in the image to erase.

End
Task

Task 12: Changing Painting Tool Settings

Each tool, including the painting tools, has special settings accessible in the Options palette. The palette changes its name and its controls depending on what tool is selected, and the Options palette for each tool can be displayed by double-clicking that tool.

Double Click

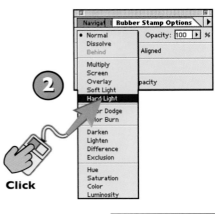

Click

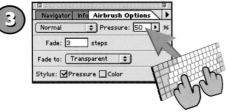

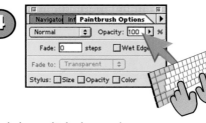

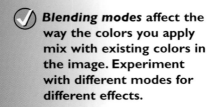

✓ **Blending modes** affect the way the colors you apply mix with existing colors in the image. Experiment with different modes for different effects.

 Double-click any tool to display the **Options** palette, and then click the tool you want to use.

② When using the Paintbrush, Airbrush, History Brush, or Pencil, choose a **blending mode**.

③ When using the Airbrush, choose a **Pressure** percentage.

④ When using the Paintbrush, History Brush, or Rubber Stamp, choose an **Opacity** percentage.

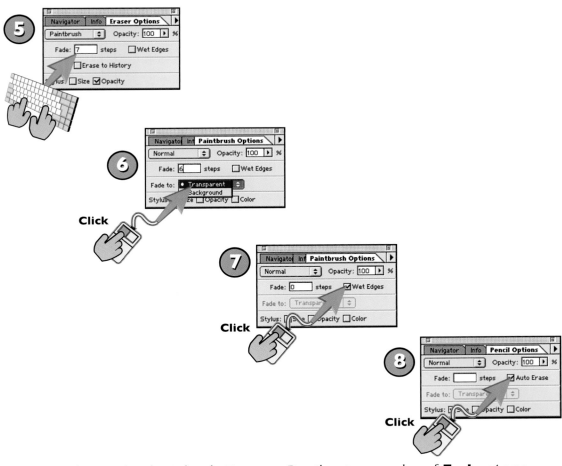

5. When using the Paintbrush, Airbrush, Eraser, or Pencil, enter a number of **Fade steps** to fade the ends of strokes.

6. When using the Paintbrush or Airbrush with more than zero Fade steps, choose **Transparent** or **Background** from the **Fade to** menu.

7. When using the Paintbrush or the Eraser in Paintbrush mode, click **Wet Edges** to simulate watercolor painting.

8. When using the Pencil, click **Auto Erase** to draw the background color when clicking pixels of the foreground color.

Editing Images

With the "digital darkroom" represented by the powerful capabilities of Photoshop, it's easy to make any existing image look just the way you want. You can quickly remove, add, or modify details of an image with Photoshop's painting and editing tools. Transformation commands allow you to rotate, skew, scale, and apply perspective to an object or entire image. Each of the commands explained in this part can be applied to the entire image or just to a selected area.

Part 6 shows you how to transform an image in several ways, sharpen and blur details, darken or lighten areas, duplicate an image, and remove the moiré pattern that sometimes shows up in scanned images.

Tasks

The Move tool is designed for moving pixels from one point in an image to another. But if you need to move pixels a specific distance from their starting point, Photoshop's Numeric Transform command contains a Move function.

✓ Just as in high-school geometry, the **X** and **Y** values indicate horizontal and vertical position respectively. Photoshop places the zero point of the two axes at the upper-left corner of the image.

✓ To avoid moving the background along with the selected object, that object must be on a separate layer surrounded by transparent pixels.

Task 1: Moving an Object a Specified Distance

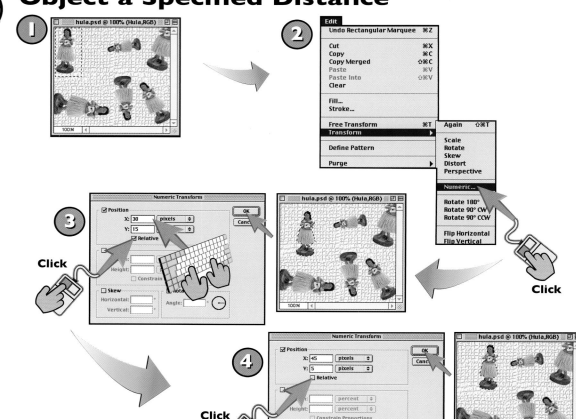

1. Select the area you want to move; all selected pixels on the active layer will be moved.

2. Choose **Edit**, **Transform**, **Numeric**.

3. Click **Relative**, and then enter **X** and **Y** distances in pixels and click **OK**.

4. To move the selection to a designated position, click off **Relative**, enter new coordinates, and click **OK**.

Task 2: Aligning Objects with One Another

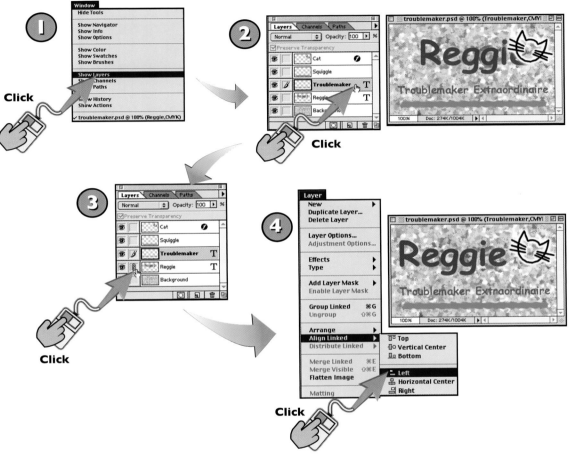

Photoshop can align objects on different layers. It looks for non-transparent pixels to tell it where the edges of objects are, so the **Align** commands really only work when each object is on its own layer and surrounded by transparent pixels.

---

1. Choose **Window**, **Show Layers**.

2. Click the name of the layer to which you want to align objects.

3. Click in the blank box to the left of each layer you want to align to the active layer.

4. Choose **Layer**, **Align Linked** and choose an option from the submenu.

 Make sure you press **Cmd+D/Ctrl+D** to drop any active selection before aligning layers; when a selection is active, Photoshop aligns layers with respect to the selection.

Task 3: Rotating an Object

Transformations are actions that change the shape of a selected area. One of the most useful transformations is rotation. Photoshop allows you to rotate selected areas in either direction, as far as you want to.

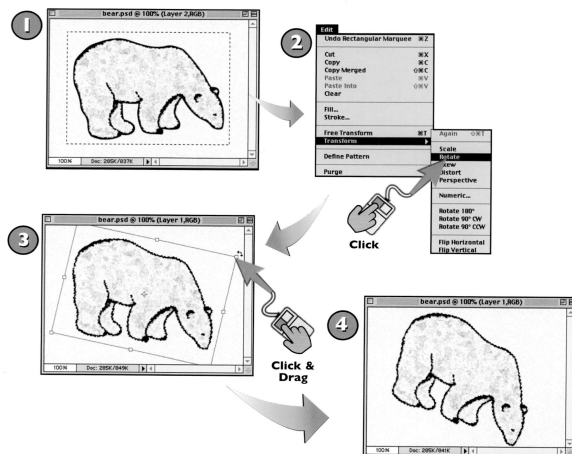

✓ If the Transform command isn't available, check to make sure the image is in Grayscale or a color mode. Transformations don't work in Bitmap mode.

1 Select the area to rotate.

2 Choose **Edit**, **Transform**, **Rotate**.

3 Click outside the transformation box and drag to rotate.

4 Press **Enter** to apply the rotation or **Esc** to cancel it.

Task 4: Skewing an Object

Start Here

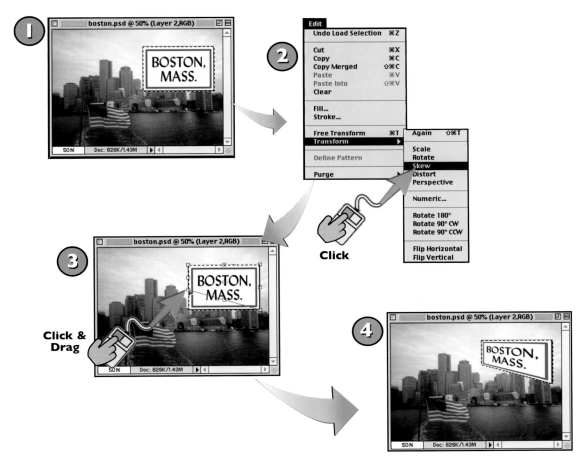

Click

Click & Drag

Skewing an object ordinarily involves tilting it to one side while keeping its top and bottom level. In Photoshop, you can apply skew in any direction by dragging transformation handles, and you can skew a selection in more than one direction with one operation.

① Select the area to skew.

② Choose **Edit**, **Transform**, **Skew**.

③ Drag any handle of the transformation box to skew the selected area.

④ Press **Enter** to apply the skew or **Esc** to cancel it.

✓ Applying skew to two adjacent corners of a selection is the same as applying perspective to the selection; applying skew to all four corners of a selection is the same as resizing the selection.

End Task

Task 5: Scaling an Object

While the Image Size command allows you to change the size of an entire image, the Scale command resizes only the selected area. You can resize proportionally or nonproportionally, as required.

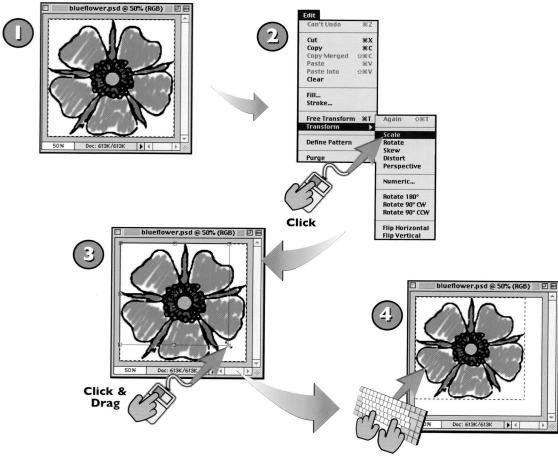

Click

Click & Drag

✓ To make sure that you're resizing the selected area proportionally, hold down **Shift** as you drag the transformation handle.

✓ Until you press Enter to apply the transformation, you can choose **Edit, Undo** or press **Cmd+Z/Ctrl+Z** to undo the latest change made to the transformation box. Undo works with any transformation, not just Scale.

① Select the area to resize.

② Choose **Edit**, **Transform**, **Scale**.

③ Drag any handle of the transformation box to resize the selected area.

④ Press **Enter** to apply the change in size or **Esc** to cancel it.

Task 6: Rotating an Image

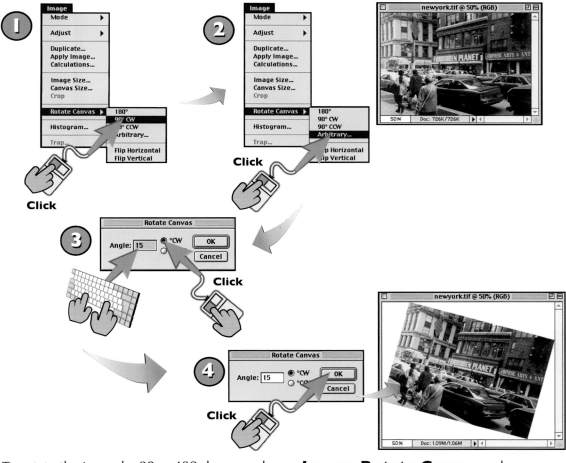

Click

Click

Click

Click

Click

When you need to rotate an entire image, use the **Rotate Canvas** command. You can choose three built-in options—useful if you've scanned an image sideways and just need to rotate it 90 degrees—or you can specify an arbitrary number of degrees clockwise or counterclockwise.

✓ Photoshop automatically adjusts the Canvas Size to fit the entire rotated image; that's why the command is called Rotate Canvas instead of Rotate Image.

✓ The Flip Horizontal and Flip Vertical commands in the Rotate submenu do just what you'd think they would do—flip (or "flop," in prepress-speak) the image from side to side or top to bottom.

1 To rotate the image by 90 or 180 degrees, choose **Image**, **Rotate Canvas** and choose from the submenu.

2 To rotate the image an arbitrary number of degrees, choose **Image**, **Rotate Canvas**, **Arbitrary**.

3 Enter a number of degrees in the **Angle** field and click **CW** or **CCW**.

4 Click **OK** to rotate the image.

Quick artistic perspective effects are within your grasp with Photoshop's Perspective transformation. Applying perspective is like skewing two corners of a selected area by exactly the same amount.

Task 7: Applying Perspective to an Object

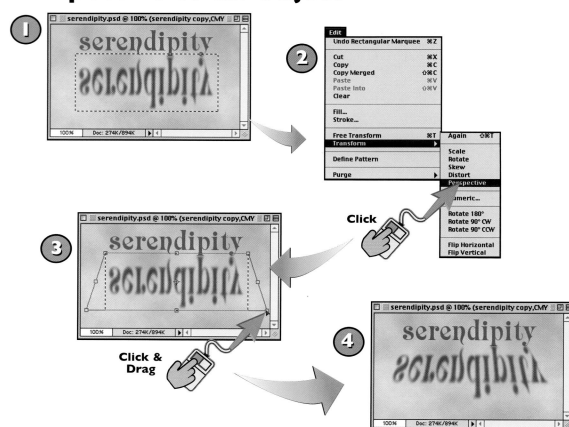

✓ By using perspective, you can blend added elements into an image, such as a sign or book that needs to be at an angle to the viewer.

(1) Select the area to which perspective will be applied.

(2) Choose **Edit**, **Transform**, **Perspective**.

(3) Drag any handle of the transformation box to create the perspective effect.

(4) Press **Enter** to apply the perspective or **Esc** to cancel it.

Task 8: Smudging an Area

Start Here

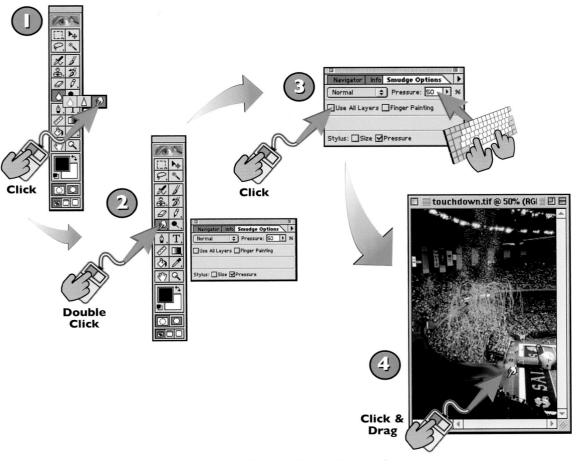

Click

Double Click

Click

touchdown.tif @ 50% (RGI

Click & Drag

To help you get rid of unwanted details in an image, Photoshop provides a Smudge tool that looks and works just like a finger through wet paint. It can be used for image touch-ups, to eliminate scratches and dust, or for special effects, to focus attention on the unsmudged areas of an image.

① Click the **Blur** tool and slide over to select the **Smudge** tool.

② Double-click the **Smudge** tool to show the Smudge Options palette.

③ Enter a **Pressure** percentage, and then click **Use All Layers** if you want to smudge more than one layer at a time.

④ Click and drag in the image to smudge.

✓ The Smudge tool's Finger Painting option—a checkbox on the Smudge Options palette—adds the foreground color to the mix, letting you paint in new colors with the Smudge tool's finger.

End Task

Task 9: Sharpening or Blurring Details

Photoshop's Sharpen filters allow you to sharpen entire images or selected areas. When you need to sharpen a few details here and there, such as the sparkle of an eye or the reflection in a mirror, you can use the Sharpen tool to apply the effect right where you want it.

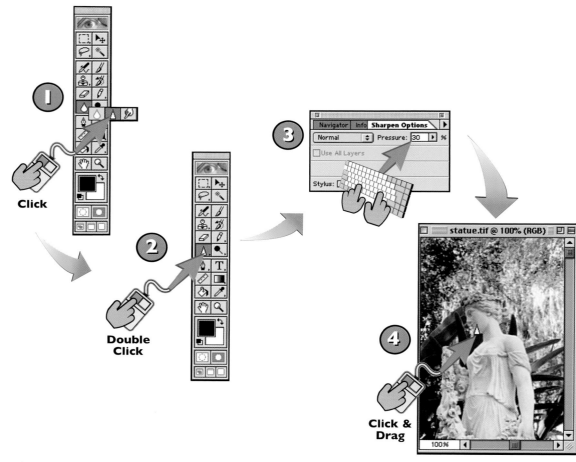

Click

Double Click

statue.tif @ 100% (RGB)

Click & Drag

✓ The active area of the Sharpen tool's cursor is the point at the top.

✓ The Sharpen tool really is intended for close-up detail work, not for sharpening entire images. If you find yourself using it in more than two or three places in an image, consider using a Sharpen filter.

1 Click the **Blur** tool and slide over to select the **Sharpen** tool.

2 Double-click the **Sharpen** tool to show the Sharpen Options palette.

3 Enter a **Pressure** percentage; higher pressure produces more sharpening.

4 Click and drag in the image to sharpen.

Task 10: Intensifying or Toning Down an Area

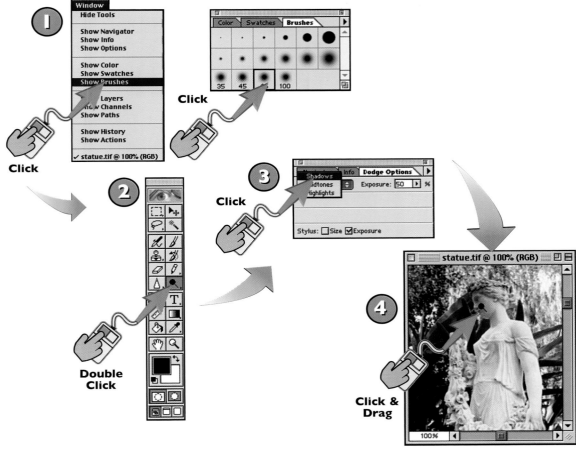

Click

Click

Click

Double Click

Click & Drag

Two darkroom techniques can emphasize or de-emphasize areas of an image: *burning* and *dodging*. Photoshop has equivalent tools with the same names. The Burn tool allows you to intensify details of an image, while the Dodge tool fades areas you want to tone down.

✓ Shadows, Midtones, and Highlights are the gray levels that are darkened by the Burn tool or lightened by the Dodge tool. To reduce the effect of shadows on a face, for instance, you'd use the Dodge tool and choose Shadows.

1 Choose **Window**, **Show Brushes** and choose a brush from the **Brushes** palette.

2 Double-click the **Dodge** or **Burn** tool to display the Dodge or Burn Options palette.

3 Choose **Shadows**, **Midtones**, or **Highlights** from the pop-up menu on the palette.

4 Click and drag in the image to dodge or burn.

Task 11: Duplicating an Image

Photoshop can create a new file that duplicates an existing open file. Use the **Duplicate** command if you need two versions of a file, or to create a testing ground for new effects. You can compare multiple versions side-by-side by using duplicate files.

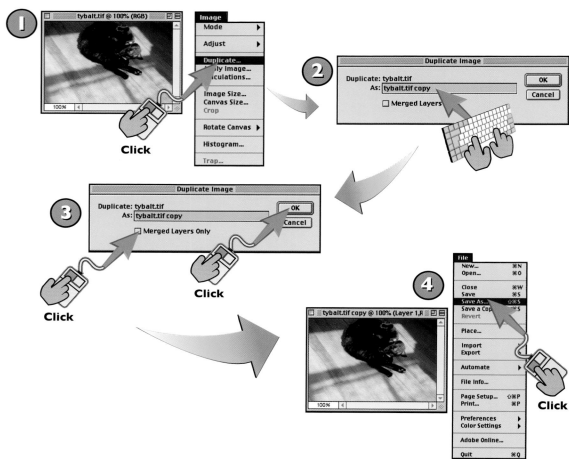

✓ Leave **Merged Layers Only** unchecked to duplicate the individual visible layers, rather than merging them into one layer in the new file.

✓ Hidden layers aren't included in the duplicated file—only visible ones.

① Choose **Image**, **Duplicate**.

② Enter a name for the new file.

③ Click **Merged Layers Only** to duplicate all visible layers as one layer, and then click **OK**.

④ Choose **File**, **Save As** to save the file.

Task 12: Saving a Snapshot of an Image for Later Use

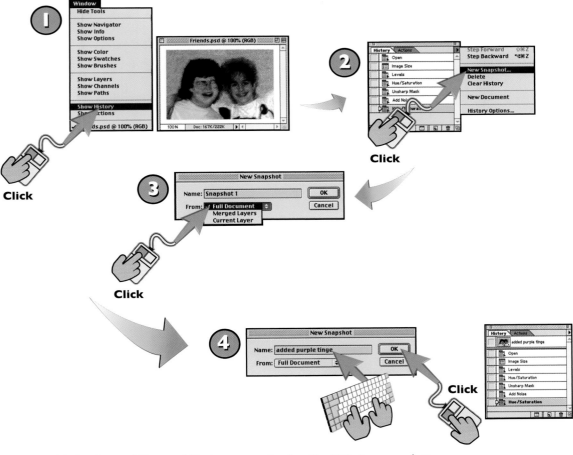

Click

Click

Click

Click

Click

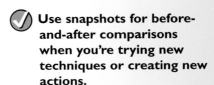

When you need to return to a specific point in the history of an image, the History palette can be a little confusing. Snapshots, the alternative, are just what they sound like—previous versions of an image. You can assign names to snapshots and return the image to each snapshot state at any time.

✓ Use snapshots for before-and-after comparisons when you're trying new techniques or creating new actions.

✓ Snapshots go away when you close a file, so if you need to save versions of an image for another session, use the **Save a Copy** command.

① Choose **Window, Show History** to display the **History** palette.

② Choose **History palette menu, New Snapshot**.

③ Choose **Full Document**, **Merged Layers** (to merge all layers in the snapshot), or **Current Layer** (to include only the active layer).

④ Enter a name for the snapshot and click **OK**.

Combining two images is much easier in Photoshop than in the darkroom—no double exposures required. Blending modes allow you to jazz up a double image quickly, and you can size each image as required for the effect you seek.

✓ Linking the two layers keeps them in the same relative positions, even if you move one of them later.

✓ Before you link the layers, press **Cmd+T/Ctrl+T** to resize or reshape them, if required. Hold down the **Shift** key and drag any corner to resize proportionally.

Task 13: Laying an Image Over Another Image

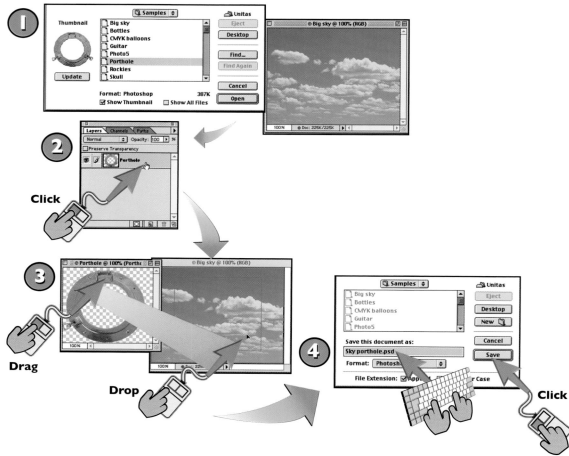

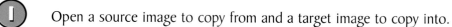

① Open a source image to copy from and a target image to copy into.

② In the source image, choose **Window, Show Layers** and click the layer you want to copy.

③ Choose the **Move** tool and drag the source layer into the target image.

④ Choose **File, Save As** to save the combined image with a new name, and click **Save**.

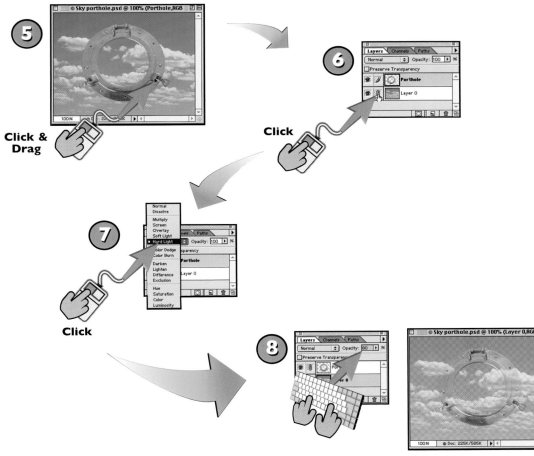

**Click &
Drag**

Click

Click

(5) Use the **Move** tool to position the new layer as you want it.

(6) Click the blank square next to the target layer's name in the Layers palette to link the layers.

(7) Click the source layer's name and choose a blending mode in the Layers palette.

(8) In the Layers palette, enter an **Opacity** percentage for each layer.

✓ **Blending modes determine how the colors in the two layers combine. Experiment with different modes for different effects—the most useful ones in this context are Normal (with a lowered Opacity), Hard Light, Diffuse, and Difference.**

End Task

A moiré pattern is a checkerboard pattern that occurs when a pattern in the image isn't correctly reproduced by the scanner. The most common cause of moiré patterns is scanning printed images that contain halftone patterns, but they also show up in scans of objects such as cloth, house siding, and shingled roofs.

Task 14: Removing a Moiré Pattern from a Scan

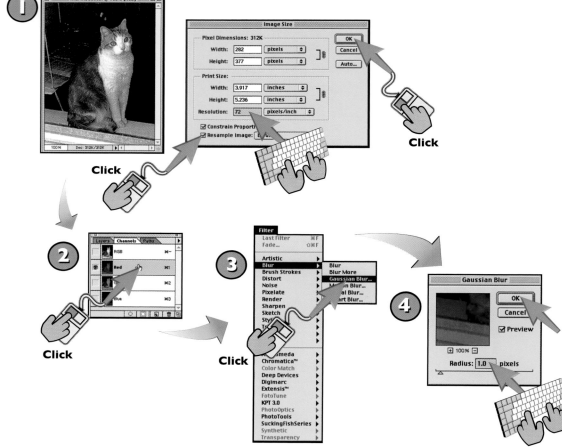

For best results, scan the image as straight as possible and at the highest possible resolution. Then adjust the resolution before trying to remove the moiré.

1 Choose **Image**, **Image Size**; enter the desired resolution, click **Resample Image**, and click **OK**.

2 Choose **Window**, **Show Channels**, and click the first color channel in the palette.

3 Choose **Filter**, **Blur**, **Gaussian Blur**.

4 Enter a **Radius** of 1–2 pixels and click **OK**.

Next Step

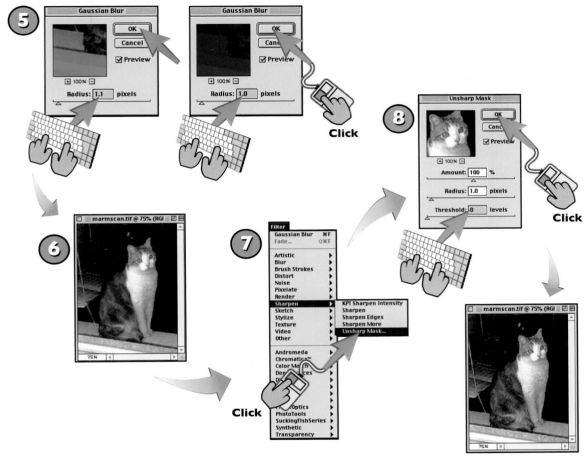

5 Repeat steps 3 and 4 for each color channel.

6 Press **Cmd+~/Ctrl+~** to display the composite image—all the color channels at once.

7 Choose **Filter**, **Sharpen**, **Unsharp Mask**.

8 Enter an **Amount** of 100%, **Radius** of 1-2, and **Threshold** of 0, and then click **OK**.

✓ When applying the Gaussian Blur filter, check **Preview** and watch the image as you adjust the Radius value. Use the lowest value that removes the moiré.

✓ Use approximately the same Radius value with the Unsharp Mask filter as you did with the Gaussian Blur filter.

Task 15: Restoring Part of the Image to an Earlier Stage

Both snapshots and the History palette allow you to return to an earlier stage in an image's creation. The History Brush does the same thing, but it operates on only part of the image at a time, leaving the rest at its current appearance.

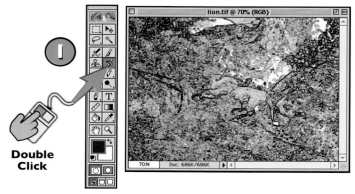

Double Click

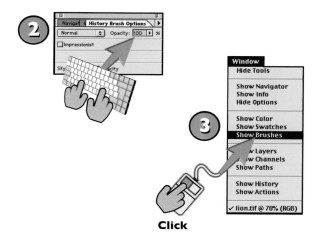

Click

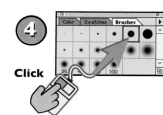

Click

(1) Double-click the **History Brush** to display the **History Brush Options** palette.

(2) Enter an **Opacity** percentage.

(3) Choose **Window**, **Show Brushes** to display the Brushes palette.

(4) Choose a brush.

Next Step

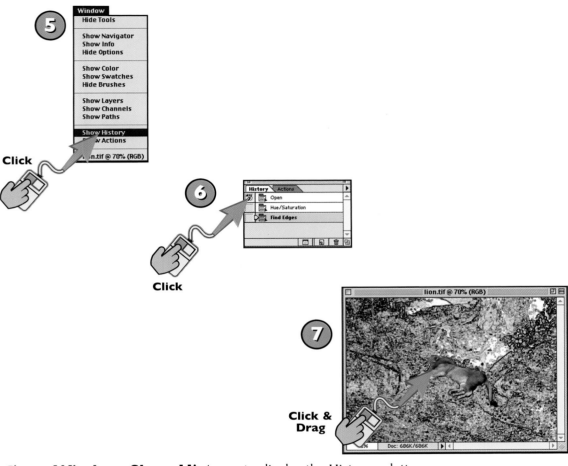

Click

Click

Click &
Drag

5 Choose **Window**, **Show History** to display the History palette.

6 Click in the **blank square** to the left of the History state you want to restore.

7 Click in the image and drag to restore.

✓ The History Brush Options palette includes a checkbox labeled Impressionist; click **Impressionist** to smear the pixels as you paint, giving an effect that actually doesn't look very impressionist at all.

✓ The History Brush doesn't work on images you've just opened, since they don't have a history.

Adjusting Colors and Tones

As an image editor, perhaps Photoshop's most commonly used function is to improve the color, contrast, and sharpness of existing images, such as scanned photographs. Several tools provide ways to make these adjustments with varying levels of complexity. Like any effect, these changes can be applied to the entire image or just to selected areas; for example, you can remove shadows that fall on a person's face or tone down a background to focus attention on a figure in the foreground.

Part 7 shows you how to adjust an image's bright, dark, and medium areas; correct colors for printing; change a file's color mode for use with a different medium; and make multiple adjustments at one time based on changes previewed in small thumbnail images.

Tasks

Although Photoshop includes tools for adjusting each individual gray or color level in an image, sometimes all you need is a quick tweak. In this case, you can turn to the **Brightness/Contrast** command—just don't overdo it.

Task 1: Brightening or Darkening an Image

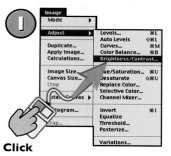

Click

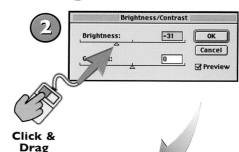

Click & Drag

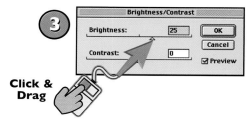

Click & Drag

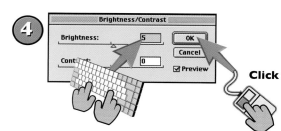

Click

✓ If you want to adjust a group of images exactly the same way, use the slider to adjust the first image, and then enter the resulting number in the dialog box for each of the other images.

1 Choose **Image**, **Adjust**, **Brightness/Contrast**.

2 Drag the slider left to darken the image.

3 Drag the slider right to lighten the image.

4 Enter a positive or negative numeric value to lighten or darken the image, and then click **OK**.

End Task

Task 2: Increasing Contrast

Start Here

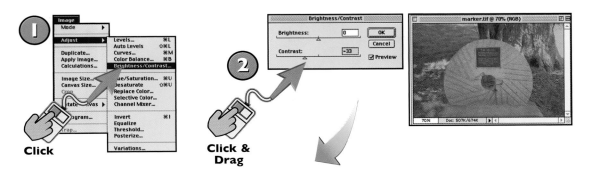

Click

Click & Drag

Photoshop's Brightness/Contrast dialog box allows you to bump up the contrast in an image with a simple slider. Watch out, though; it's easy to turn a lovely photograph into a cartoon with a contrast adjustment.

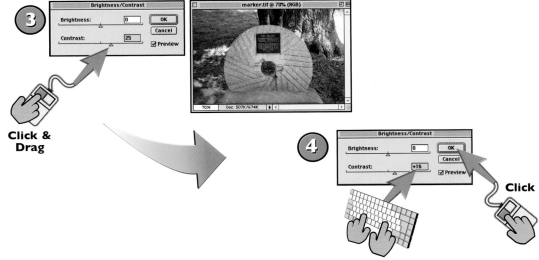

Click & Drag

Click

1. Choose **Image**, **Adjust**, **Brightness/Contrast**.

2. Drag the slider left to reduce contrast.

3. Drag the slider right to increase contrast.

4. Enter a positive or negative numeric value to increase or reduce contrast, respectively, and click **OK**.

✓ **Try adjusting the Contrast all the way up or most of the way down for some cool special effects. These are things you wouldn't normally do to an image, but they have their uses.**

End Task

Photoshop's Levels dialog box is the professional's favorite way to quickly adjust all the tones within an image, whether it's color or grayscale. With Levels, you can show Photoshop the lightest and darkest areas in an image and force the software to remap areas in between for a smooth range of brightness throughout the image.

Task 3: Adjusting an Image's Overall Tones

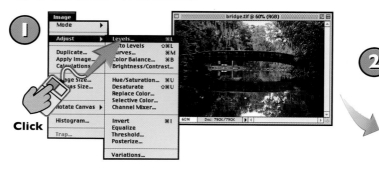

Click

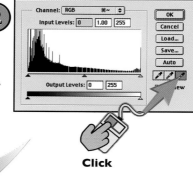

Click

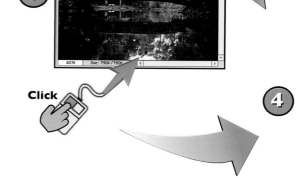

Click

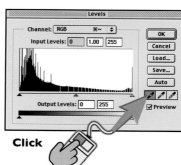

Click

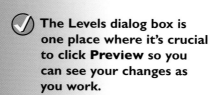

The Levels dialog box is one place where it's crucial to click **Preview** so you can see your changes as you work.

1 Choose **Image**, **Adjust**, **Levels**, or press **Cmd+L/Ctrl+L**.

2 Click the **white eyedropper** tool.

3 Click in the lightest area of the image.

4 Click the **black eyedropper** tool.

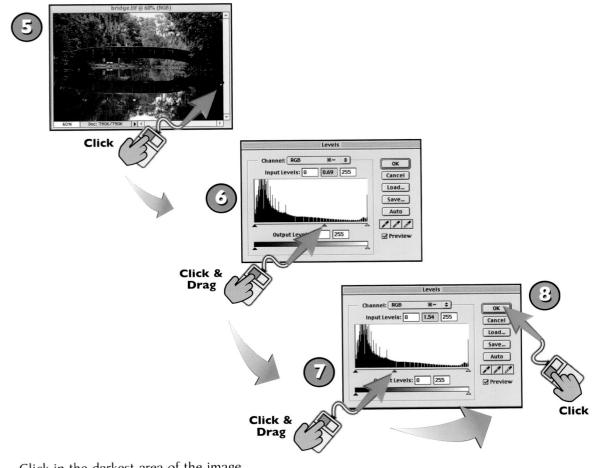

Click

Click & Drag

Click & Drag

Click

✓ Press **Cmd+Shift+L/ Ctrl+Shift+L** to automatically adjust an image's levels without opening the Levels dialog box.

✓ To apply the same adjustments to multiple images, click **Save** in the Levels dialog box to save a file containing the settings you've just made. Click **Load** to load those settings back into the dialog box at any time.

5 Click in the darkest area of the image.

6 Drag the middle slider to the right to darken the image.

7 Drag the middle slider to the left to lighten the image.

8 Click **OK** to apply the changes.

End Task

Equalizing distributes an image's brightness values evenly so that there are as many white pixels as black and gray. It's an occasional fix for an image that's too light or dark, but it will do bad things to an image that's supposed to be high-contrast.

Task 4: Equalizing an Image's Bright and Dark Areas

Click

Click

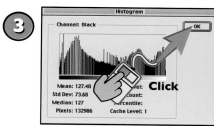

Click

✓ The Histogram command isn't required when you're equalizing an image—it's just a good way to get an idea of what the Equalize command is doing.

(1) Choose **Image**, **Histogram** to see a graph of the image's brightness values, and then click **OK** in the Histogram dialog box.

(2) Choose **Image**, **Adjust**, **Equalize**.

(3) Choose **Image**, **Histogram** and then click **OK** in the Histogram dialog box to view the adjusted histogram.

Task 5: Inverting an Image

Start Here

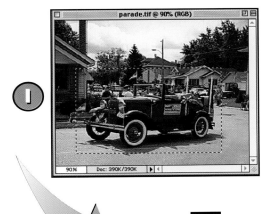

Most often useful for special effects, the Invert command creates a negative image— or turns a negative into a positive. A common technique is to invert half of an image, leaving the other half as a positive.

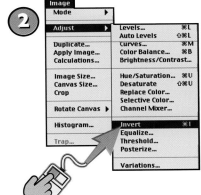

Click

This negative image is not truly like a film negative because of the compensation in film for the orange-colored base of film. But it can be a neat effect.

To invert part of an image select that part.

Choose **Image**, **Adjust**, **Invert** or press **Cmd+I/Ctrl+I**.

Warning
The Invert command is often confused with the Inverse command (**Cmd+Shift+I/ Ctrl+Shift+I**), which reverses a selection.

End Task

For some designs, a black and white image is more desirable than a color one. The Threshold command turns images into areas of solid black and white with no grays. It's useful for creating images that will photocopy well or even for designing screen printing images.

Task 6: Creating a High-Contrast Black and White Image

Start Here

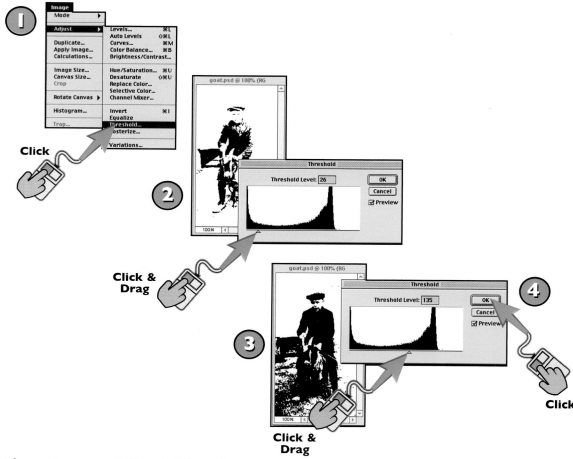

Click

Click & Drag

Click & Drag

Click

✓ When using the Threshold dialog box, it's important to click **Preview** so you can see the effects of your changes as you make them.

✓ You can apply the Threshold command to just part of the image by selecting that part before choosing **Image, Adjust, Threshold.**

① Choose **Image**, **Adjust**, **Threshold**.

② Drag the slider to the left to increase the amount of white in the image.

③ Drag the slider to the right to increase the amount of black in the image.

④ Click **OK**.

End Task

Task 7: Locating and Correcting Colors that Won't Print Correctly

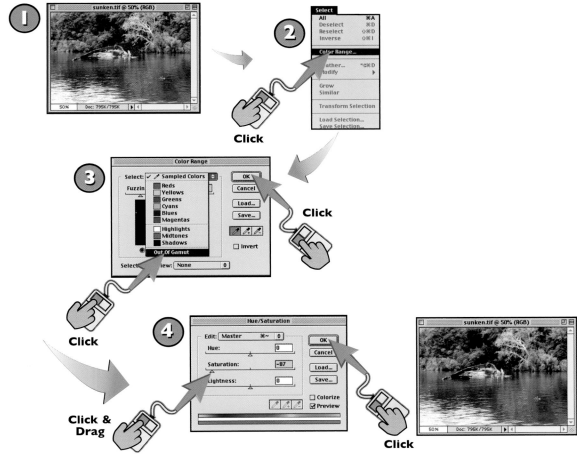

Click

Click

Click

Click

Click & Drag

Click

One of the biggest problems in working with color images is trying to make color prints match what you see on your monitor. Colors that won't print correctly are called out of gamut colors, and Photoshop can help you identify and fix them.

✓ Press **Cmd+D/Ctrl+D** to drop the selection.

✓ It's easier to see the gamut alarm color while you're working in the Hue/Saturation dialog box if you press **Cmd+H/Ctrl+H** to hide the selection first.

✓ The gamut alarm color is gray by default, but it's easier to see if you change it to a bright color that doesn't appear in your image. Choose **File, Preferences, Transparency and Gamut,** and click the color swatch to choose a new color.

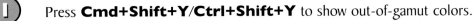

① Press **Cmd+Shift+Y/Ctrl+Shift+Y** to show out-of-gamut colors.

② Choose **Select, Color Range**.

③ Select **Out of Gamut** from the pop-up menu and click **OK**.

④ Press **Cmd+U/Ctrl+U,** drag the **Saturation** slider left to get rid of the gamut alarm color, and click **OK**.

Task 8: Desaturating an Area

Converting an entire image to grayscale involves changing its color mode (see Task 10), but you can choose to "drain" the color from just part of an image with the Desaturate command.

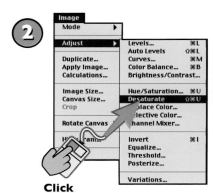

Click

✅ If you decide to put some of the color back into the desaturated area, choose **Filter, Fade Desaturate** and drag the slider left; then click **OK**.

 Select the area you want to desaturate.

 Choose **Image**, **Adjust**, **Desaturate**.

✅ To make an image *more* colorful, use the Hue/Saturation command (see the next task).

End Task

Start Here

Task 9: Increasing the Color Saturation of an Area

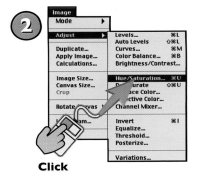

Click

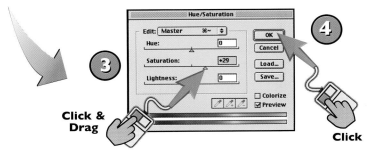

Click & Drag

Click

Color intensity is referred to as *saturation* in Photoshop—the more intense a color is, the more saturated it is. An image with no saturation at all is a grayscale image with no color. Highly saturated images look like cartoons.

✓ To adjust the saturation of an entire image, don't make a selection before choosing **Image, Adjust, Hue/Saturation.**

✓ Avoid increasing the saturation too much in images that will be printed—most color printers can't reproduce highly saturated images anyway.

1. Select the portion of the image to adjust.

2. Choose **Image**, **Adjust**, **Hue/Saturation**.

3. Drag the **Saturation** slider right to increase the saturation.

4. Click **OK** to apply the change.

End Task

Task 10: Changing a File's Color Mode

Photoshop's color modes allow you to define color in different ways. Different image formats also require specific color modes, and even Bitmap and Grayscale are considered color modes. Changing color mode has a permanent effect on an image, so always save a copy first. The options covered here are the most common color modes.

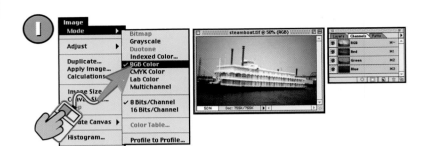

Click

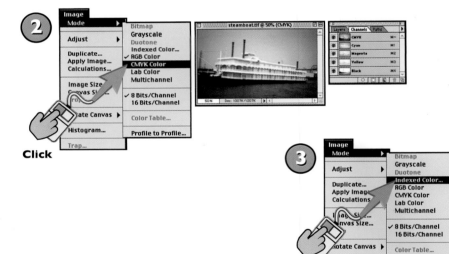

Click

Click

(1) Choose **Image**, **Mode**, **RGB Color** to create images for onscreen display.

(2) Choose **Image**, **Mode**, **CMYK Color** to create images for printing.

(3) Choose **Image**, **Mode**, **Indexed Color** to convert images for display on the Web.

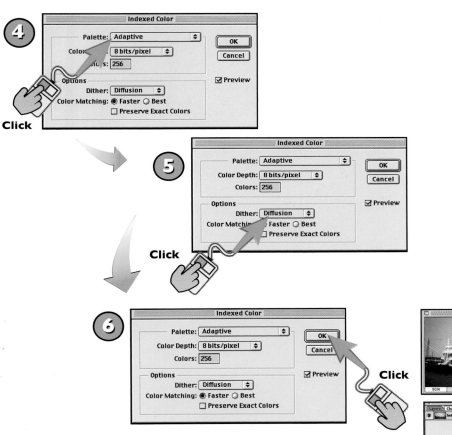

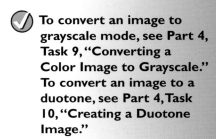

4 Choose **Adaptive** from the **Palette** pop-up menu.

5 Choose **Diffusion** from the **Dither** pop-up menu.

6 Click **OK** to convert the image.

✓ **To convert an image to grayscale mode, see Part 4, Task 9, "Converting a Color Image to Grayscale." To convert an image to a duotone, see Part 4, Task 10, "Creating a Duotone Image."**

End Task

Often image colors tend toward one extreme, such as being too magenta or too yellow. The Color Balance command allows you to adjust distorted colors—called **color casts**—by moving the colors in the image more toward the opposite side of the color spectrum.

Task 11: Adjusting an Image's Color Balance

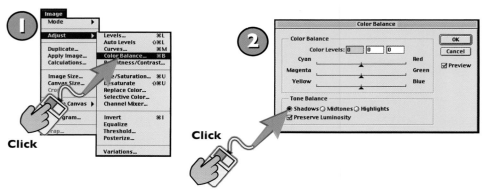

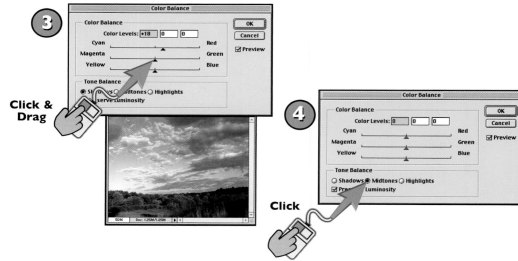

✓ To make sure the overall lightness or darkness of the image isn't affected, click **Preserve Luminosity**.

✓ Not every image will need adjustments in all three tonal areas: highlights, midtones, and shadows. Before using Color Balance, determine what areas contain color casts.

1 Choose **Image**, **Adjust**, **Color Balance** or press **Cmd+B/Ctrl+B**.

2 Click **Shadows** to adjust the image's dark colors.

3 Adjust the cyan, magenta, and yellow tones in dark areas by dragging the sliders.

4 Click **Midtones** to adjust the image's medium colors.

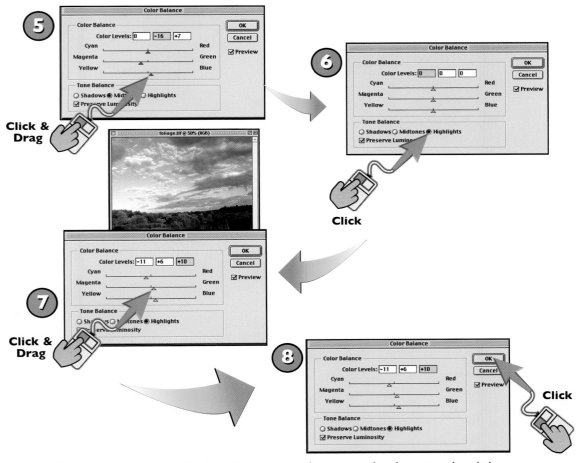

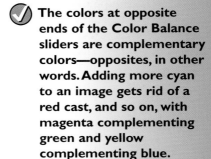

Click & Drag

Click

Click & Drag

Click

The colors at opposite ends of the **Color Balance** sliders are complementary colors—opposites, in other words. Adding more cyan to an image gets rid of a red cast, and so on, with magenta complementing green and yellow complementing blue.

⑤ Adjust the cyan, magenta, and yellow tones in medium areas by dragging the sliders.

⑥ Click **Highlights** to adjust the image's light colors.

⑦ Adjust the cyan, magenta, and yellow tones in light areas by dragging the sliders.

⑧ Click **OK** to apply the changes.

When you're working with color images, a big step in the adjustment process is the Hue/Saturation dialog box. It also controls the brightness of the image.

Task 12: Changing an Image's Hue and Saturation

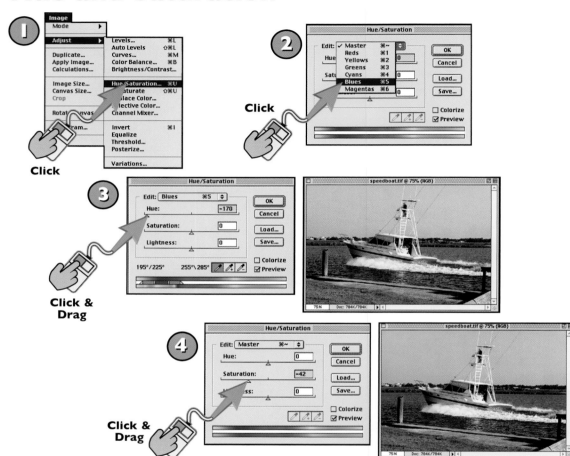

1 Choose **Image**, **Adjust**, **Hue/Saturation**, or press **Cmd+U/Ctrl+U**.

2 Choose a group from the **Edit** pop-up menu to adjust only certain groups of colors.

3 Drag the **Hue** slider to change the image's hue.

4 Drag the **Saturation** slider left to make the image's colors less intense.

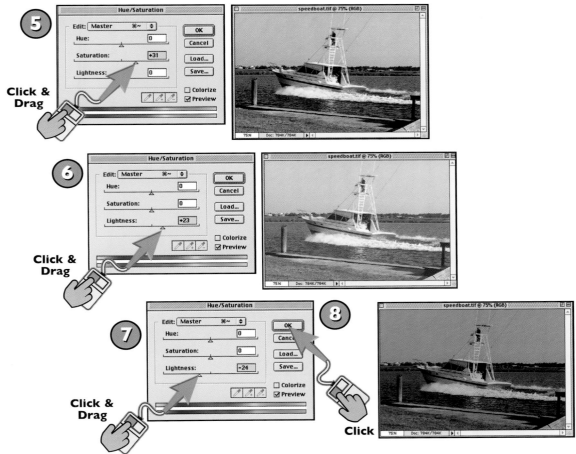

Click & Drag

Click & Drag

Click & Drag

Click

Hue/Saturation operates on all the colors in an image, light and dark—if you need to adjust just one color, use **Selective Color** (see Task 13). If you need to adjust only light colors, for example, use **Levels** (see Task 3).

Click the **Colorize** checkbox to change all the colors in the image to the color indicated by the Hue slider.

If you don't know which group in the Edit menu contains the colors you want to change, choose any group and then click the eyedropper tool and click the color in the image to specify the correct group.

5 To make the image's colors more intense, drag the **Saturation** slider right.

6 Drag the **Lightness** slider right to lighten the image.

7 Drag the **Lightness** slider left to darken the image.

8 Click **OK** to apply the changes.

End Task

Task 13: Changing Individual Colors

Photoshop allows you to change colors in an image, either all at once or one at a time. The latter situation is where **Selective Color** comes in—choose this command to change just the reds or just the blues in an image.

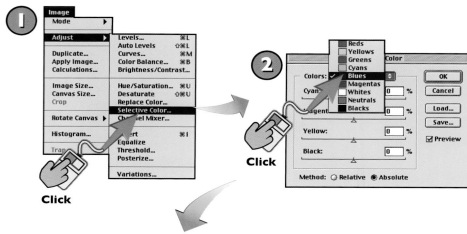

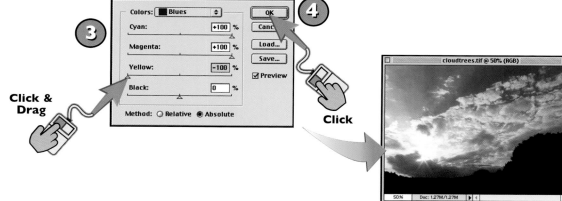

Click Relative to change colors proportionally with respect to how much of the target color they contain, or click **Absolute** to change colors by adding the specified percentage of color to all the colors in the target group.

1. Choose **Image**, **Adjust**, **Selective Color**.

2. Choose the colors to adjust from the **Colors** pop-up menu.

3. Drag the four sliders to adjust the colors.

4. Click **OK** to apply the changes.

Task 14: Reducing the Number of Colors in an Image

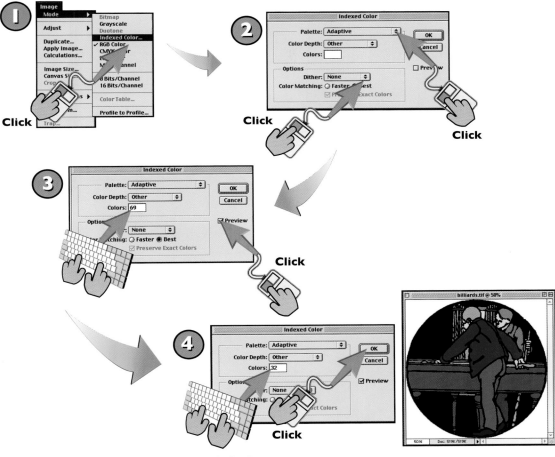

When you're creating images for use on the World Wide Web, you need to use as few colors as possible so that the image files will be as small as possible. Converting images to Indexed Color mode allows you to specify how many colors are used in an image.

The number of colors you use in an image depends on how important it is that the image look exactly like the original. Photos generally need more colors; logos and other "flat" artwork can do with fewer colors.

1 Choose **Image**, **Mode**, **Indexed Color**.

2 Choose **Adaptive** from the **Palette** pop-up and **None** from the **Dither** pop-up menu.

3 Click **Preview** and enter a number of colors.

4 Adjust the number of colors if necessary and click **OK** to apply the change.

Photoshop 5 introduces a fascinating new way to make color adjustments. It takes a little experimentation to get used to the **Channel Mixer** command, but it can produce great special effects and make lovely hand-tinted effects.

Task 15: Adjusting Colors by Mixing Channels

Start Here

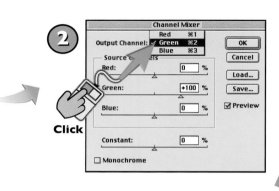

Click

Click

Click

✓ **What's really happening when you use the Channel Mixer?** Photoshop changes the grayscale image contained in one of your image's color channels by overlaying the images from the other color channels in the percentages you specify.

(1) Choose **Image**, **Adjust**, **Channel Mixer**.

(2) Choose the channel to "mix" in from the **Output Channel** pop-up menu.

(3) Click **Monochrome** to make a grayscale image.

(4) Drag the color sliders right to add those channels to the mix.

Next Step

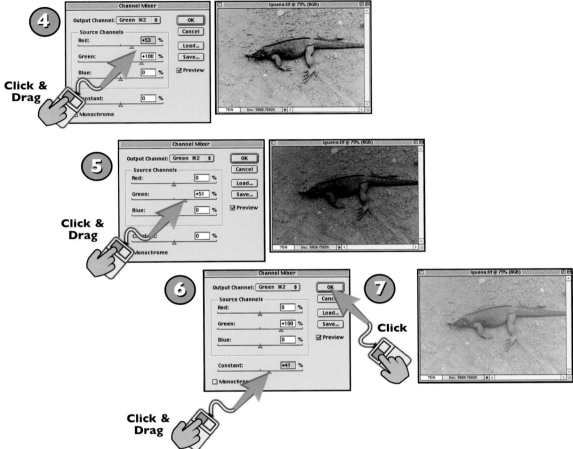

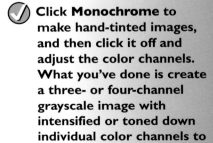
(5) Drag the color sliders left to subtract those channels from the mix.

(6) Drag the **Constant** slider right to lighten the channel or left to darken it.

(7) Click **OK** to apply the changes.

Photoshop contains a lot of very technical tools, and it's not always possible to predict in advance what their effect will be. The Variations command allows you to adjust images based on tiny thumbnails that show you exactly what effect your changes will have.

Task 16: Adjusting an Image Based on Thumbnail Images

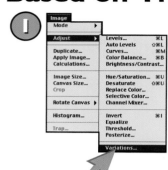

Start Here

Click

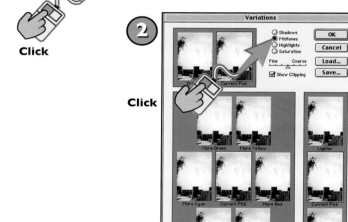

Click

**Click &
Drag**

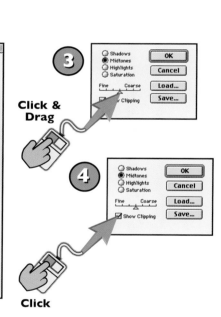

Click

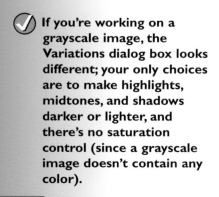

If you're working on a grayscale image, the Variations dialog box looks different; your only choices are to make highlights, midtones, and shadows darker or lighter, and there's no saturation control (since a grayscale image doesn't contain any color).

1 Choose **Image**, **Adjust**, **Variations**.

2 Click **Shadows**, **Midtones**, or **Highlights** to adjust dark, medium, or light colors.

3 Drag the slider to change the amount each click changes the image.

4 Click **Show Clipping** to see colors that will change to black or white.

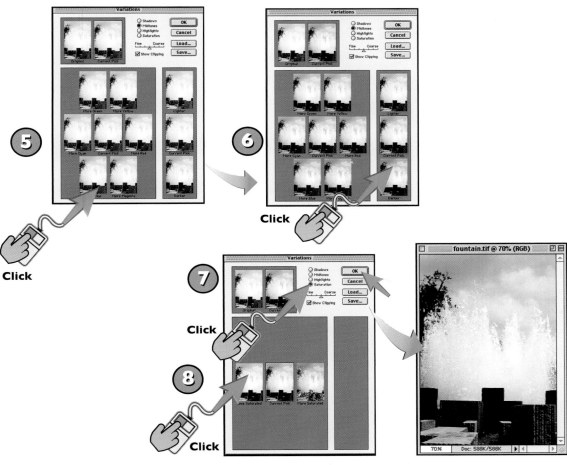

Click

Click

Click

Click

Click

End Task

(5) Click the thumbnails on the left to change the image's hues.

(6) Click the thumbnails on the right to change the image's brightness.

(7) Click **Saturation** to adjust the image's color intensity.

(8) Click the left thumbnail to reduce saturation or the right one to increase it, and then click **OK**.

  Watch for the colors that indicate clipping; Photoshop uses different colors depending on what tones you're adjusting, but they'll always be very noticeable.

Working with Layers

Layers allow you to keep different elements within an image organized so you can move, hide, duplicate, and edit them without affecting the rest of the image. Photoshop's Layers palette is the control center for layers, enabling you to reorder layers, hide them, and create new ones. Special *adjustment layers* can contain effects that exist independent of image elements, which allows you to revise the effects throughout the image creation process.

Part 8 shows you how to view the Layers palette, create and name layers, mask layers, and make selections based on the contents of one or more layers. Other tasks in this part explain how to apply *layer effects*—embossing, beveling, shadows, and glows that can be quickly created for any layer.

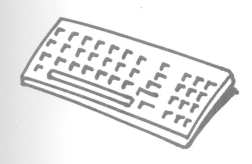

Tasks

Task 1: Using the Layers Palette

Whether you're building complex composite images or just editing scans, layers are the basis for almost all work in Photoshop. You can paint to your heart's content on a layer without affecting the pixels on any other layer, so it's easy to change your mind. The Layers palette is the key to manipulating the layers in an image.

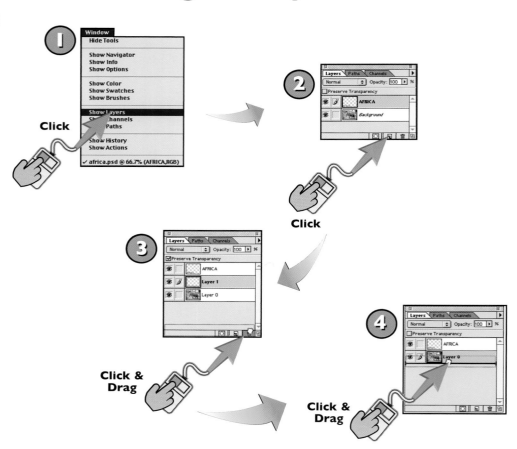

✓ In the Layers palette, top equates with front and bottom equates with back. In other words, the top layer in the palette is in front of all the layers shown under it.

① Choose **Window**, **Show Layers** to display the Layers palette.

② To add a layer, click the **Add Layer** button.

③ To delete a layer, drag it to the trash icon.

④ To change a layer's stacking order, drag it up or down in the palette.

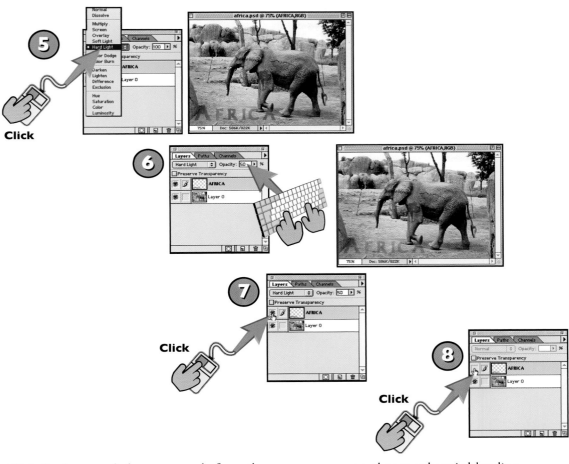

5 Click the layer and choose a mode from the pop-up menu to change a layer's blending mode.

6 Click the layer and enter a new percentage in the **Opacity** field to change a layer's opacity.

7 Click the eye icon next to a layer's name to hide it.

8 Click in the left-hand blank space next to a layer's name to show a hidden layer.

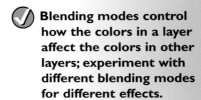

✓ **Blending modes control how the colors in a layer affect the colors in other layers; experiment with different blending modes for different effects.**

End Task

Task 2: Renaming a Layer

Photoshop assigns names to new layers that you create, whether by adding type, pasting, or clicking the New Layer button. But it's usually easier to keep track of the different layers in an image if you assign them your own names.

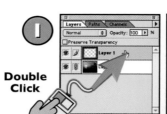

Start Here

Double Click

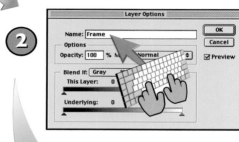

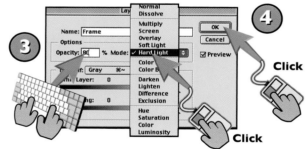

Click

Click

(✓) Layer names can be up to 250 characters, and you can widen the Layers palette to show the entire name if you've used a long one. If the entire name doesn't show in the Layers palette, hold the cursor over the part of the name that does show and after a second Photoshop displays the whole name.

1 Double-click the name of the layer you want to rename.

2 Enter a new name in the **Name** field.

3 If you wish, change the **Opacity** and blending **Mode**.

4 Click **OK** to apply the change.

End Task

Task 3: Filling an Entire Layer

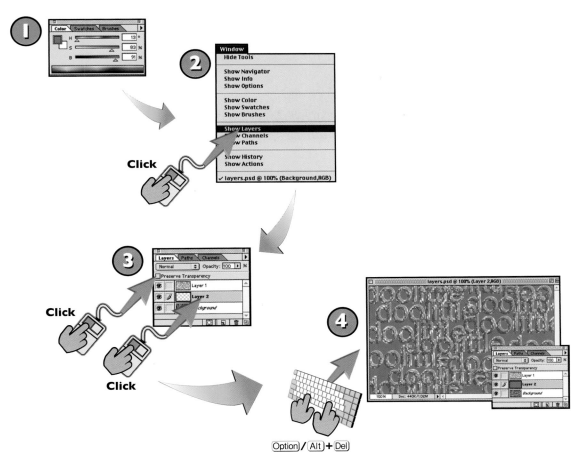

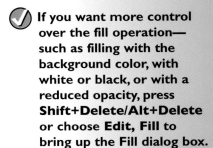

Option/Alt + Del

Some Photoshop filters need colored pixels to operate on—they won't work if you invoke them while a completely transparent layer is active. For this and other situations, you need to know how to fill an entire layer with a color.

Choose the foreground color you want to use.

Choose **Window**, **Show Layers**.

Click the layer to fill and click off **Preserve Transparency**.

Press **Option+Delete/Alt+Delete**.

If you want more control over the fill operation— such as filling with the background color, with white or black, or with a reduced opacity, press **Shift+Delete/Alt+Delete** or choose **Edit, Fill** to bring up the **Fill** dialog box.

Task 4: Creating a New Adjustment Layer

Photoshop's adjustment layers allow you to make image adjustments with tools like Levels, Hue/Saturation, and the Channel Mixer. Unlike the normal way of using these tools, though, adjustment layers allow you to go back and change settings at any time.

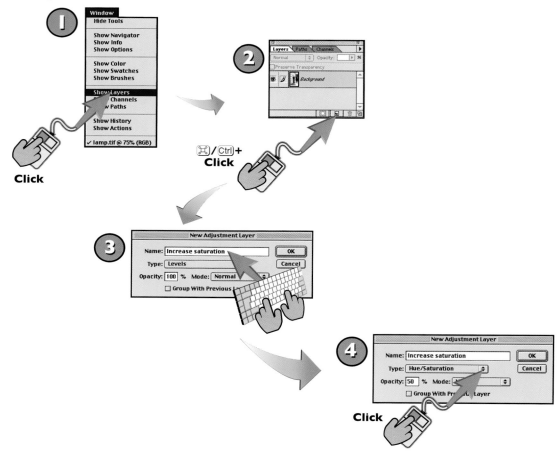

 To change the name of an adjustment layer, choose **Layers** palette menu, **Layer Options**.

(1) Choose **Window**, **Show Layers**.

(2) **Cmd+click/Ctrl+click** the New Layer button.

(3) Enter a name for the adjustment layer.

(4) Choose a **Type** (some types aren't available for some kinds of images).

Next Step

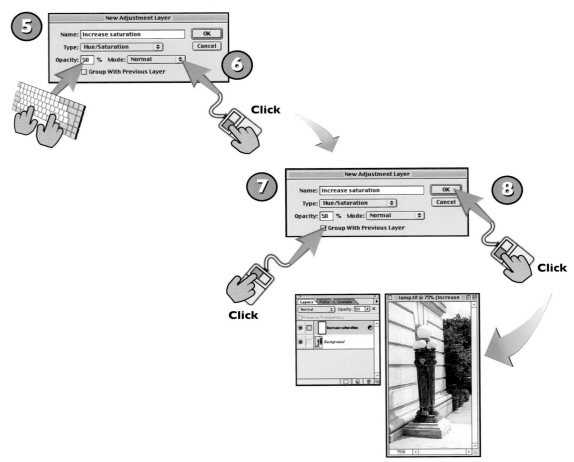

Click

Click

Click

Click

✓ As soon as you've created an adjustment layer, you'll see the appropriate dialog box, such as Levels for a levels adjustment layer. Make the image adjustments and click **OK**.

✓ To change the settings at any time, double-click the name of the adjustment layer.

(5) Enter an **Opacity** for the layer.

(6) Choose a blending mode—usually **Normal**.

(7) To apply the layer's adjustments only to the layer below it, click **Group With Previous Layer**.

(8) Click **OK** to create the layer.

End
Task

Task 5: Creating and Editing a Layer Mask

A layer mask, as its name indicates, masks off portions of a layer that are then hidden from view but not deleted. Using layer masks is a great way to create composite images while preserving each component image in its entirety.

Click

Click

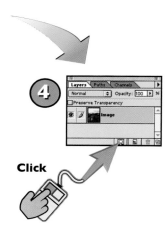

Click

✓ Gray areas of the mask only mask partially, black areas mask the image completely, and white areas allow the image to show through completely.

(1) Choose **Window**, **Show Layers**.

(2) Click the layer that you want to mask.

(3) Make a selection in the image to define the area that will show through the mask.

(4) Click the **Add Layer Mask** button in the **Layers** palette.

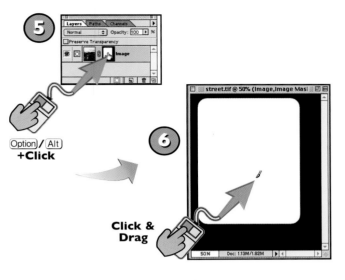

**Option)/ (Alt)
+Click**

**Click &
Drag**

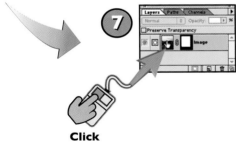

Click

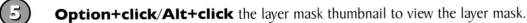

5   **Option+click/Alt+click** the layer mask thumbnail to view the layer mask.

6   Paint on the layer mask with black, white, or gray to edit it.

7   Click the layer image thumbnail to return to viewing the layer.

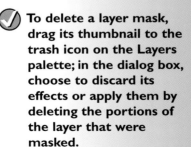

To delete a layer mask, drag its thumbnail to the trash icon on the Layers palette; in the dialog box, choose to discard its effects or apply them by deleting the portions of the layer that were masked.

In addition to layer masks, Photoshop allows you to use one layer to mask another. This is useful for special effects. For example, you could use a seashell image to mask an image of a beach; the shell wouldn't show at all, and the beach image would only show inside the shape of the shell.

Task 6: Masking a Layer with the Contents of Another Layer

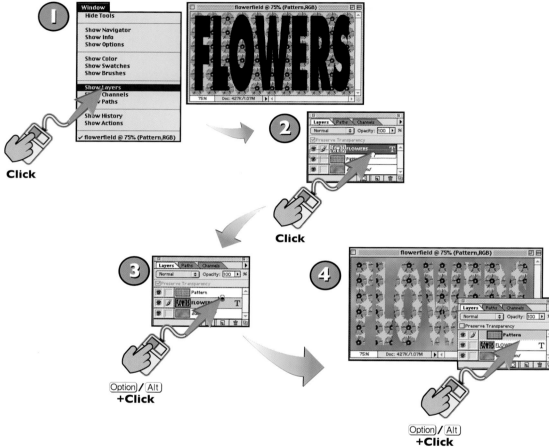

Start Here

Click

Click

③ Option / Alt +Click

④ Option / Alt +Click

✓ Photoshop calls this technique "grouping" layers and refers to the grouped layers as a "clipping group." To ungroup a layer, **Option+click/Alt+click** again on the border between the two layers in the **Layers** palette.

✓ You can group as many layers as you want—there's no limit.

① Choose **Window**, **Show Layers**.

② Drag the masking layer so that it's below any layers you want to mask.

③ **Option+click/Alt+click** the line separating the masking layer from the next layer.

④ **Option+click/Alt+click** the lines between any other layers to be masked.

End Task

Task 7: Converting a Layer Effect to Individual Layers

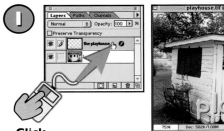

Click

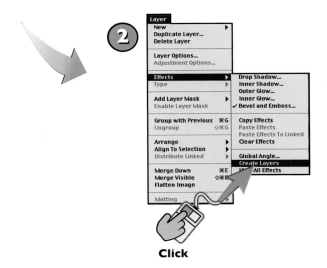

Click

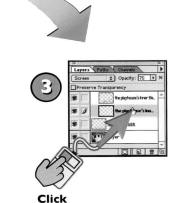

Click

Layer effects can't be edited except via the Effects dialog box. But if you do need to change a layer effect in some way—such as to cut out a piece of shadow so it won't overlap another element—you can convert a layer effect to its constituent pieces, each on a layer of its own.

1. Make sure the layer with the effect you want to convert is active.

2. Choose **Layer**, **Effects**, **Create Layers**.

3. To edit an effects layer, click it in the **Layers palette**, as you would any layer.

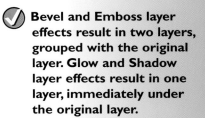 **Bevel and Emboss layer effects result in two layers, grouped with the original layer. Glow and Shadow layer effects result in one layer, immediately under the original layer.**

Task 8: Adding a Shadow to a Layer

New to Photoshop 5 are several layer effects—special effects that you can apply to layers with (almost) just one click. The Drop Shadow layer effect creates a drop shadow behind an object on a transparent layer.

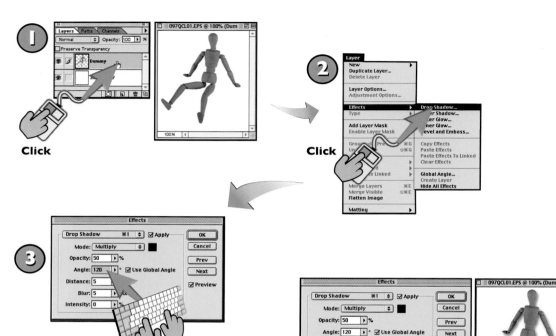

Click

Click

✓ The Distance value determines the amount of the shadow that sticks out from behind the object casting the shadow, and the Blur value determines how "fuzzy" the shadow is.

(1) Make sure the desired layer is active.

(2) Choose **Layer**, **Effects**, **Drop Shadow**.

(3) Enter an **Opacity** and an **Angle** for the shadow.

(4) Enter a **Distance** value and a **Blur** value, then click **OK** to create the shadow.

Task 9: Adding a Glow to a Layer

Start Here

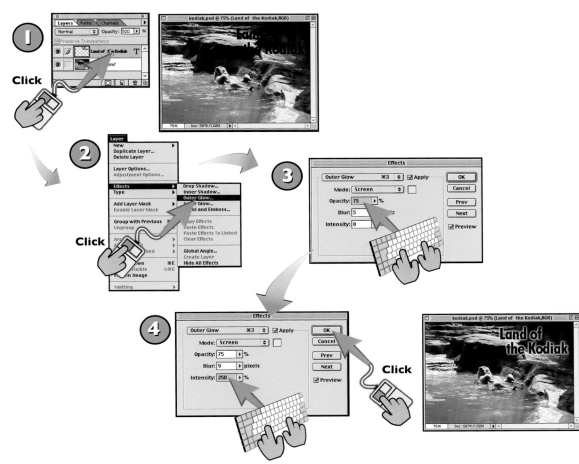

Click

Click

Click

The Inner Glow and Outer Glow layer effects work the same way; both add a colored glow to an object on an otherwise transparent layer. They work with both images and type, and unlike filters they can be applied to type without rendering the type into pixels.

✓ You can change the color of the glow by clicking the color swatch in the Effects dialog box and choosing a different color in the Color Picker.

✓ Try choosing different blending modes from the Mode pop-up menu for different effects; Exclusion makes a particularly neat-looking glow.

1. Make sure the desired layer is active.

2. Choose **Layer**, **Effects**, **Outer Glow** or **Inner Glow**.

3. Enter an **Opacity** for the glow.

4. Enter a **Blur** value and an **Intensity** value. Click **OK** to create the glow.

End Task

Task 10: Beveling a Layer

Creating a bevel used to require a lot of work with selections, channels, and the Levels controls. With Photoshop 5, beveling an object or type is much easier. Like all layer effects, this technique is designed to work with an image or type on an otherwise transparent layer.

Start Here

Click

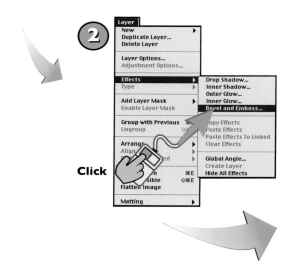

Click

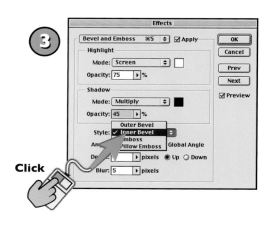

Click

① Make sure the desired layer is active.

② Choose **Layer**, **Effects**, **Bevel and Emboss**.

③ Choose a bevel style from the **Style** menu.

Next Step

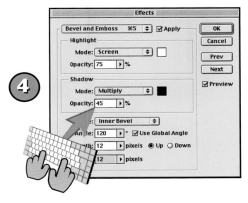

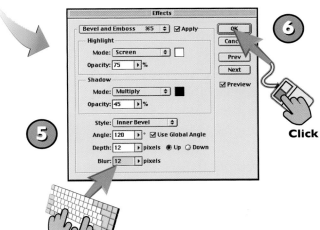

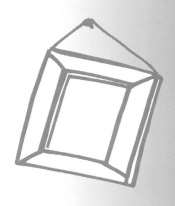

Click

Enter **Opacity** values in the **Highlight** and **Shadow** areas.

Enter values for the **Angle**, **Depth**, and **Blur**.

Click **OK** to create the bevel.

✓ The Bevel layer effect comes in two flavors; choose **Outer Bevel** or **Inner Bevel** from the Style pop-up menu to switch between them.

✓ You can change the colors of the "light" that creates the bevel effect by clicking the white and black color swatches and choosing new colors in the **Color Picker**.

Task 11: Embossing a Layer

Photoshop's built-in Emboss filter doesn't produce very attractive results. Fortunately, the Emboss layer effect is much more useful. It creates a three-dimensional embossing effect that can be any height you desire, or even a reverse emboss (sometimes called debossing).

Start Here

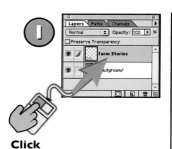

Click

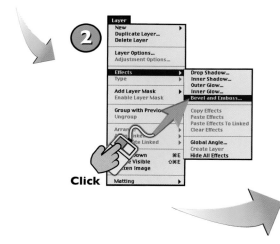

Click

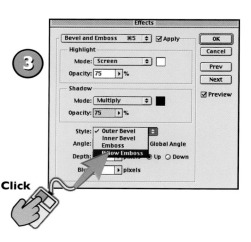

Click

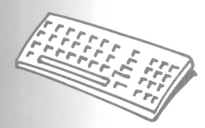

 Make sure the desired layer is active.

 Choose **Layer**, **Effects**, **Bevel and Emboss.**

 Choose an embossing style from the **Style** menu.

Next Step

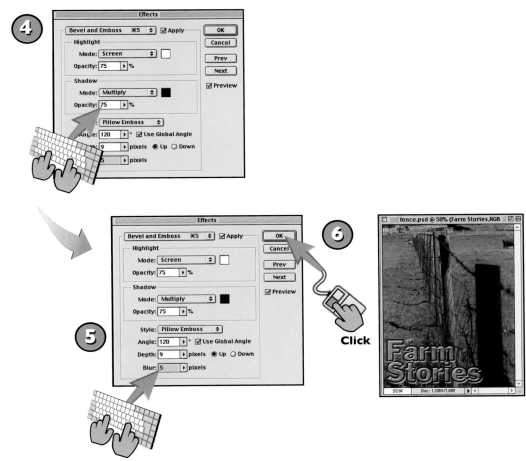

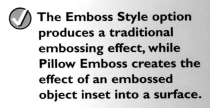

Click

④ Enter **Opacity** values in the **Highlight** and **Shadow** areas.

⑤ Enter values for **Angle**, **Depth**, and **Blur**.

⑥ Click **OK** to create the embossing.

✓ **The Emboss Style option produces a traditional embossing effect, while Pillow Emboss creates the effect of an embossed object inset into a surface.**

Task 12: Copying an Area from More than One Layer

Start Here

Photoshop's Copy command works only on the active layer; to copy from more than one layer at a time, you need to use the Copy Merged command. Copy Merged copies non-transparent pixels from all visible layers at one time.

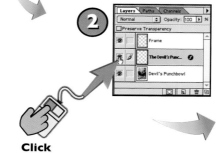

Click

Click

Click

✓ When only transparent pixels are selected, neither the Copy nor the Copy Merged command is available. They're also unavailable if the active layer is hidden.

(1) Select the area to copy.

(2) Hide all layers from which you don't want to copy.

(3) Make one of the layers you're copying active.

(4) Choose **Edit**, **Copy Merged**.

 End Task

Task 13: Merging Layers

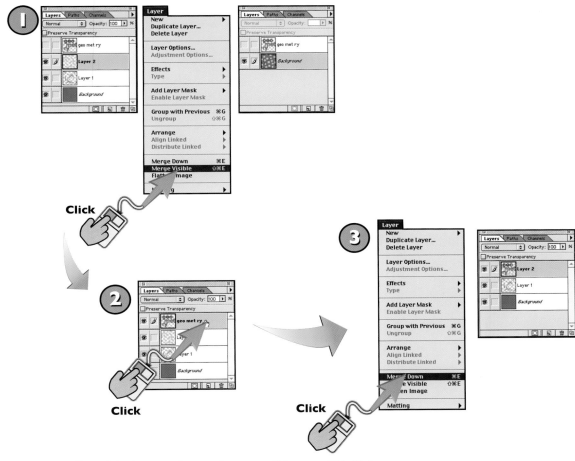

Click

Click

Click

Layers are convenient, but the number of them can get out of hand. When you're sure that you won't need objects to exist on separate layers any more, you can combine the layers to simplify your life. You have a choice of merging layers two at a time or all visible layers at once.

1 To merge all visible layers, choose **Layer**, **Merge Visible**.

2 To merge two layers, make the upper (frontmost) of the two layers active.

3 Choose **Layer**, **Merge Down**.

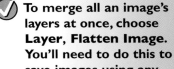 To merge all an image's layers at once, choose **Layer, Flatten Image**. You'll need to do this to save images using any format other than Photoshop.

Creating and Editing Type

Even in Photoshop, the king of image editors, there's a place for type. Photoshop's type tools allow you to create editable type that can be formatted character by character and edited as many times as you wish. Photoshop allows you to use any font installed on your computer system; it offers the usual text-formatting options such as bold and italic along with more sophisticated controls such as kerning and tracking.

Once you've got the words you want just the way you want them, you convert them to pixels—at that point you can apply filters and other effects to them just like any other part of the image. This Part shows you how to create and edit type, how to render it into pixels, and how to create a couple of fun special effects with type, such as flaming type.

Tasks

Task 1: Creating Type

Even in Photoshop, the king of image editors, type has a place. The type controls in Photoshop 5 are greatly improved—you can edit type after it's created, and you can apply different formatting to individual words and characters. Type is always added to an image on a new layer.

✓ It's hard to predict exactly where the type will end up when you click in the image with the Type tool. After you've created the type, while you're still in the Type Tool dialog box, you can reposition it with the Move tool.

✓ By default, the current foreground color is shown in the Type Tool dialog box's color swatch, so the fastest way to choose a type color is to change the foreground color before using the Type tool. For type over photographs, use the Eyedropper tool to choose a color from the image—this guarantees that the color will complement the image.

Click

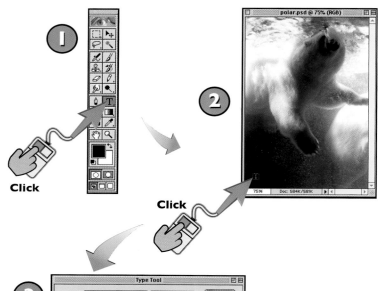

Click

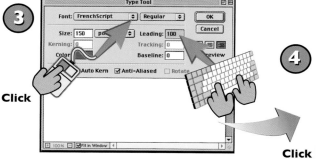

Click

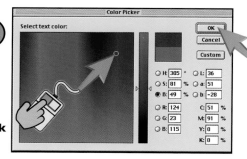

Click

1 Click the **Type** tool in the **Tool** palette.

2 Click in the image where you want the type to be.

3 Choose a font, size, and leading.

4 Choose a color by clicking the color swatch. Click **OK**.

Next Step

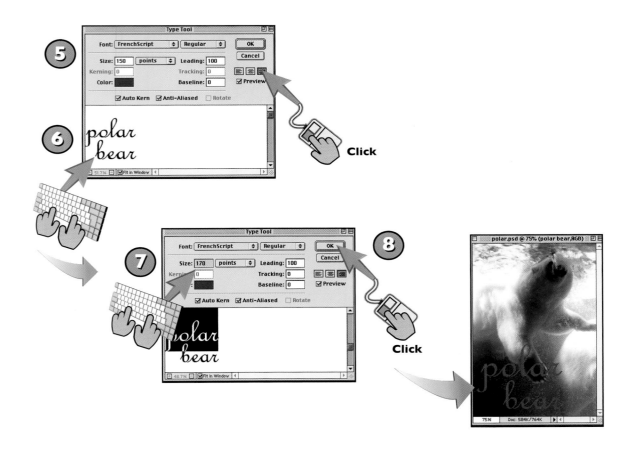

Click

Click

5. Choose an alignment option by clicking the **Left**, **Center**, or **Right Justified** button.

6. Enter the text in the bottom half of the dialog box.

7. To reformat some of the type, select that portion and change its settings.

8. Click **OK** to create the type.

✅ Tracking refers to spacing between a selected range of characters, and kerning refers to spacing between two specific characters.

✅ Click **Auto Kern** to have Photoshop adjust the spacing between letters for the most even visual effect. Click **Anti-aliased** to smooth the edges of the type by blurring them slightly.

End
Task

Page
185

Task 2: Editing Type

Photoshop 5's new type features are a big improvement over those in earlier versions. The biggest advance is the fact that type remains editable until you render it into pixels. Via a return trip to the Type Tool Options dialog box, you can change the color, formatting, and content.

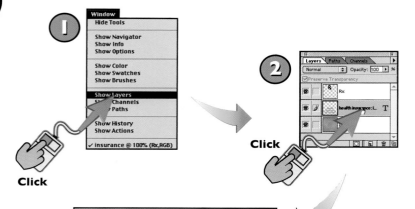

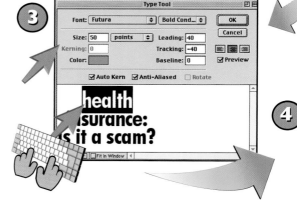

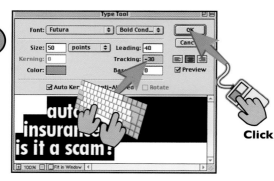

✓ You can tell which type layers haven't yet been rendered into pixels because of the distinctive "T" symbol next to their names in the Layers palette.

① Choose **Window**, **Show Layers**.

② Double-click the type layer you want to edit.

③ To edit the text, click in the bottom half of the dialog box and make the changes.

④ To change formatting, select all or some of the text, change the settings, and then click **OK**.

Task 3: Rendering Type into Pixels

Start Here

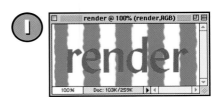 

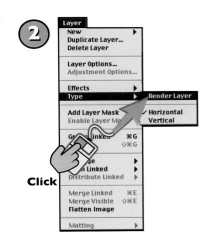 

Click

To make sure you can edit type after it's created, Photoshop doesn't *render* the type into pixels until you tell it to. You can't run filters on type until you render it, because filters operate on the individual pixels of the object to which they're applied.

(✓) Although you can't run filters on unrendered type, you can fill it with a color, and you can apply layer effects to create glows, shadows, and bevelling or embossing effects.

(✓) Before you render a type layer, create a copy of it, and then make it invisible. Later, if you realize you need to edit the type, you can make it visible and don't have to start from scratch.

1 Create the type.

2 Choose **Layer**, **Type**, **Render Layer**.

End Task

Task 4: Creating Distressed Type

Type doesn't have to be clean, clear, and boring. Photoshop's fun filters can be applied to type as well as to images, and an unlimited number of effects can be achieved by combining two or more filters. Distressed type looks as though it's really been through the wringer.

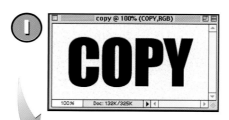

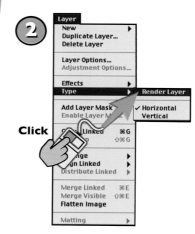

Click

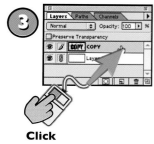

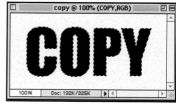

Click

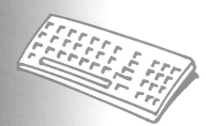

1 Create the type.

2 Choose **Layer**, **Type**, **Render Layer** to turn the type into pixels.

3 **Cmd+click/Ctrl+click** the type layer to select the type.

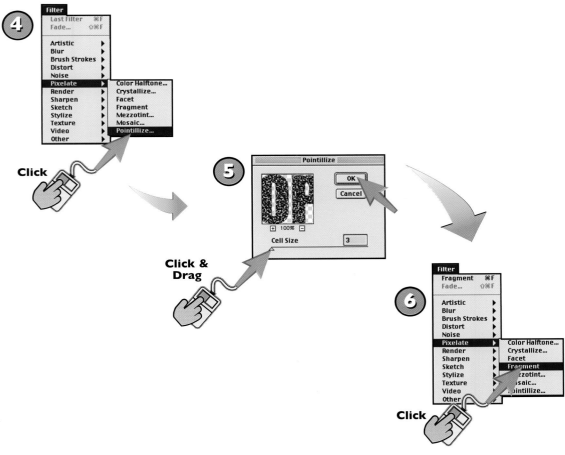

Click

Click & Drag

Click

4 Choose **Filter**, **Pixelate**, **Pointillize**.

5 Enter the lowest setting and click **OK**.

6 Choose **Filter**, **Pixelate**, **Fragment**.

If you're working in a color image, your type will turn out rainbow colored. To change its color, choose **Image**, **Adjust**, **Hue/Saturation**, click **Colorize**, drag the **Hue** slider until you like the color, and then click **OK**.

Next Step

Creating Distressed Type Continued

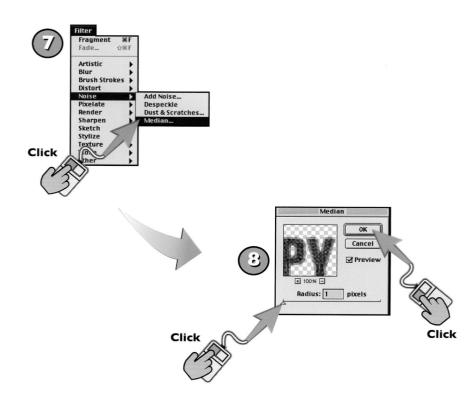

⑦ Deselect and choose **Filter**, **Noise**, **Median**.

⑧ Use a very low setting and click **OK**.

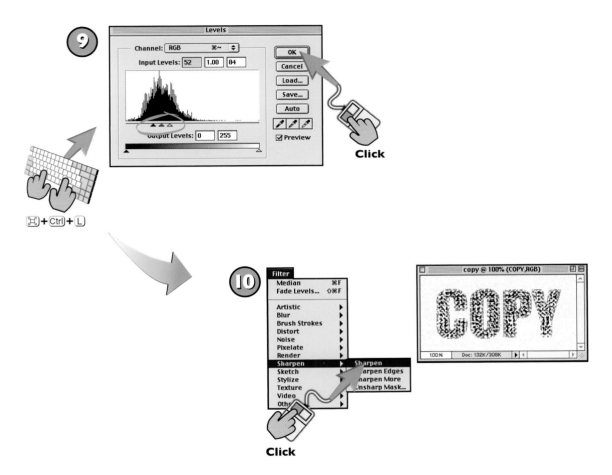

Click

$\mathbb{H}$ + Ctrl + L

Click

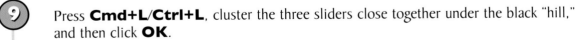

⑨ Press **Cmd+L/Ctrl+L**, cluster the three sliders close together under the black "hill,"
and then click **OK**.

⑩ Choose **Filter**, **Sharpen**, **Sharpen**.

Task 5: Creating Flaming Type

Flaming type is one of the coolest type effects Photoshop has to offer, yet it's very easy to accomplish—for the most part. You just run several filters with their default settings. You need to start with an empty image in Grayscale mode.

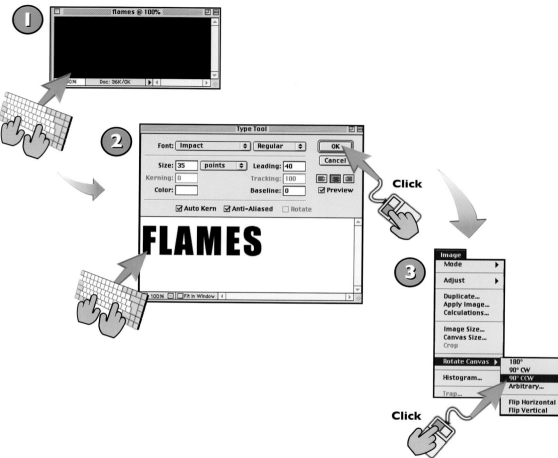

Start Here!

Click

Click

FLAMES

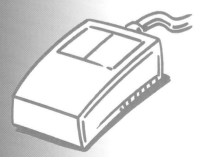

① Press **D**, and then press **Option+Delete/Alt+Backspace** to fill the image with black.

② Create the type you want to flame; use a thick font and make it white.

③ Press **Cmd+E/Ctrl+E**, and then choose **Image**, **Rotate Canvas**, **90°CCW**.

Next Step

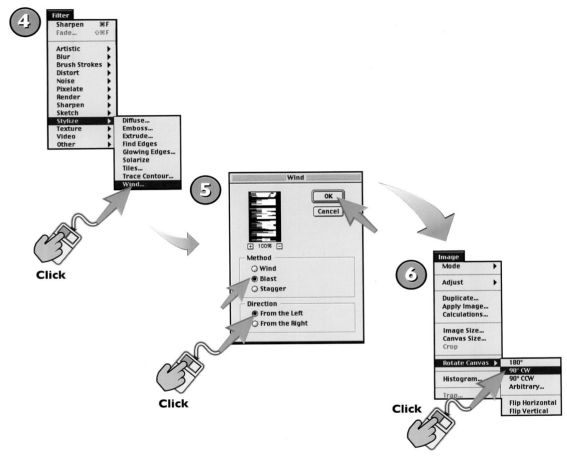

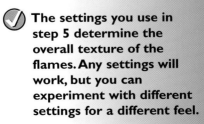

Click

Click

Click

④ Choose **Filter**, **Stylize**, **Wind**.

⑤ Select the **Blast** and **From the Left** settings and click **OK**.

⑥ Choose **Image**, **Rotate Canvas**, **90°CW**.

The settings you use in step 5 determine the overall texture of the flames. Any settings will work, but you can experiment with different settings for a different feel.

Creating Flaming Type Continued

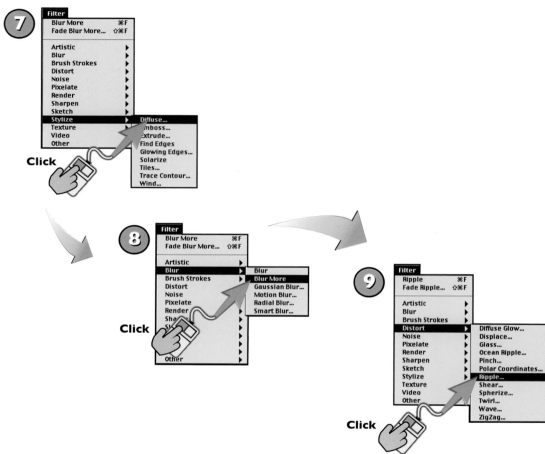

You can make black type with flaming edges with a bit more work. After step 3, select the transparency mask of the type layer and save the selection. After step 6, load the selection, contract it a bit and feather it a bit, and fill it with black. Then go on to steps 7 and 8.

For more information on selecting transparency masks, see Part 3, Task 14, "Selecting the Non-Transparent Areas of a Layer." To feather selections, see Part 3, Task 18, "Feathering the Edges of a Selection." To contract selections, see Part 3, Task 13, "Making a Selection Smaller or Larger."

7 Choose **Filter**, **Stylize**, **Diffuse**.

8 Choose **Filter**, **Blur**, **Blur More**.

9 Choose **Filter**, **Distort**, **Ripple**.

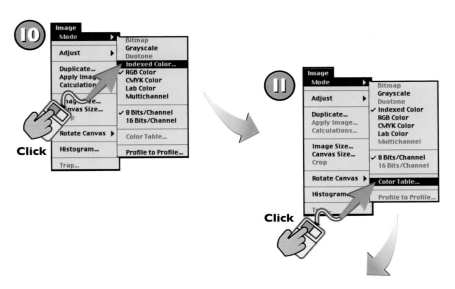

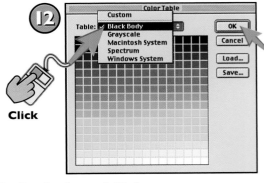

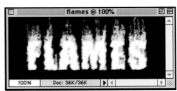

10 Choose **Image**, **Mode**, **Indexed Color**,

11 Choose **Image**, **Mode**, **Color Table**.

12 Choose **Black Body** from the **Table** pop-up menu and click **OK**.

✓ If you like this effect, create an Action to apply these steps to any type with one click. (See Part 1, Task 16, "Automating a Series of Steps," for information on making actions.)

✓ Your results will vary depending on the resolution of the image and the size of the type; the images shown here were created with 80-point Futura Bold type in a 150-ppi image.

Creating Special Effects

Playing with Photoshop's filters is probably the most fun you'll have using the program. Adobe includes dozens of plug-in filters with Photoshop, ranging from purely functional (Unsharp Mask, for example) to truly unusual (Polar Coordinates). But each one has a useful function—the challenge is to keep working until you find it.

Photoshop's filters are arranged in logical groups; for example, all the filters in the Distort submenu apply some kind of distortion effect to an image, such as rippling or twirling it. This Part shows you how to use several of the most useful filters, both for creating new effects within an image and for cleaning up flaws such as blurriness or dust. Also included in this Part are instructions for fading the effects of a filter after it's been applied.

Tasks

Task 1: Adding Noise

"Noise" is an electronic term more than it is a photographic one; it refers to randomly colored pixels added throughout an image. Photoshop's Add Noise filter allows you to insert colored or monochrome noise and determine how it's placed in the image.

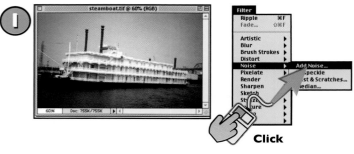

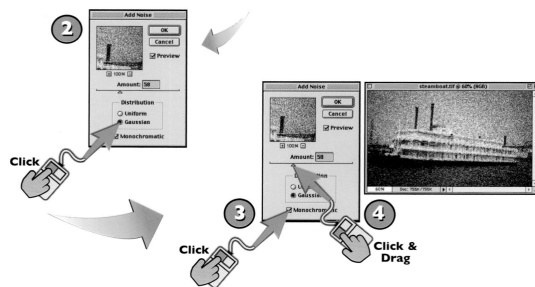

Adding noise is a good starting point for many special effects, and it's a quick fix for boring, flat images. If you're creating a background pattern for a Web page or other use, try a plain color with a little noise added—subtle and classy.

1 Choose **Filter**, **Noise**, **Add Noise**.

2 Click **Uniform** for a noise pattern or **Gaussian** for random distribution.

3 Click **Monochromatic** for black and white noise or click it off for colored noise.

4 Choose an **Amount** and click **OK** to apply the filter.

Task 2: Blurring a Selection or Layer

Start Here

Click

Blurring gets rid of detail by softening transitions between different colors. You can blur entire images for a soft-focus effect, you can blur backgrounds to point up the foreground, and you can blur to remove details by "averaging" colors.

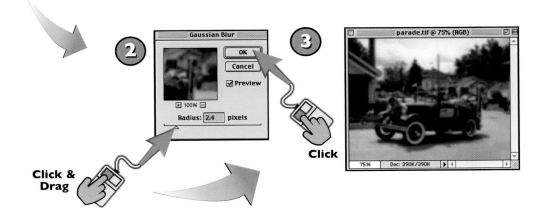

Click

Click & Drag

1. Choose **Filter**, **Blur**, **Gaussian Blur**.

2. Drag the **Radius** slider to control the amount of blurriness.

3. Click **OK** to apply the change.

 Radius refers to the distance from each color transition that the blur effect is applied; smaller Radius settings result in less blurring.

Task 3: Sharpening a Selection or Layer

Sharpening works by "hardening" the transitions between one color and another. While sharpening can't correct a photo that was blurry before it was scanned, it's a good way to correct some of the inevitable image degradation that comes from scanning an image and using that second-generation copy.

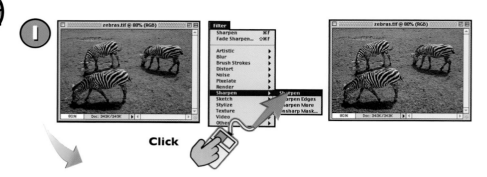

Start Here

Click

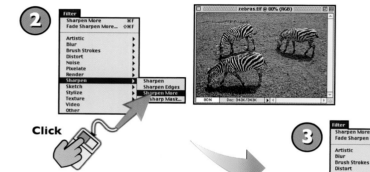

Click

Click

✓ Use a light touch with the **Unsharp Mask** filter; it's better to go back and sharpen more than to sharpen too much at one time.

1 Choose **Filter**, **Sharpen**, **Sharpen** to apply a quick sharpening effect to an image.

2 Apply **Filter**, **Sharpen**, **Sharpen More** for more sharpening.

3 Choose **Filter**, **Sharpen**, **Unsharp Mask** to apply a variable amount of sharpening.

Next Step

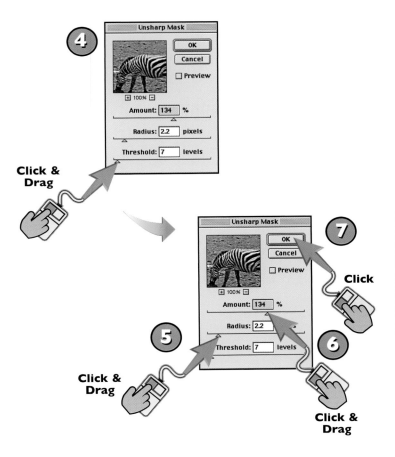

Click & Drag

Click

Click & Drag

Click & Drag

(4) Drag the **Threshold** slider to control how different colors must be for their edges to be affected.

(5) Drag the **Radius** slider to control how much of the area around transitions is sharpened.

(6) Drag the **Amount** slider to determine how much sharpening is applied.

(7) Click **OK** to apply the filter.

✓ If you apply too much sharpening with the Unsharp Mask filter (or with any filter), choose **Filter, Fade Unsharp Mask** and drag the **Opacity** slider to reduce the impact of the filter.

✓ The Unsharp Mask filter takes its name from a darkroom technique that involves combining multiple negatives to create the final, sharper image.

End Task

Task 4: Removing Dust and Scratches from a Scan

Even with the best of intentions and lots of rubbing alcohol, it's not always possible to keep images and scanner beds clean. While it's possible to retouch each dust mote or scratch individually, the Dust & Scratches filter tackles them all at once.

Start Here

Click

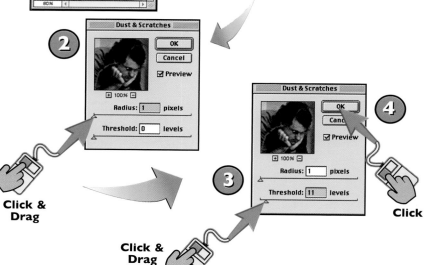

Click & Drag

Click & Drag

Click

✓ The Dust & Scratches filter has the effect of blurring the image slightly; use the smallest Radius value to avoid blurring too much.

✓ If you do decide to go after dust and scratch marks individually, the best tool to use is the Rubber Stamp. You can clone nearby areas to cover up stray marks—this is especially effective in sky areas.

① Choose **Filter**, **Noise**, **Dust & Scratches**.

② Drag the **Radius** slider to determine the size of dust to be eliminated.

③ Drag the **Threshold** slider to determine the contrast level at which dust is "noticed."

④ Click **OK**.

End Task

Task 5: Rippling an Image

Start Here

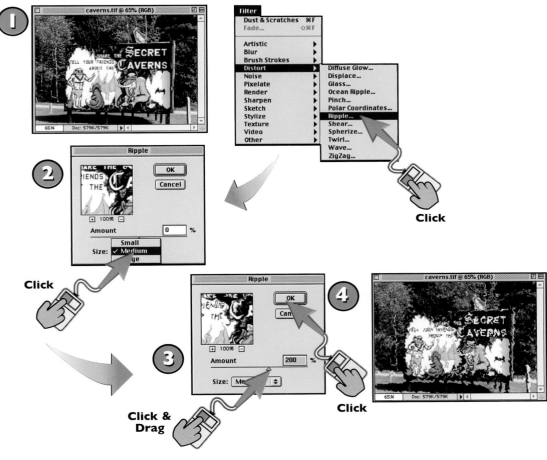

Click

Click

Click

Click & Drag

Click

Among Photoshop's Distort group of filters, Ripple is perhaps the most useful. It gives an image or type a pleasant hand-drawn feeling by rippling any straight lines in the image.

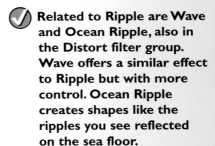

1.) Choose **Filter**, **Distort**, **Ripple**.

2.) Choose a **Size** for the ripples.

3.) Drag the **Amount** slider to raise or lower the ripples.

4.) Click **OK** to apply the changes.

✓ Related to Ripple are Wave and Ocean Ripple, also in the Distort filter group. Wave offers a similar effect to Ripple but with more control. Ocean Ripple creates shapes like the ripples you see reflected on the sea floor.

Task 6: Pinching an Image

The Pinch filter does just that, squishing an image's center so it looks as though you'd pinched together the paper on which it's printed (or the screen on which it's displayed). It's similar in operation to the Spherize filter—both look as though they're performing a 3D action on a 2D image.

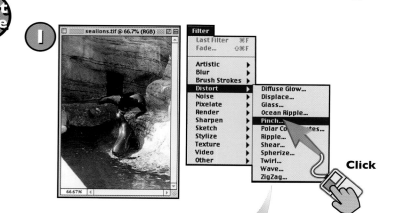

Start Here

Click

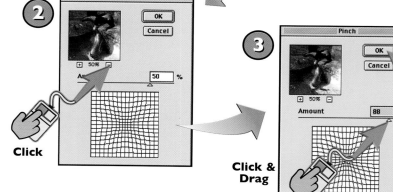

Click

Click & Drag

✓ To save time, preview filters such as Pinch by selecting a small portion of the image before applying the filter. This will give you an idea of what the filter will do, but it takes less time than applying the filter to the entire image—just in case you don't like the effect.

1 Choose **Filter**, **Distort**, **Pinch**.

2 Click the **plus** and **minus** buttons to enlarge or reduce the preview.

3 Drag the **Amount** slider right to push the image inward, left to pull it outward.

4 Click **OK** to apply the filter.

End Task

Task 7: Shearing an Image

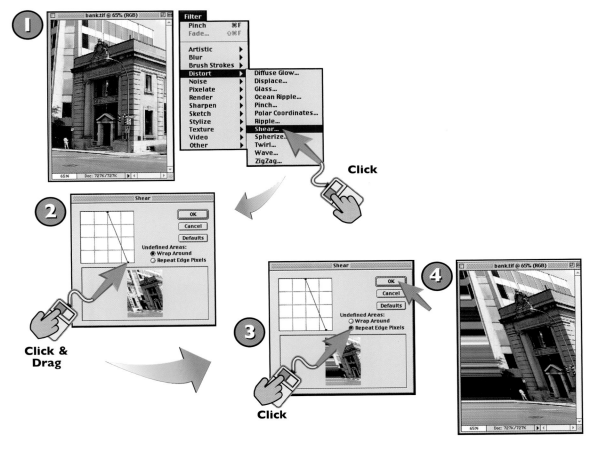

Shearing is what other programs call skewing. The image is tilted, but its base remains in place. The result is a distorted image that can wrap around or disappear off the edge of the window.

① Choose **Filter**, **Distort**, **Shear**.

② Drag either end of the line to adjust the shear angle.

③ Click **Wrap Around** or **Repeat Edge Pixels**.

④ Click **OK** to apply the filter.

✓ When using the Shear filter, don't forget that you can drag both ends of the line—you're not restricted to one at a time.

✓ This effect is similar to that of the Skew transformation (choose **Layer**, **Transform**, **Skew**), but the Skew command doesn't offer the choices of wrapping around or repeating the edge pixels.

Task 8: Twirling an Image

To imagine the effect of the Twirl filter, picture the image floating on the surface of a bowl of pudding. Now stick your finger in and drag it in circles. At high settings, Twirl wreaks havoc on an image; at low settings, it applies a rather psychedelic curvy distortion.

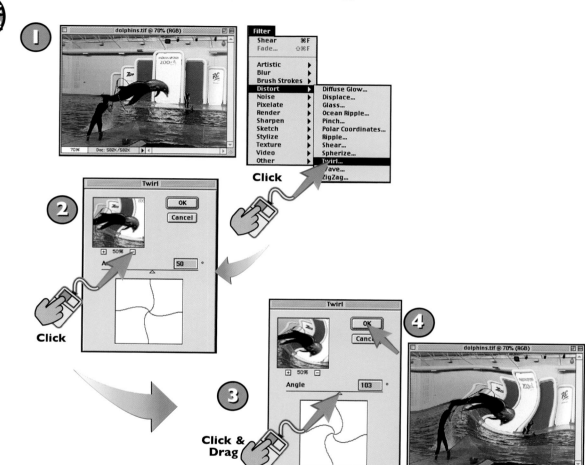

✓ For an unpredictable twirling of just an object's interior, apply the Twirl filter once and then apply it again using the opposite setting (for example, 135° and -135°). The outlines of the object will return to their original shape, but some of its interior will still be twirled.

① Choose **Filter**, **Distort**, **Twirl**.

② Click the **plus** and **minus** buttons to enlarge or reduce the preview.

③ Drag the **Amount** slider right to twirl to the right, left to twirl to the left.

④ Click **OK** to apply the filter.

Task 9: Switching Image Coordinates

Start Here

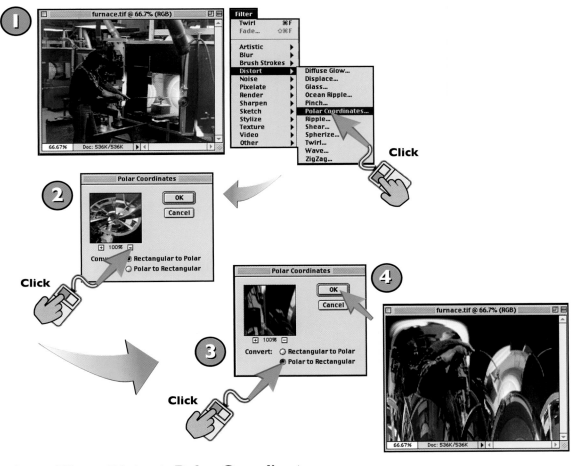

Click

Click

Click

The Polar Coordinates filter remaps an image by converting each pixel's Cartesian coordinates into polar coordinates. The effect is difficult to describe, but it distorts an image about as much as you possibly can and still recognize it.

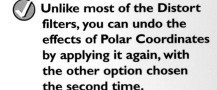

1 Choose **Filter**, **Distort**, **Polar Coordinates**.

2 Click the **plus** and **minus** buttons to enlarge or reduce the preview.

3 Click **Rectangular to Polar** or **Polar to Rectangular**.

4 Click **OK** to apply the filter.

✓ Unlike most of the Distort filters, you can undo the effects of Polar Coordinates by applying it again, with the other option chosen the second time.

End Task

Task 10: Applying a Glass Distortion Effect

The Glass filter makes your image look as though it's behind a glass shower door, and you have a choice of glass textures to use with it, including glass blocks and frosted glass.

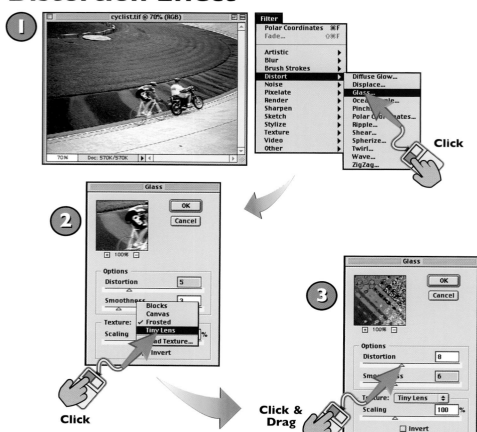

Click

Click

Click & Drag

1 Choose **Filter**, **Distort**, **Glass**.

2 Choose an option from the **Texture** menu.

3 Drag the **Distortion** slider to adjust the texture's effects on the image.

Next Step

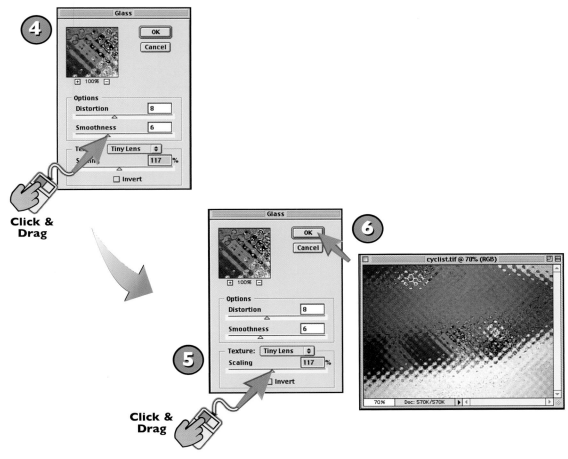

(4) Drag the **Smoothness** slider to adjust the texture's effects on the image.

(5) Drag the **Scaling** slider to scale the texture.

(6) Click **OK** to apply the texture.

✓ **You can make your own textures to use with the Glass filter; save them as grayscale files in Photoshop format. Choose Load Texture from the Texture pop-up menu to use them.**

Task 11: Creating Clouds

The Clouds filter obliterates any existing image, filling the window with a cloudy texture by using the foreground and background colors. You can't start with a transparent layer, though; the filter must have some pixels on which to work.

Start Here

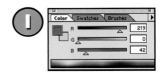

①

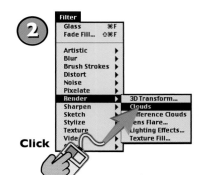

②

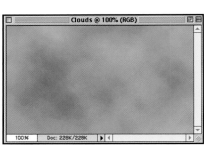

Click

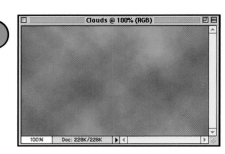

③

✓ **Difference Clouds** is a related filter that does operate on the image's existing colors. If you run the filter again, it inverts the colors it used the first time. Use Difference Clouds repeatedly on a white background to get rainbow colors.

① Choose the foreground and background colors to use.

② Choose **Filter**, **Render**, **Clouds**.

③ Press **Cmd+F/Ctrl+F** to apply the filter again to change the cloud pattern.

Task 12: Adding a Lens Flare

Start Here

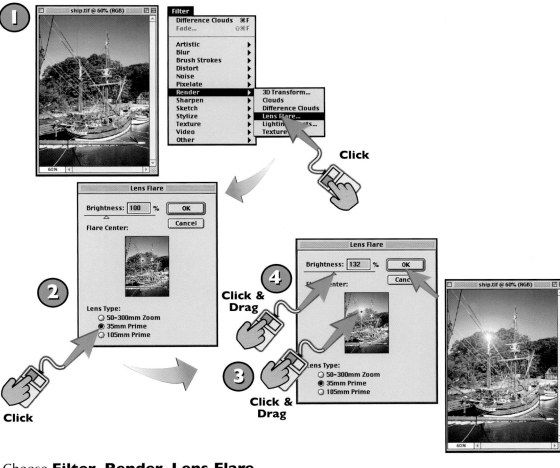

Click

Click & Drag

Click & Drag

Click

You can spice up your photos by adding an effect that photographers sometimes get accidentally: a lens flare. This bright flare of light can add a twinkle to chrome bumpers in scans of antique autos, among other things.

1 Choose **Filter**, **Render**, **Lens Flare**.

2 Choose a **Lens Type**.

3 Drag the **cross** in the preview window to move the flare.

4 Drag the **Brightness** slider to set the flare's intensity, and then click **OK**.

✓ The three lens types, from top to bottom, make successively larger flares, but they have other differences too. Try all three for variety!

End Task

Task 13: Applying a Stylized Halftone Pattern

There are several ways to achieve a pop art-style halftone effect—in other words, a halftone screen with dots so large they actually form an element of the image. This method produces a two-color halftone that uses the foreground and background colors.

Start Here

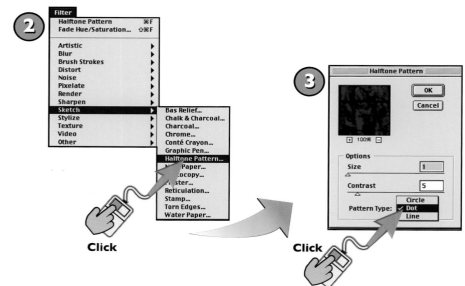

Click

Click

1 Choose the foreground and background colors to use.

2 Choose **Filter**, **Sketch**, **Halftone Pattern**.

3 Choose a **Pattern Type** from the pop-up menu.

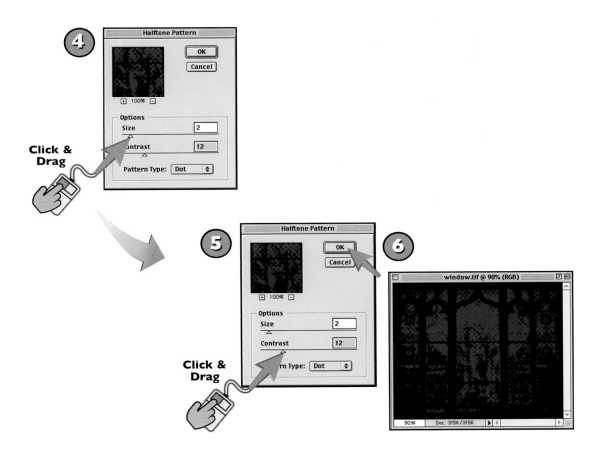

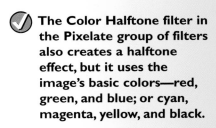

④ Drag the **Size** slider to adjust the image.

⑤ Drag the **Contrast** slider to adjust the image.

⑥ Click **OK**.

✓ The Color Halftone filter in the Pixelate group of filters also creates a halftone effect, but it uses the image's basic colors—red, green, and blue; or cyan, magenta, yellow, and black.

Task 14: Applying Texture

Want to make a photo look as though it's printed on the side of a brick wall? The Texturizer filter is your solution. It includes four built-in textures and allows you to create your own and load them into the Filter dialog box.

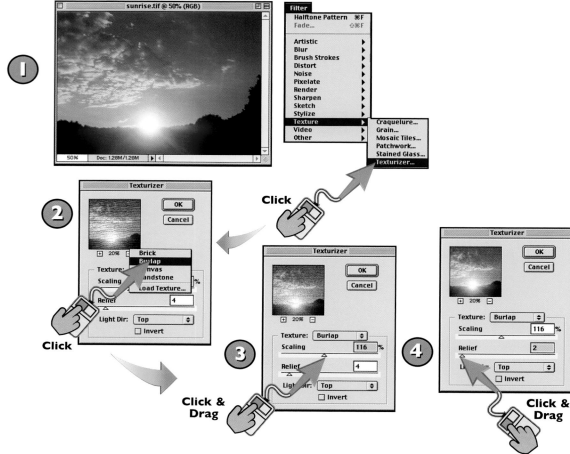

Click

Click

Click

Click & Drag

Click & Drag

1. Choose **Filter**, **Texture**, **Texturizer**.

2. Choose an option from the **Texture** pop-up menu.

3. Drag the **Scaling** slider to enlarge or reduce the texture.

4. Drag the **Relief** slider to determine the height of the texture.

Next Step

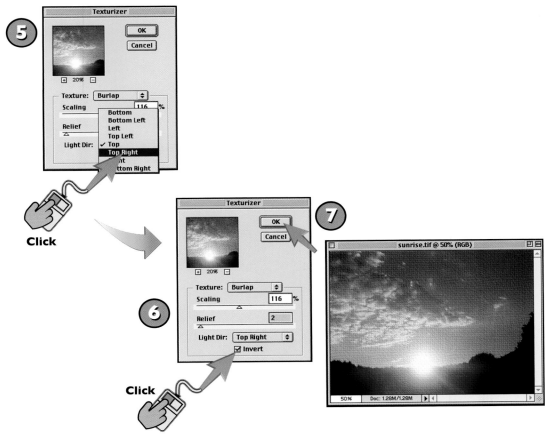

Click

Click

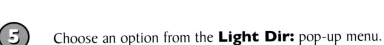

5) Choose an option from the **Light Dir:** pop-up menu.

6) Click **Invert** to reverse the high and low areas of the texture.

7) Click **OK** to apply the texture.

✓ If you're creating your own textures, be sure to save them in Photoshop format. Choose **Load Texture** in the Texture pop-up menu to use your own texture.

✓ For a 3D effect, save your image in Photoshop format and then choose **Load Texture** and select the image on which you're working. It's applied to itself as a texture, making all the light areas jump forward and the dark areas recede.

The Glowing Edges filter applies brightly colored edges to an image, darkening the image enough that any other details are effectively lost. It works best with high-contrast images.

Task 15: Converting an Image to Glowing Edges

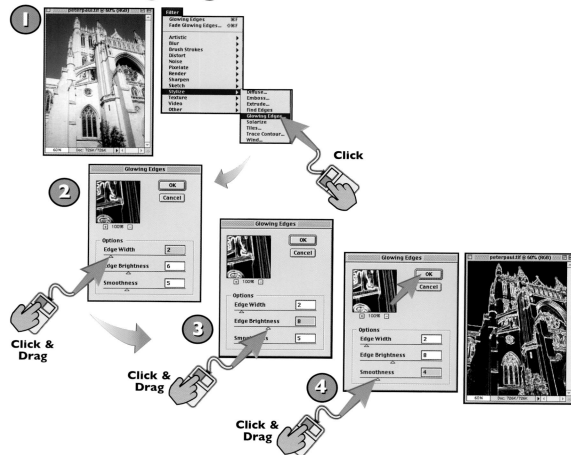

✓ Apply **Glowing Edges** and then choose **Filter, Fade Glowing Edges** for just a suggestion of glow. Drag the slider to reduce the opacity of the glowing edges.

① Choose **Filter**, **Stylize**, **Glowing Edges**.

② Drag the **Edge Width** slider to widen the edges.

③ Drag the **Edge Brightness** slider to make the edges brighter or dimmer.

④ Drag the **Smoothness** slider to add or remove detail from the edges.

Task 16: Applying a Windblown Effect

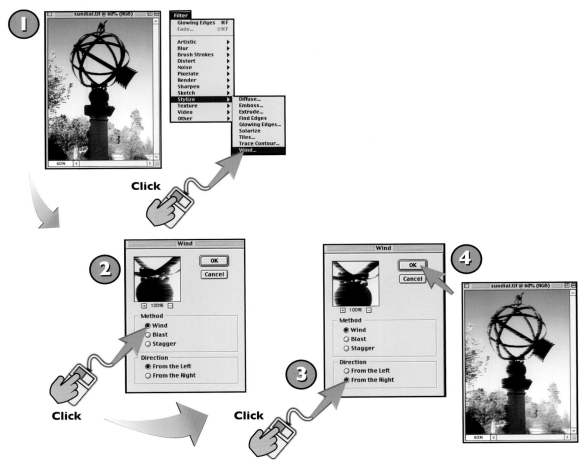

The Wind filter makes an object look as though it's being blown away by the wind, bit by bit. It works best with an object on a plain background.

Click

Click

Click

1. Choose **Filter**, **Stylize**, **Wind**.

2. Click a **Method**.

3. Click a **Direction**.

4. Click **OK** to apply the filter.

✓ The Method choices increase in intensity from top to bottom.

✓ For a fun effect that uses the Wind filter, see Part 9, Task 5, "Creating Flaming Type."

Task 17: Creating Contour Lines

Start Here

Here's an easy way to convert a normal photograph into something that looks like one of those geological survey maps with all the contour lines. This filter finds the edges in an image and draws lines along them. The simpler the image, the better Trace Contour works.

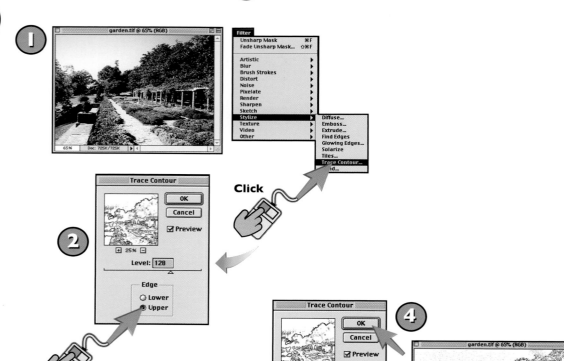

Click

Click

Click & Drag

✓ For an interesting effect, apply the Trace Contour filter and then press **Cmd+F/Ctrl+F** to apply it again—Photoshop traces the edges of the edges.

① Choose **Filter**, **Stylize**, **Trace Contour**.

② Choose an **Edge** to be traced.

③ Drag the **Level** slider to determine what brightness level is traced.

④ Click **OK** to apply the filter.

Task 18: Applying a Neon Glow

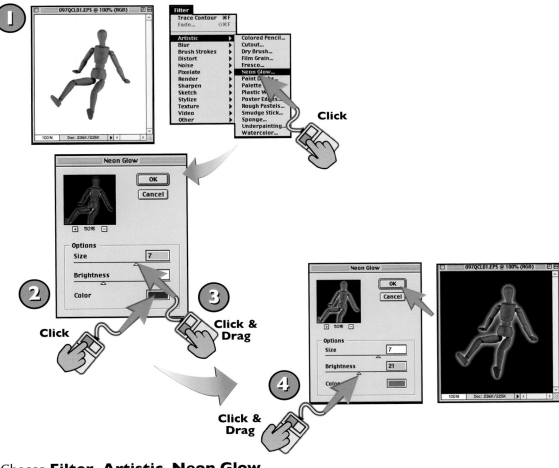

Click

Click

Click & Drag

Click & Drag

Unlike Glowing Edges, Neon Glow leaves image detail fairly intact, although it obscures image colors. This filter works best with an object on a plain white background, which will turn black.

① Choose **Filter**, **Artistic**, **Neon Glow**.

② Click the **color swatch** to choose a color.

③ Drag the **Size** slider to adjust the extent of the glow.

④ Drag the **Brightness** slider to make the glow brighter or dimmer.

✓ Negative values on the Size slider place the glow inside the object; positive ones place the glow outside it.

End Task

Task 19: Diffusing an Image

The **Diffuse** filter is similar to a blur filter in that it shuffles pixels around the edges of objects in an image. But instead of blurring them, Diffuse spreads them around to give a sort of crumbly effect. It's a good quick fix for blurry images that can't be sharpened any further.

The **Darken Only** and **Lighten Only** options only show the "shuffled" pixels that darken or lighten the image respectively. The result is that they produce a less fuzzy image that's either darker or lighter than the **Normal** mode.

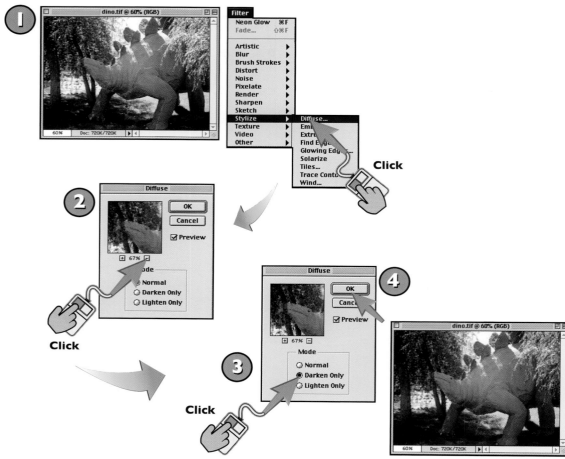

Start Here

Click

Click

Click

1. Choose **Filter**, **Stylize**, **Diffuse**.

2. Click the **plus** and **minus** buttons to enlarge or reduce the preview.

3. Click a **Mode**.

4. Click **OK** to apply the filter.

End Task

Task 20: Adding a Motion Blur to an Image

Start Here

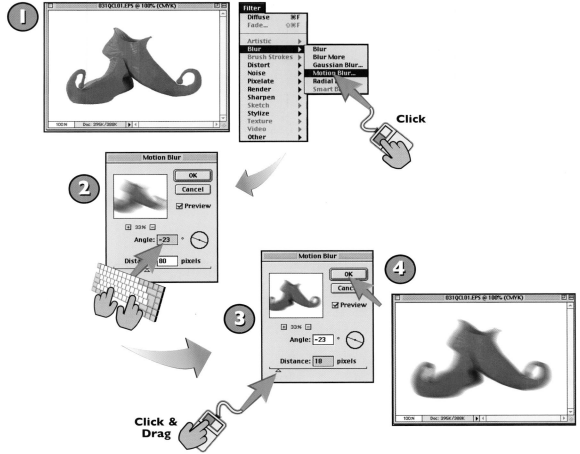

Click

Click & Drag

Motion Blur produces the same effect you get when you use slow film to photograph something that's moving fast—the image is blurred in the direction from which the object is moving. Photoshop allows you to control both the amount of blur and its direction.

1. Choose **Filter**, **Blur**, **Motion Blur**.

2. Choose an **Angle** by entering a value or dragging the circle.

3. Drag the **Distance** slider to set the size of the blur.

4. Click **OK** to apply the filter.

✔ Applying the Motion Blur filter in two different directions gives a general blurry effect.

Task 21: Adding Lighting Effects

One of Photoshop's most complex filters, **Lighting Effects** allows you to define the lighting that illuminates the image. You can also choose a channel to be added to the image's surface as a texture.

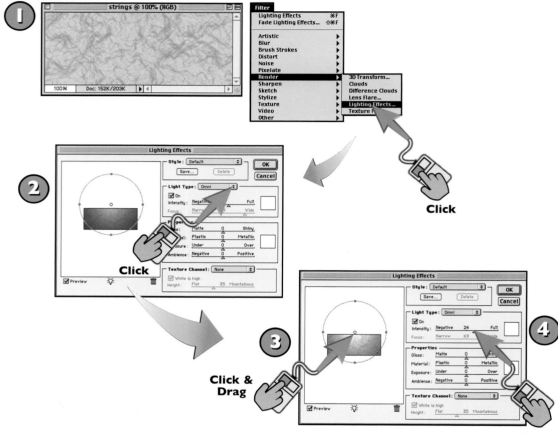

Click

Click

Click & Drag

Click & Drag

The Lighting Effects filter uses a lot of memory (RAM). If you see an alert saying that there's not enough **RAM** to run the filter, choose **Edit, Purge, All.** You'll lose the History of the image, but you'll probably clear out enough memory to run the filter.

(1) Choose **Filter, Render, Lighting Effects.**

(2) Choose a **Light Type** from the pop-up menu.

(3) Drag to position the light in the preview window.

(4) Drag the **Intensity** slider to brighten or dim the light.

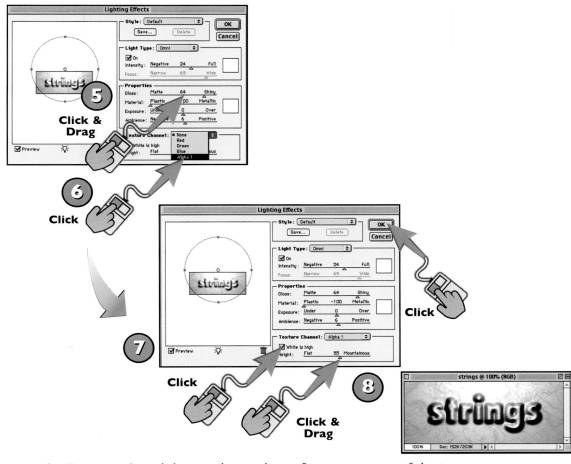

5 Drag the **Properties** sliders to change the surface appearance of the image.

6 Choose a **Texture Channel**.

7 Click **White is high** on or off.

8 Drag the **Height** slider to adjust the texture's depth, and then click **OK**.

Like the Texturizer filter, Lighting Effects can apply any grayscale image to the existing image—only with a lot more control over surface and lighting properties. To create an image to be applied by using Lighting Effects, store it in an alpha channel of the image and choose that channel from the Texture Channel pop-up menu.

End Task

Task 22: Crystallizing an Image

The **Crystallize** filter, like all the **Pixelate** filters, turns an image into chunks of pixels all the same color. In this case, the resulting image looks as though it's made of rock candy.

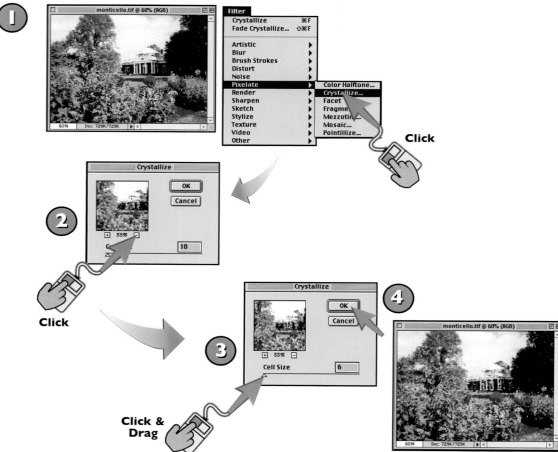

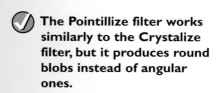

The **Pointillize** filter works similarly to the **Crystalize** filter, but it produces round blobs instead of angular ones.

1 Choose **Filter**, **Pixelate**, **Crystallize**.

2 Click the **plus** and **minus** buttons to enlarge or reduce the preview.

3 Drag the **Cell Size** slider to adjust the size of the crystals.

4 Click **OK** to apply the filter.

Task 23: Fading an Effect

Start Here

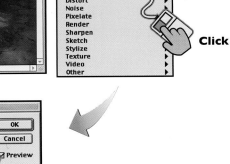

Click

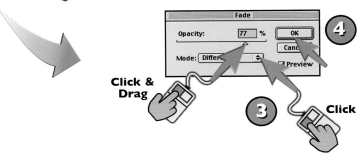

Click

Click & Drag

Click

Fading a filter leaves the filter's effects in place but reduces its opacity so you can see the original image underlying the filtered image. It's usually not quite the same as using a lower intensity setting in the filter.

✓ Like Undo and Redo, the exact text of the Fade command depends on the filter or adjustment you're fading—the menu will say **Fade Levels** or **Fade Shear**, for example. Fade affects only the most recently used filter, and you must have already used at least one filter in a session for this command to be active.

✓ The Fade command also works with image adjustment commands such as **Hue/Saturate, Levels,** and **Selective Color.**

(1) Choose **Filter, Fade [command]** or press **Cmd+Option+F/Ctrl+Alt+F**.

(2) Click **Preview** to show the effects of the Fade command as you work.

(3) Choose a **blending mode** to be applied to the filtered image.

(4) Drag the **Opacity** slider to fade the filter, and then click **OK**.

End Task

Creating Artistic Effects

The other half of Photoshop's dual personality—image editor versus paint program—takes the fore in the program's collection of artistic filters. These filters simulate effects ordinarily achieved by fine artists by using natural media such as oils, watercolors, chalks, pencils, crayons, and plaster. You can use Photoshop's more artistic filters on their own or in combination with other filters to extend the range of possible effects. Many of the controls used by the artistic filters are similar; for example, several of the filters include texture controls so that you can apply a background texture such as canvas or burlap along with the "brushstrokes" or other effects.

Part II shows you how to use the controls for several of Photoshop's most popular artistic filters, including Watercolor, Rough Pastels, and Craquelure.

Tasks

Task 1: Applying a Pen-and-Ink Effect

Photoshop's Ink Outlines filter creates the effect of an ink drawing with a watercolor wash. Details are outlined in black "ink" and colors are softened and blurred. You can control the amount of detail retained in the effect, as well as how much of the image's original color is preserved.

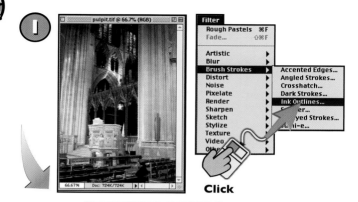

Click

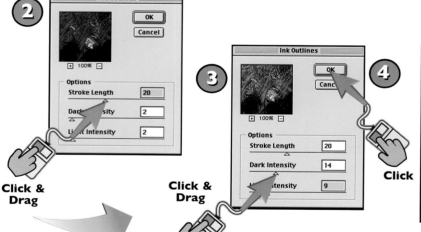

**Click &
Drag**

**Click &
Drag**

Click

✓ Higher Stroke Length settings decrease the image's detail. Higher Dark and Light Intensity settings increase the image's color saturation; lower settings allow a "rainbow" color effect to show through the image's colors.

1 Choose **Filter**, **Brush Strokes**, **Ink Outlines**.

2 Drag the **Stroke Length** slider to adjust the amount of detail.

3 Drag the **Dark Intensity** and **Light Intensity** sliders to adjust the color intensity.

4 Click **OK** to apply the filter.

End
Task

Task 2: Applying a Crayon Effect

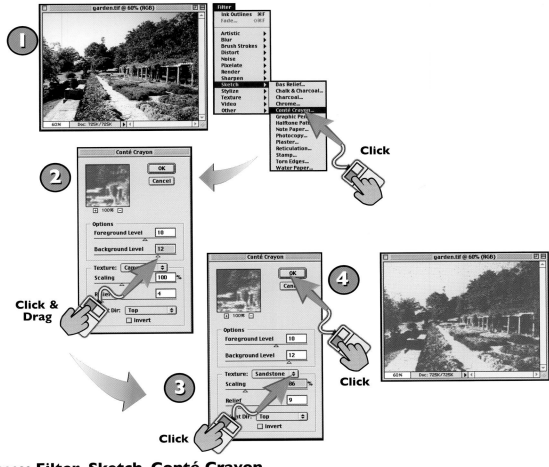

Click

Click & Drag

Click

Click

The Conté Crayon filter creates an effect similar to that of a crayon rubbing, with a choice of "paper" textures. The filter uses the foreground and background colors, combined with a neutral gray, to create the image.

1. Choose **Filter**, **Sketch**, **Conté Crayon**.

2. Drag the **Foreground Level** and **Background Level** sliders to adjust the amount of color used.

3. Choose a **Texture** from the pop-up menu.

4. Click **OK** to apply the filter.

 The Conté Crayon filter's Texture settings are the same as those used in Part 10, Task 14, "Applying Texture."

Task 3: Applying a Watercolor Effect

Included in the Artistic filter group is the **Watercolor** filter, which is supposed to simulate the effect of a medium-sized watercolor brush, very wet, with lots of paint. Don't expect to get light, frothy pastel images from this filter—it tends to produce rather dark colors.

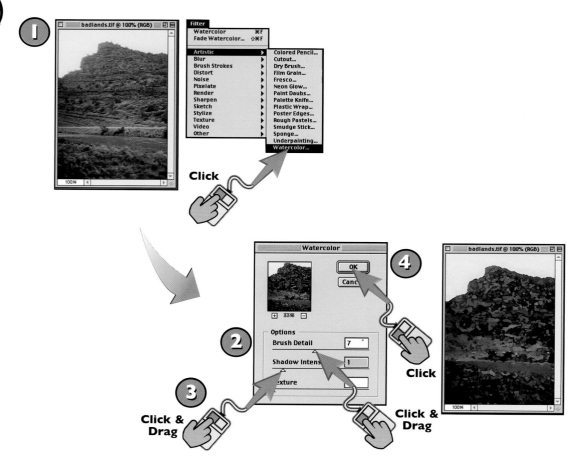

(✓) Dragging the **Texture** slider to the right "simplifies" the colors in the image, making them brighter and clearer.

1 Choose **Filter**, **Artistic**, **Watercolor**.

2 Drag the **Brush Detail** slider to adjust the amount of image detail that is preserved.

3 Drag the **Shadow Intensity** slider to lighten or darken shadows.

4 Click **OK** to apply the filter.

Task 4: Applying a Rough Pastels Effect

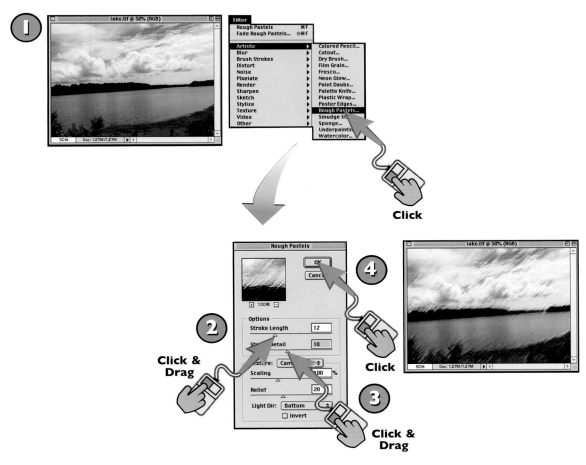

Click

Click & Drag

Click

Click & Drag

Click

Some of Photoshop's Artistic filters are more convincing than others. While Rough Pastels produces an interesting effect, it doesn't actually make an image look as though it's been drawn with pastels—the result is more like a chalky texture laid over the existing image.

① Choose **Filter**, **Artistic**, **Rough Pastels**.

② Drag the **Stroke Length** slider to adjust the length of the chalk strokes.

③ Drag the **Stroke Detail** slider to control how much image detail is preserved.

④ Click **OK** to apply the filter.

✔ The Rough Pastels filter's Texture settings are the same as those used in Part 10, Task 14, "Applying Texture."

End Task

Task 5: Applying a Colored Pencil Effect

Photoshop's Colored Pencil filter does a credible job of producing an image that looks as though it's been done with colored pencils, except for the fact that you have no control over the angle of the pencil strokes. You can control how much the paper shows through and how bright the paper is.

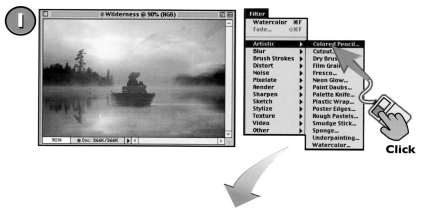

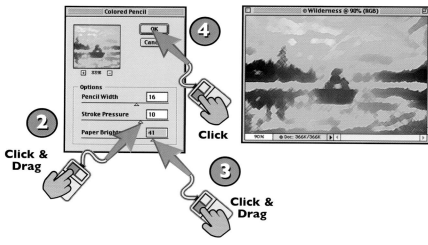

✓ Photoshop uses the current background color for the color of the paper when applying the Colored Pencil filter.

1 Choose **Filter**, **Artistic**, **Colored Pencil**.

2 Drag the **Pencil Width** and **Stroke Pressure** sliders to control the "pencil strokes."

3 Drag the **Paper Brightness** slider to lighten or darken the "paper."

4 Click **OK** to apply the filter.

End Task

Task 6: Applying a Photocopy Effect

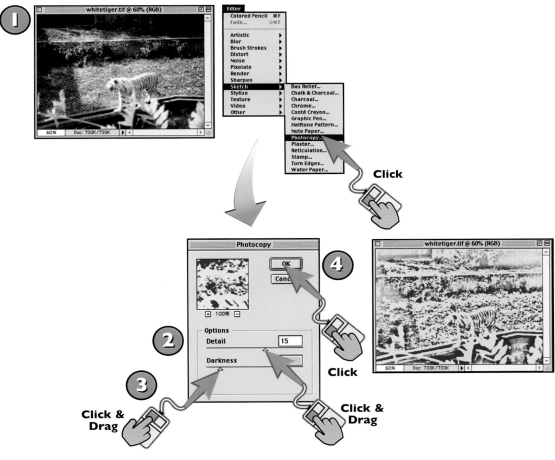

The Photocopy filter has one big advantage over using a real photocopier to create images—it works in color, converting an image by combining the current foreground and background colors. Like a real photocopier, the filter allows you to adjust the brightness of the copy.

Click

Click

Click & Drag

Click & Drag

1. Choose **Filter**, **Sketch**, **Photocopy**.

2. Drag the **Detail** slider to control the amount of image detail that is preserved.

3. Drag the **Darkness** slider to lighten or darken the image.

4. Click **OK** to apply the filter.

✓ Photoshop uses the current foreground color for dark areas and the current background color for light areas when applying the Photocopy filter.

Task 7: Applying a Bas Relief Effect

Photoshop can simulate three-dimensional effects with several filters, including **Bas Relief.** This filter "raises" light areas of the image, "lowers" dark areas, and replaces the image's colors with the current foreground and background colors.

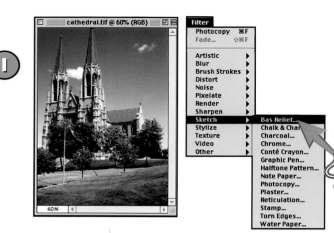

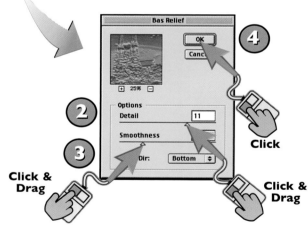

Click

Click

Click & Drag

Click & Drag

✓ Photoshop uses the current foreground color for dark areas and the current background color for light areas when applying the Bas Relief filter.

① Choose **Filter**, **Sketch**, **Bas Relief**.

② Drag the **Detail** slider to control the amount of image detail that is preserved.

③ Drag the **Smoothness** slider to control the image's surface texture.

④ Click **OK** to apply the filter.

End Task

Task 8: Applying a Craquelure Effect

Start Here

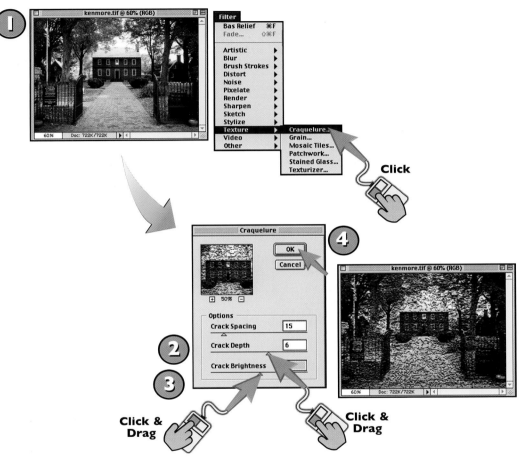

Click

In craquelure, images are painted on highly textured plaster surfaces with many tiny cracks. Photoshop's Craquelure filter produces an attractive embossed effect with as much cracking as you want (or as little).

Click & Drag

Click & Drag

Choose **Filter**, **Texture**, **Craquelure**.

Drag the **Crack Spacing** and **Crack Depth** sliders to adjust the cracks' size and positioning.

Drag the **Crack Brightness** slider to make the cracks brighter or darker.

Click **OK** to apply the filter.

Like most filters that incorporate an embossing effect, the Craquelure filter raises light areas of the image and sinks dark areas.

End Task

Task 9: Applying a Film Grain Effect

The Film Grain filter is similar to the non-Gaussian version of the Add Noise filter, except that it applies different noise patterns to the highlights of an image and to the darker areas. It simulates the film grain you can see when you overenlarge a slide.

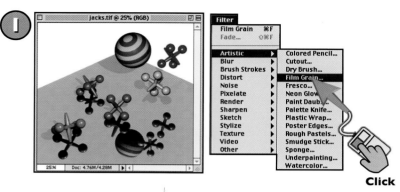

Click

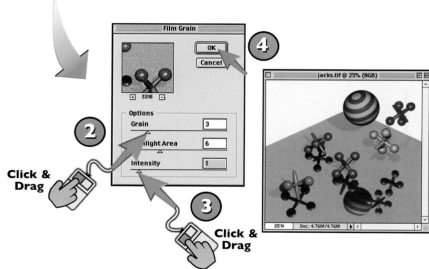

✓ The Highlight Area slider controls how much of the image's lighter areas are considered highlights for the purposes of adding grain—a different pattern is used for grain in highlight areas.

✓ To apply noise to an image, see Part 10, Task 1, "Adding Noise."

① Choose **Filter**, **Artistic**, **Film Grain**.

② Drag the **Grain** slider to adjust the amount of grain added.

③ Drag the **Intensity** slider to adjust the intensity of the image's colors.

④ Click **OK** to apply the filter.

Task 10: Applying a Stained Glass Effect

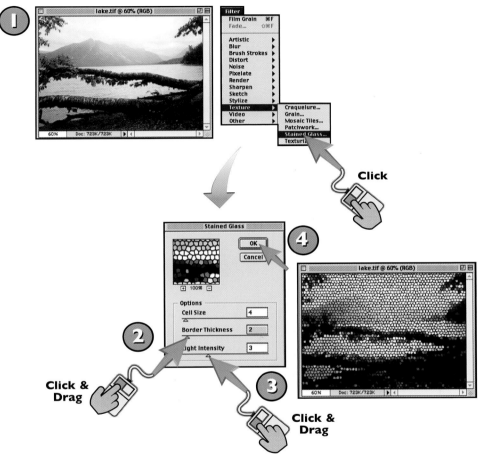

Click

Click & Drag

Click & Drag

Do the results of Photoshop's Stained Glass filter look like stained glass? Not really, but this filter can be useful nonetheless. It produces a honeycomb effect with a single color in each "cell." The Stained Glass filter works best with large, simple images.

1. Choose **Filter**, **Texture**, **Stained Glass**.

2. Drag the **Cell Size** and **Border Thickness** sliders to adjust the cells and the space between them.

3. Drag the **Light Intensity** slider to control the image's brightness.

4. Click **OK** to apply the filter.

✓ The current foreground color is used for the "lead" between the pieces of colored glass.

The Mosaic Tiles filter doesn't produce a traditional mosaic effect; rather, it creates images that look as though they've been painted on top of irregularly shaped tiles. You can control the size and spacing of the tiles, but they're always based on a square grid.

Task 11: Applying a Mosaic Effect

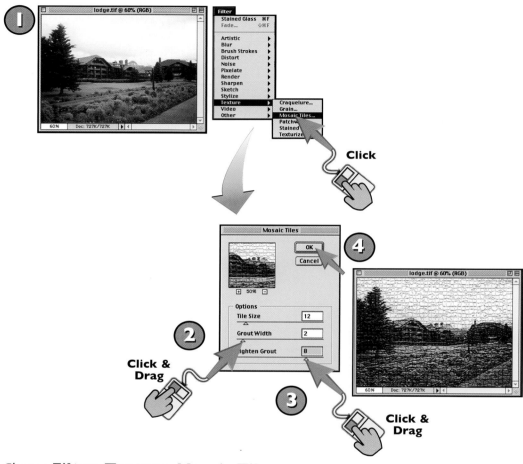

Click

Click & Drag

Click & Drag

✓ The results of the Mosaic Tiles filter are much improved by following the filter with a light application of noise. To apply noise to an image, see Part 10, Task 1, "Adding Noise."

① Choose **Filter**, **Texture**, **Mosaic Tiles**.

② Drag the **Tile Size** and **Grout Width** sliders to adjust the tiles' size and spacing.

③ Drag the **Lighten Grout** slider to control the brightness of the spaces between tiles.

④ Click **OK** to apply the filter.

End Task

Task 12: Applying a Stamped Effect

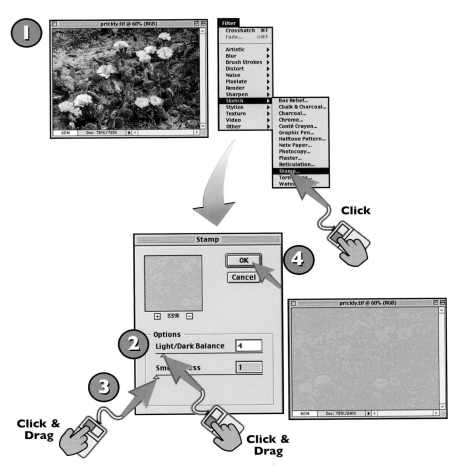

Click

Click & Drag

Click & Drag

The name of this filter is somewhat misleading—the effect is really more like a silkscreen print. Using the foreground and background colors, the Stamp filter converts the image to a somewhat abstract representation of its former self that resembles the results of the Photocopy filter.

① Choose **Filter**, **Sketch**, **Stamp**.

② Drag the **Light/Dark Balance** slider to adjust the ratio of the two colors.

③ Drag the **Smoothness** slider to smooth or roughen the image's edges.

④ Click **OK** to apply the filter.

✓ Photoshop uses the current foreground color for dark areas and the current background color for light areas when applying the Stamp filter.

Task 13: Applying a Plaster Effect

The Plaster filter molds your image onto a plaster wall by using the current foreground and background colors to indicate highlights and shadows. The effect is three-dimensional and works best on simple images without a lot of small details.

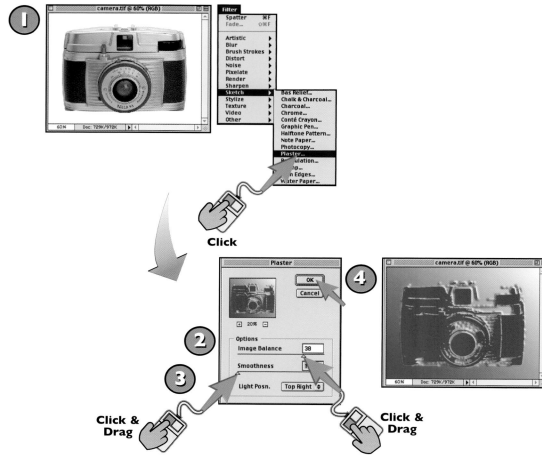

Click

Click

Click & Drag

Click & Drag

✓ The **Light Posn.** pop-up menu controls the direction of the light casting the shadows in the plaster image. Changing this setting can make a big difference in which details show up in the final image.

1 Choose **Filter**, **Sketch**, **Plaster**.

2 Drag the **Image Balance** slider to control the light and dark areas.

3 Drag the **Smoothness** slider to determine the "cragginess" of the plaster.

4 Click **OK** to apply the filter.

Task 14: Applying an Extruded Effect

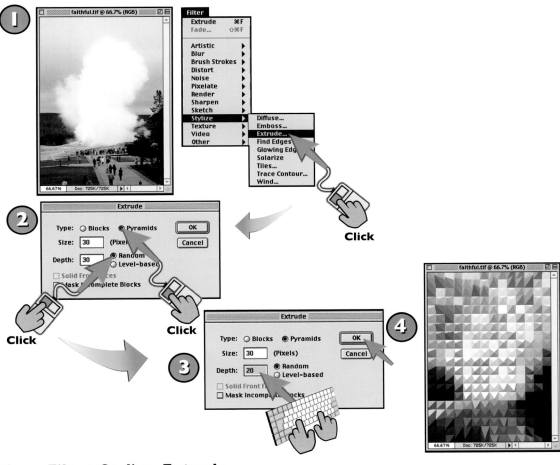

Click

Click

Click

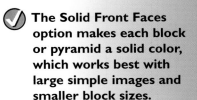

How about creating a picture from stacks of colored blocks or pyramids? That's the effect the Extrude filter produces. You can choose the size and depth of the blocks, but they always appear to be stacked from below your feet to over your head.

① Choose **Filter**, **Stylize**, **Extrude**.

② Click a **Type** option, and click **Random** or **Level-based**.

③ Enter a **Size** setting and a **Depth** setting.

④ Click **OK** to apply the filter.

✓ The Solid Front Faces option makes each block or pyramid a solid color, which works best with large simple images and smaller block sizes.

End Task

Task 15: Applying a Spatter Effect

The Spatter effect turns a photo into an impressionist painting—sort of. You can control how far from its original location each pixel is spattered, and you can control the overall amount of spattering. The effect preserves image colors and is fairly attractive.

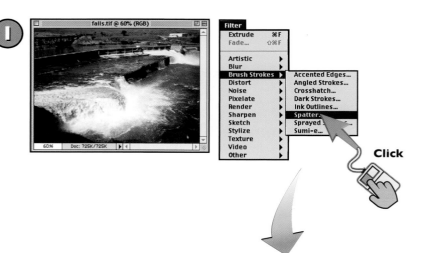

Click

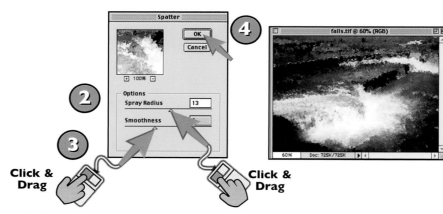

**Click &
Drag**

**Click &
Drag**

✓ To minimize the spatter effect, drag **Spray Radius** all the way to the left and **Smoothness** all the way to the right. This is a good place to start—from there, move the sliders back toward the middle to add more spattering.

① Choose **Filter**, **Brush Strokes**, **Spatter**.

② Drag the **Spray Radius** slider to spatter each pixel less or more.

③ Drag the **Smoothness** slider to determine how much spattering takes place.

④ Click **OK** to apply the filter.

**End
Task**

Task 16: Applying Crosshatching

Click

Click &
Drag

Click &
Drag

Don't confuse Photoshop's version of crosshatching with the pen-and-ink technique by the same name. The results of the Crosshatch filter are soft and chalky, with distinct diagonal "strokes." This is another way to achieve a "fine art" effect with little effort.

① Choose **Filter**, **Brush Strokes**, **Crosshatch**.

② Drag the **Stroke Length** slider to determine the length of the strokes.

③ Drag the **Sharpness** and **Strength** sliders to adjust the strokes' prominence.

④ Click **OK** to apply the filter.

 The higher the Strength setting, the more the crosshatching strokes obscure the image.

A

Action   Named series of Photoshop commands that can be executed by simply invoking the Action.

alpha channel   Channel that contains a mask image, as opposed to a color channel.

anti-aliasing   Smoothing the edges in an image by adding pixels of intermediate colors between contrasting pixels.

B

batch processing   Applying changes to a specified group of images automatically through the use of Actions.

Bézier path   A path in which each curve is defined by three points, one indicating position and the others indicating direction; used in drawing programs such as FreeHand, CorelDraw, and Illustrator and also in Photoshop's paths.

bicubic   Highest-quality method of interpolation.

bilinear   Moderate-quality method of interpolation.

bitmap mode   Photoshop's term for a black-and-white (as opposed to grayscale) image.

bitmapped image   Image created from colored, gray, or black pixels, each occupying a predetermined position on a grid.

blending mode   Mathematically based way of combining colors on two or more layers or in a new element and an existing one; the most commonly used blending mode is Normal.

BMP   Bitmapped file format commonly used on PCs.

burn   To intensify by darkening the image details.

C

channel   Component of an image; each file contains a number of color channels (such as red, green, and blue channels) and potentially a number of alpha channels used for masking portions of the image.

clipping path   Path that is used to mask portions of an image that lie outside the path's boundaries.

CMYK   Cyan (light blue), magenta (bright pinkish-red), yellow, and black—the four colors used in process printing to create full-color images.

color mode   Way of defining color within Photoshop, such as CMYK, Grayscale, or Bitmap.

color model   Another term for color mode that is more commonly used when not referring to Photoshop.

color-separated   Broken into component images that reflect the amount of ink required from each ink color to produce a full-color printed image. A color-separated file contains separate grayscale images for each of the four process ink colors.

compression   Method of encoding image data more efficiently to decrease file size.

crop   To delete any portion of the image that lies outside a rectangular cropping selection.

curve handles   Imaginary points that can be moved to define the shape of a Bézier path.

D

DCS   Desktop Color Separation, an EPS file format option that creates five files to form a preseparated color image (one for each process color and one containing a full-color preview).

dodge   De-emphasize by lightening image details.

E

EPS Encapsulated PostScript; a file format used for both bitmapped images, as in Photoshop, and vector images, as in draw programs like Illustrator.

F

feathered Refers to a selection that "fades out" around the edges for a specified distance. In a feathered selection, the outer pixels are only partially selected, and any change made to that selection will be only partially applied to those pixels.

filter Command that changes the appearance of an image by applying a mathematical equation to each pixel in the image.

G

gamut Range of colors that can be reproduced by a particular device or process.

Gaussian Refers to a mathematical method of redistributing pixels randomly; used to blur and add noise to images in Photoshop.

GIF Graphic Interchange Format, a file format originated by CompuServe and widely used on the Internet.

Grabber Hand Tool that moves the image within the window; to access the Grabber Hand, press the spacebar, and then click and drag.

gradient Color fill that shades from one color to another; gradients can include multiple colors and even transparency.

grayscale Composed completely of shades of gray.

grid Non-printing rows and columns that can be used to position objects within an image more precisely.

guides Non-printing lines that can be placed anywhere within an image.

H

highlights Brightest (closest to white) points in an image.

HSB Method of defining colors in terms of hue (color), saturation (purity), and brightness (intensity).

I

imagesetter High-resolution printing device that prints on coated paper (used for paste-up) or film (used for making printing plates).

interlaced Refers to an image whose data is saved in an order that will allow the image to be displayed in a low resolution, even before all the image data is delivered to the viewing computer; commonly used on the World Wide Web.

J-K

JPEG Joint Photographic Experts Group—a compression method and lossy file format that allows for extremely high compression levels.

L

layer Part of an image that can lie above or below other parts of the image and that can be modified without affecting the rest of the image.

layer mask Grayscale image that determines what parts of a layer are visible and what parts do not show.

lossless compression Compression method that does not affect the quality of the image compressed.

lossy Compression method that reduces the quality of the image compressed.

LZW Lempel-Ziv-Welch—lossless image compression method used in the TIFF format.

M

marching ants Common term for the moving selection marquee.

midtones Middle (between white and black) tones in an image.

N-O

nearest neighbor Lowest-quality (but quickest) method of interpolation.

P-Q

path See *Bézier path*.

PDF Portable Document Format—the format used by Adobe's Acrobat software.

Photo CD File format used to store multiple resolutions of an image within one file.

pixel "Picture element," a square portion of an image that can be only one color.

PostScript Page description language that defines images in mathematical terms; used by printers and imagesetters. PostScript fonts are defined in terms of their character outlines.

preview Low-resolution version of an image stored within the image file so that the image can be viewed in programs into which it is imported, such as page layout applications.

process color One of the four ink colors used to print CMYK images, that is, cyan magenta, yellow, or black.

progressive Refers to an image that displays at gradually higher resolutions as more image data is downloaded to the viewer's computer.

R

RAM Random Access Memory—the computer memory in which currently active programs are stored.

rasterize Convert from Bézier paths to pixels.

resample Add or delete pixels and rearrange existing pixels to resize or change the resolution of an image.

resolution The number of pixels per measurement unit; usually measured in pixels per inch or pixels per centimeter.

resolution-independent Stored in a format that can be printed at any size or resolution.

RGB Red, green, and blue, the colors displayed by computer monitors and combined to create the illusion of full-color images.

RIP Raster Image Processor—the "brain" of a printing device; usually used in reference to high-resolution imagesetters.

rulers Measurement guides along the top and left edges of the image window.

S

selection Currently active area of the image, to which any changes will be applied; indicated by "marching ants" along the outer edges of the selection.

shadows Darkest (closest to black) points in an image.

spot color   Printed color that will be reproduced by a single ink, rather than by a combination of the four process ink colors.

spot color channel   Channel that contains image data to be printed with a spot color rather than with the process colors.

swatchbook   Book of printed ink samples showing what common colors look like on paper rather than onscreen.

T-U

TIFF   Tag Image File Format; bitmapped file format commonly used in prepress applications.

transform   Modify an image by rotating, skewing, or otherwise reshaping it.

transparency mask   The selection that includes all non-transparent pixels on a layer.

V

vector image   Image created from points, lines, and fills and defined in terms of the mathematical characteristics of those elements. Drawing programs such as Illustrator, CorelDraw, and FreeHand create vector images.

W-Z

work path   The currently active path.

Filter menu commands

Levels dialog box

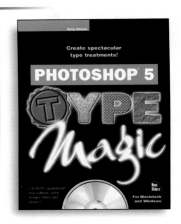

Photoshop 5 Type Magic

by Greg Simsic

This is the perfect resource for typographers, designers, and Photoshop users looking to spice up their work. Every page makes a visual promise: you will be able to create this exciting artwork! The book's highly effective, recipe-style approach walks you through the procedures of creating special effects with type, and the stunning four-color illustrations are sure to inspire any designer.

New Riders $39.99
1-56830-465-X
264 pages, CD, 4-color

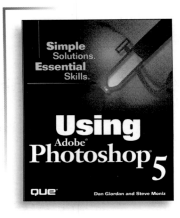

Using Adobe Photoshop 5

by Dan Giordan and Steve Moniz

A task-based reference that puts the answers to professionals' problems at their fingertips. Learn to create stunning graphics, correct and enhance tonality and focus of your images, and achieve professional results quickly with concise, step-by-step directions.

July 1998
Que $29.99
0-7897-165-9
600 pages, 2-color

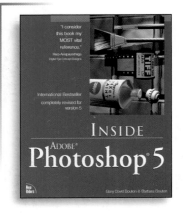

Inside Adobe Photoshop 5

by Gary David Bouton and Barbara Bouton

Inside Adobe Photoshop 5 reads like a knowledgeable neighbor who has dropped by to show you the way around the world's most popular image editing program. The Bouton's easy-to-follow style and technical know-how provide comprehensive coverage of Photoshop's newest and traditional features.

Whether you're a professional or a hobbyist, after your intimate visit with the Boutons you'll walk away with the skills needed to accomplish fantastic, advanced image manipulation.

ISBN:1-56205-884-3
$44.99 USA/$64.95 CAN

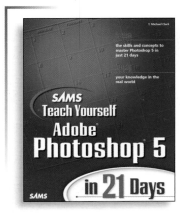

Sams Teach Yourself Adobe Photoshop 5 in 21 Days

by T. Michael Clark

In just three weeks, you'll understand the fundamentals of Photoshop 5, master professional imaging techniques, learn how to effectively use all the tools and features, and get tips on creating spectacular designs quickly and easily. Using the step-by-step approach of this easy-to-understand guide, you'll be up to speed with Photoshop 5—in no time!

Sams $39.99
0-672-31300-6
500 pages, CD, color insert